THE MYSTERY NEXT DOOR

Michael Rodney Moore

Copyright © 2023 Michael Rodney Moore

All rights reserved

The characters and events portrayed in this book are fictitious. Any similarity to real persons, living or dead, is coincidental and not intended by the author.

No part of this book may be reproduced, or stored in a retrieval system, or transmitted in any form or by any means, electronic, mechanical, photocopying, recording, or otherwise, without express written permission of the publisher.

CONTENTS

Title Page
Copyright
Dedication
Acknowledgements
PROLOGUE ... 1
CHAPTER 1 • A NEW HOME ... 5
CHAPTER 2 • THE HOUSE IN THE WOODS ... 13
CHAPTER 3 • OAK HARBOR ... 21
CHAPTER 4 • MISS ROSE ... 29
CHAPTER 5 • LIGHTS IN THE NIGHT ... 37
CHAPTER 6 • INTRUDER ... 44
CHAPTER 7 • DISCOVERIES IN THE HOUSE ... 54
CHAPTER 8 • CAMERAS & BOOKS ... 64
CHAPTER 9 • CONFESSIONS & OATHS ... 78
CHAPTER 10 • YOUNG DUPREE ... 85
CHAPTER 11 • A NEW BEGINNING IN WILMINGTON ... 97
CHAPTER 12 • CAMERAS & BEARS ... 104
CHAPTER 13 • MEEMA ... 112
CHAPTER 14 • A PIRATE'S TALE ... 118
CHAPTER 15 • THE TRAP IS SPRUNG ... 127
CHAPTER 16 • THE BIRTH OF OAK HARBOR ... 137
CHAPTER 17 • ESCAPES & SUSPECTS ... 150
CHAPTER 18 • REWARDS & REGRETS ... 158

CHAPTER 19 · FOUR BODIES	167
CHAPTER 20 · WAR, SPIES & GOODBYES	179
CHAPTER 21 · DEAD MEN TELL NO TALES	189
CHAPTER 22 · LOVE?	196
CHAPTER 23 · THE THIRD BOOK	206
CHAPTER 24 · FOUL MURDERS	214
CHAPTER 25 · SINS OF LONG PAST	220
CHAPTER 26 · SINS OF TODAY	227
CHAPTER 27 · RETURN TO THE TOMB	236
EPILOGUE	243
AFTERWORD FROM THE AUTHOR	246
About The Author	249
Books By This Author	251

DEDICATION

*This book is dedicated to my granddaughter, Haleigh Rose!
Thank you for giving me the inspiration to write this story. It was written for you!*

Love Pap

ACKNOWLEDGEMENTS

I want to thank my sweet wife and best friend, Debbie Rose for all of her encouragement in my writing efforts. She has spent countless hours reading my first drafts, discussing the colloquialism of eastern North Carolina and the development of characters that form in my imagination. None of my writing would be possible without her!

I also want to thank my editor Deborah Louis for all of her time and effort to make my story better. I truly believe that the "red pen" is my friend!

PROLOGUE

It was a dark night off the coast of North Carolina on that long-ago day in 1852. Dupree Durant tried to discern the difference between the night sky and the horizon of the water but the heavy cloud cover did not allow enough ambient light for even an experienced mariner, such as himself, to see the horizon. He felt his nerves stand on end as he waited for the arranged signal.

"They should have been here by now," hissed his chief mate who stood next to him.

"They'll be here," Dupree replied confidently even as doubts ate into his sureness as he pondered all the things that could go wrong or that may have already gone wrong.

"Why did I ever get myself tied up in this?!" he said to himself but then he thought of just how wealthy he would be after tonight and smiled.

This had all started when Meredith Williams, an old shipmate from his whaling days, tracked him down. His old friend had recently looked him up and said that he was now the chief mate on the Seahorse, a schooner that voyaged between Panama and Philadelphia. Mostly they hauled bananas, which were becoming all the rage with the rich folk up north. Of much greater interest was that their cargo also included a consignment of gold from California on a regular basis.

When he had asked his old friend just how much gold was on the ship, he only smiled and held up two fingers.

"Two hundred pounds?" Dupree had asked in astonishment.

His old friend shook his head from side to side and said "Tons," laughing like a mad man.

The plan was simple enough. His friend said that the crew of the Seahorse wanted to participate in stealing the gold. They planned on subduing the captain and tying him up in his cabin. They would then rendezvous near Ocracoke Island and offload the gold onto Dupree's ship, the Audacia. When finished they would leave the other ship at anchor to be found by a fisherman or another passing ship. By that time, they would have sailed to New Bern, where they would divide the gold and everyone would go on their way as wealthy men.

"Lights four points off starboard!" thundered the voice of the lookout above, who was watching to the east.

Dupree raised his telescope, scanned the area, and picked up the running lights of a ship about a mile away. The two red lights indicated that the ship was moving on a northerly heading. Then there were three quick flashes from a signal lamp.

"Flash two long back, if you would, Mr. Brown," Dupree ordered his chief mate, to make the agreed upon reply.

There was the clatter of shutters opening and closing on the signal lamp. In just a few seconds there was one long and four short flashes from the other schooner, which was obviously the Seahorse.

"That is them! Get ready to transfer cargo!" he ordered and his crew of seven men began to scurry about.

Dupree was relieved that the two ships had found each other on such a large ocean but now a new worry set in as he considered the complicated process of moving 4,000 pounds of gold bullion between two ships on the open sea. He had placed his ship on the leeward side of the island and thanked God that it was a calm night here on the Outer Banks. Even with those advantages it would still take more than ten trips by his launch to bring the gold across. He noted that the Seahorse was slowing to drop anchor nearby as his crew rushed to get their small boat in the water and to rig the block and tackle to hoist the gold onto his ship.

"Ahoy!" came a shout across the forty yards separating the two vessels. Dupree was glad that no name was given for the imprisoned captain to hear.

"Ahoy, my men will bring the launch alongside," he replied. "Transfer the cargo in no more than 400-pound lots. Can you also put your launch in the water to cut the number of trips down?"

"Avast! We have had casualties. There are just three of us," Meredith's voice replied.

Dupree was shocked. Something serious must have gone wrong aboard the Seahorse. He knew that there were supposed to be eight men on the other schooner. That meant that four men had been killed or seriously injured. That was bad but how they got that way was a more important issue that immediately began to nag at Dupree's suspicious mind. Piracy was one thing but murder was another! Then it occurred to him that he would be hanged either way if he were caught.

"Just keep the men moving!" he thought to himself.

The next two hours were spent unloading the launch of crates that contained the gold bars and sending them down into the cargo hold. Finally the last of the crates was being stowed below and his launch was making one final journey to gather the three men from the other ship. He watched intently as the launch began its return journey. Dupree was anxious to get away before the Audacia was spotted near the scene of the crime.

Finally the launch was secured to its divots to be raised back to its storage hooks while the men scrambled up the rope ladder. Meredith was the first to step on deck. Then two other sailors joined him. Dupree felt the hair on the back of his neck stand up as he had an uneasy feeling about his former shipmate's two

3

companions. As he looked them over, he noticed that they both appeared to be extremely nervous as they glanced back at the other ship. Something was not right about all of this!

"What happened to the rest of your men?" Dupree asked as his suspicions grew.

"I'll tell you all about it after we get underway. The quicker we're away from that ship the safer we will be," Meredith said as he also looked back across the way.

Dupree continued to study the crew of the Seahorse but he knew that Meredith was right and that they needed to get away as quickly as they could, so he gave the order to get underway. "Make ready to sail! Man the capstan and weigh the anchor!" he commanded.

"Go and help get us underway," Meredith said quietly to the other two men who immediately raced to help weigh the anchor.

"Set the sails and make your course for New Bern, Mr. Brown!" Dupree commanded.

Slowly the schooner began to make way as the gentle breeze filled her sails. They had moved about a half-mile when there was a blinding flash followed by a thundering roar. Dupree felt himself thrown violently to the deck along with all the other crewmen. Then water and bits of wreckage began to land on the deck. Slowly Dupree stood up and looked to where the Seahorse should have been but all that was there were smoke and debris.

"What the hell happened?" Dupree asked, turning towards Meredith to find two pistols aimed at his chest.

"Just do what you're told and you and your men will stay alive!" Meredith said.

CHAPTER 1 • A NEW HOME

Zoey Morganton watched the countryside of eastern North Carolina roll by as her mom's car sped down the highway toward what would be her new home. Zoey had mixed feelings about moving. She was going to miss her friends and her old school, which made her a little sad. On the other hand, she was curious as to what new things she would get to experience.

She smiled as she remembered her Meema saying; "Zoey, you are the happiest child I have ever seen. You always make the best out of everything."

It was true. Zoey knew that she always tried to see the best in people and events in her life even when things did not go the way she wished.

Somewhere in her young life she realized that not everything would go as she wanted. When things did not work out for some kids they would whine and complain about it. Zoey could not understand why so many kids did that, since it would never fix the problem and it only made them even more miserable along with everyone around them. Her attitude was to focus on the good things that she had and to get on with life. Even at the age of thirteen she knew this was the secret to being happy.

Her mom would start her new job as a nurse practitioner at a small clinic in New Bern next Monday. Zoey was proud of her mom for putting in all those years of hard work to earn her degree in order to help people live healthier and longer lives.

"I hope you like our new home, Zoey," her mom said cheerfully from the front seat. "We should be there in just a few minutes!"

"I can't wait to see it!" Zoey replied.

"It's got a really big yard and we'll live out in the country. I wish I could have afforded something in town but the rents were so high there!" her mom said a little defensively.

"It will be an adventure," she reassured her mom. "Besides, I'll have a lot of places to ride my bike."

A few minutes later her mother turned off the highway onto a country road. There were stands of pine trees and then flat farm fields with crops that neither Zoey or her mom could identify. They passed over a small river that flowed through marshland. Zoey could see long-legged birds walking through green growth and occasionally putting their long beaks under the surface to eat some unknown creature. It was so different from living in Raleigh!

"Here we are!" her mom said with excitement in her voice.

Zoey carefully looked at the house they were moving into. It was a single story that she had heard her mom describe as a ranch-style house. The exterior walls were the reddish-brown color of brick. The house had a large covered porch on the front and there was an attached carport on the side.

The yard was well tended with many flowering trees and shrubs. Zoey liked it right away.

Her mom pulled into the driveway and parked off to one side.

"I got a text message from the movers and they should be here in thirty minutes. Let me show you the inside!" Her mom said eagerly.

It was not a big house but it had three bedrooms, a living room, kitchen, and two-and-a-half bathrooms. A set of French doors opened out onto a screened porch with a step down onto a small patio shaded by a large live oak with Spanish moss hanging from its limbs. As promised, there was a large open backyard that backed up against the woods that were just beginning to change color.

Zoey loved this new home!

Just then there was knock on the front door.

"That must be the movers!" her mom said as she rushed to answer it.

Zoey decided to walk into the backyard and get familiar with her new home. It was warm outside in the mid-October weather. She looked at the many flowering plants with growing wonder. Whoever had lived there before them must have truly loved the yard and had tended it with great care.

She walked past the patio and into the large lawn with its neatly-mowed green grass. There were many large trees providing patches of shade that kept it from becoming too hot. Then she came to the back boundary where the property ended and the woods began. The forest felt old to Zoey as if it had been there undisturbed for more than a hundred years. It was not like the pine woods she had seen earlier. Those woods look organized, as if the trees had been planted in straight lines. While the trees were tall, she could tell they were not that old. These trees by comparison seemed to be randomly placed. They were mostly oak, sweetgum, and poplar trees. Their leaves were a myriad of colors and shapes.

It was then that she noticed an old fence maybe ten yards into the woods. It, too, was very old! It was made of wrought-iron and a brick post every ten feet had vines growing all over them. It felt scary to the thirteen-year old girl and she was curious about why the fence was there. She began to walk along the length of the backyard to see how far the mysterious fence went. When she reached the end of the yard the fence marched on, paralleling the farm field next door.

Zoey shrugged her shoulders and decided the fence really did not matter. She lowered her head and turned toward the house. It was then that she saw the dusty boots standing in her way. She looked up to see a very tall black man looking down at her. She let out a small startled sound, as she was surprised to see him, but then relaxed as he smiled in a friendly way.

"Sorry to have startled you, Miss," he said in a deep baritone voice, tipping his old floppy farm hat. "I was looking to be introduced to the new folks that are moving in."

"That would be my mom and me," Zoey replied and smiled up at the man.

He had a kind face that was lined with age and a lifetime of hard work in the outdoors.

"My name is Moses Jones and I'm your closest neighbor. I live over yonder across the road," he said as he smiled at her again.

"My Mama is in with the movers. Come with me and I'll introduce you," Zoey said as she started towards the patio.

"Thank you kindly, Miss!" he replied.

Zoey opened the door and waited for Moses to follow behind her. He removed his hat and carefully wiped his feet before he stepped into the house. She watched as several men moved boxes and furniture into the house while she looked for her mom.

"Mama! I have someone that wants to meet you!" Zoey said with a raised voice trying to locate her mom.

Her mother appeared with a smile but Zoey could see that she was obviously preoccupied, trying to tell the movers where everything needed to go.

"May I help you?" her mother asked with a polite tone even as she tried to keep track of what was being put where.

"Sorry to interrupt you ma'am but I wanted to introduce myself. I'm Moses Jones and I'm your neighbor from across the road." The old black man said in his deep molasses voice.

Zoey watched her Mama smile warmly as she reached out and shook his hand. "Pleased to meet you Mr. Jones! I'm Hannah

Morganton and this is my daughter, Zoey."

"Please call me Moses, Mrs. Morganton."

"As long as you call me Hannah!" her mother replied quickly. "Is there something I can do for you? I'm afraid that I'm rather busy at the moment."

"I surely do understand, Miss Hannah, but there is one thing I wanted to talk with you about. I tended the yard for the previous owner, Miss Rose. I was wondering if you would allow me to continue doing so?" he asked, gripping his hat in his hands.

"I hadn't thought about the yard but it is quite beautiful. How much would you charge?" her mom asked with a little hesitation.

Zoey watched as Moses seemed to be looking at something that was far away and she thought his eyes glistened as if he were about to cry.

"Don't want no money," the old black man said as he shook his head. "Miss Rose was my friend. I worked with her for more than fifty years tending her gardens. She always took such pleasure in her flowers and lawn; it would be my pleasure to continue to do so in her memory." There was a definite sadness in his voice.

Her mom stood there, obviously surprised by the request from Moses. "That is very generous of you but..." her mom started but was interrupted before she could finish.

"Please, Miss Hannah. I promise to take good care of everything and if you want something changed you just tell ole Moses about it," he pleaded with urgency in his voice.

Her mom looked at Zoey with surprise at the offer and then back at the old black man and said, "Okay, but I insist that I will pay you something. Would fifty dollars a week be all right?"

Moses's face went from one of pleading to joy. His smile grew large as he said, "That'll be just fine, Miss Hannah! I'll get out of your way but if you need help with anything just come on across the road."

With that said, Moses left through the same door he had entered.

Her mom continued to look at the door after he had left. Then she sighed, looked at Zoey, and said, "That was interesting but we need to get everything into the right places while we have the help of the movers. I want you to make sure the boxes get in the right rooms."

The next several hours were spent making sure that all the furniture went where it should be. Zoey rushed from room to room checking that boxes were getting to where they belonged based on their labels. On several occasions she would find a mover putting a box in the wrong room and she would have to politely ask that it be moved to the right room. Boxes that were not labeled went to the spare bedroom to be sorted out when opened later. Despite what had seemed to be never ending chaos, the movers were finished before supper.

Zoey's mom collapsed onto the sofa in the living room with a groan and said, "Well, we're here and we still have all these boxes to unpack but that will have to wait until tomorrow. I'm plumb worn out! We still need to have supper so why don't we get in the car and head into town to see what we can find to eat?"

"All right with me," Zoey replied.

"Maybe we can find a place to get a pizza," her mom said with an exhausted sigh.

"That's okay with me," Zoey replied but she really did not feel like going anywhere.

A moment later there was a knock on the front door. Her mom opened it to find an older black woman standing there holding a basket.

"Hello Miss Hannah. My name is Zipporah and I'm Moses's wife. I know that you both must be exhausted after the busy day y'all have had, what with moving and all, so I brought you some supper. Here's some fried chicken, biscuits, green beans, and some dirty rice. I also put plates and such in there just in case you don't know where your things are," the woman said as she handed the large basket to Zoey's mom.

"You didn't have to do that!" her mom said with genuine gratitude.

"No trouble at all, Miss Hannah. Not after you made my Moses so happy!" Zipporah said as she reached out and touched the other woman's hand with a squeeze. "I'll stop by tomorrow and get the basket and dishes back."

With that the woman turned away and walked towards the road.

"Looks like we're having chicken instead of pizza," Hannah said happily as she carried the basket to the table.

The food was fantastic. Zoey had never tasted better chicken in her entire young life.

After dinner they sat on the screened porch listening to the crickets chirping in the dark backyard and the even darker woods beyond.

"So, what do you think of our new home?" her mother asked with curiosity.

"I really like it. Our new neighbors seem really nice too," Zoey replied. After few seconds she asked, "I wonder why Moses was so close to Miss Rose?"

"He did say that he had worked with her on her gardens for over fifty years. That's a long time to know someone. He also said that keeping the yard in good shape is his way of paying respect to her memory," her mother said thoughtfully.

For a while they just sat quietly in their own thoughts.

"Is Miss Rose who you are renting the house from?" Zoey asked. "No, our landlord is a man by the name of Nathaniel Smithers," her mother replied.

There was the sound of thunder in the distance.

"I think that's our sign to head to bed," her mom said with a sigh. "We still have a lot of unpacking to do tomorrow!"

CHAPTER 2 • THE HOUSE IN THE WOODS

Zoey was sound asleep when there was a tremendous crash of thunder that made her bed shake. She woke up with a start and could hear the rain beating against the window. Suddenly there was another bright flash that was instantly followed by the loud rumble of thunder. She felt afraid and started to get up and run to her Mama's bed. She glanced towards the window and a more distant flash of lighting illuminated the woods behind the house. She was surprised that she was able to see into the normally dark woods as the trees danced in the wind of the violent storm.

There was a house in those woods! From the brief illumination of the lighting, an image was captured by Zoey's eyes. She closed them and tried to recall what it had looked like. She could see that it was two or more stories tall and it was a large house, like a mansion. She thought it was made of brick or stone but was not sure.

Zoey got up from the bed and looked out the window waiting for the next flash. It was dark outside and she could hear the rain pelting the roof and window. Then it happened again. There was another flash on the other side of the woods and for a second Zoey could once again see the shape of a large house. There were definitely two floors and it looked as if it had columns in the front. Then there was another flash and Zoey could see the light reflect off the windows of the old house.

The rain slowed as the storm began to move away but Zoey continued to look into the darkness of the woods. As she stood there in her bedroom looking into the darkness, her curiosity began to grow about the house.

Who did it belong to? Did anyone live there? She finally lay back down on her bed and slowly drifted off to sleep.

Sometime during the night Zoey found herself in a dream where she realized that she was lost in the woods. She could not recall how she came to be in the woods or why. All she knew was that she was not welcome there and was certain that she had to get out of there quickly. She felt the woods closing in on her. She suddenly found herself by the fence but realized that she was on the wrong side and could not get home. She became ever more frantic and felt that if she did not get out of the woods soon, she would never leave.

Zoey woke with a start. The dream had seemed so real! Her heart was beating like a drum and she was sweaty all over as if she had been running a race. She looked at the clock, which informed her that it was almost six in the morning. She sat up in the bed and looked out into the woods in the early morning light. She could see the fence and as she looked at the tops of the trees, she could just make out the roofline of the house. Then she thought she saw movement near the fence. She was not sure what she had seen and perhaps she had not seen anything at all. She got out of the bed and walked to the window, studying the woods carefully. She wanted to see something move but she only saw the trees gently swaying in a light breeze. Then she thought she saw something out of the corner of her eye to the right side of the property. She concentrated on that spot trying to figure out what she might have seen.

"Good morning, Zoey!" her mom said and Zoey about jumped out of her skin and screamed. "I'm sorry, did I startle you?" her mother said apologetically.

"I thought I saw something in the woods. I guess I was concentrating on that too much and didn't hear you behind me!" Zoey said with a chuckle about her own surprise.

"I was surprised to see you up so early," her mom said as she joined Zoey by the window. Hannah looked at the woods for a moment and then said, "I want to get an early start on opening the boxes so that we can begin getting organized today. You get dressed and start opening the kitchen boxes while I wipe out the cabinets and drawers. After that we can go find some breakfast."

"Yes, ma'am." Zoey replied with a sigh as her mom headed for the kitchen.

As she got dressed Zoey's mind once again went back to movement in the woods. She was certain that she had seen someone.

"Someone?" she asked herself quietly.

She replayed it again in her mind and became convinced that she had seen a person moving in the woods near the fence!

"Get a move on, Zoey!" her mom said, making it clear that she needed to get started on her chores.

"Coming!" she replied but again walked to her window and looked at the woods but saw nothing.

The next hour was spent opening boxes and telling her mom what was in them. Her mom would then tell her where to put the box. Hannah was wearing rubber gloves and using a bucket with water that smelled strongly of bleach to clean the inside of each drawer, cabinet, and shelf before she would allow anything from the boxes to go into them. When she had finished cleaning, she quickly began putting things into their new places.

Finally the kitchen was done. Hannah drew a deep breath and said, "Let's go find a place to get a bite to eat."

A short time later her mom pulled into a small local dinner. There was a good number of cars in the parking lot, which indicated that the food must be good. Zoey and her mom stepped through the entrance and were greeted by the hum of conversations and smell of breakfast.

"Good morning! Will it be just the two of you this morning?" asked an older woman who wore an apron.

"That's right," said Zoey's mom with a smile.

The waitress picked up two menus and showed them to a booth.

"What would you like to drink?" she asked as she handed each of them a menu that had breakfast on one side and lunch on the other.

Zoey's mom looked at her, indicating that she should go first. "I'll have a coke, please," she said.

"I'll have a coffee with cream and sugar, ma'am," her mom added.

A few minutes later the waitress returned with their drinks and politely asked, "Are you ready to order?"

"Are you ready, Zoey?" her mom asked.

"I would like the French toast with sausage, please," Zoey said respectfully as she handed the menu back to the waitress.

"And for you, honey?" asked the waitress, turning to Hannah.

"I would like two eggs lightly scrambled, bacon crisp, and grits," Zoey's mom replied.

"Would you like toast or a biscuit with that?" "Wheat toast, please," she said.

The waitress wrote the order down and walked off to give it to the short order cook.

"That was quite the storm we had last night. Did it scare you?" Zoey's mother asked as they sipped their drinks.

"It woke me up. I think a lightning bolt hit something nearby," Zoey replied.

"My little girl must be growing up. You used to be scared to death of lightning and thunder!" her mother said with a slight smile that conveyed that she was both proud of her daughter for being grown up but also was a little sad for the same reason.

Zoey thought about what had happened during the storm and how she had discovered the house in the woods. In one way it seemed like a secret that she should keep but on the other hand she wondered if her mom had already noticed the house.

Finally she made up her mind and asked, "Did you notice that there's an old house in the woods behind us?"

"No, you'll have to point it out to me when we get home," her mom replied without any real interest as she sipped her coffee.

Just then the waitress returned with their food and placed everything on the table. She topped off the coffee and asked Zoey, "Do you need refill, sweetie?"

"No thank you, ma'am," she answered politely, then turned back to her mom to her mom. "There's an old fence in the woods that I think goes all the way around the house. It looks kind of creepy."

"You mean the old plantation house out there on Durant Road?" asked the waitress, lifting an eyebrow.

"Yes, we live on Durant Road," her mom said with growing curiosity.

"You couldn't have picked a spookier place to live in Craven County!" the waitress replied.

"Why would you say that?" Zoey asked wanting to hear what the waitress knew of the house in the woods.

"Nobody knows for sure but there was an old plantation there in the 1800's and it's said the man that owned it went crazy and killed a bunch of people. I heard it was haunted and that people have gone missing or worse, been murdered there. You take my advice and don't go into those woods!" the waitress said as she put the check on the table and left.

"Mom?" Zoey said as she looked to her mom with fear in her

eyes.

"Don't take it too seriously," Hannah said in a calming voice. "Most small towns have local legends like that. I'll bet she was told that story out by a camp fire by someone trying to scare her!" but Zoey did not look so convinced. "It is all going to be just fine, baby," she added as she squeezed her daughter's hand.

After the meal was over, they drove back to their new home where they continued to open boxes and put things away. Zoey was just carrying out another batch of moving boxes that had been broken down for recycling when there was a gentle knock on the front door. She opened the door to see her neighbor, Zipporah standing there.

"Good day Miss Zipporah," Zoey said with her normal good manners. "And a good day to you as well, Miss Zoey! I came to take the basket

back home," she said as a pleasant smile crossed her face.

Just then her mom entered the room and greeted Zipporah. "Please come in, Zipporah. I must say that was the most wonderful fried chicken! Maybe someday you'll teach me how to cook it. However, I'll warn you that you'll have your work cut out for you. You see, I'm afraid that I'm not much of a cook!"

Zipporah seemed to swell with pleasure at the compliment.

"I'm so pleased that you liked my chicken! As for cooking fried chicken, that's simple enough and it would be my pleasure to teach you and maybe Miss Zoey as well," she said as she glanced around the house. It was obvious that she was curious to see what might have been changed since she was last there.

"I'm afraid that we're still trying to get everything put away," said Hannah, indirectly apologizing for the mess as she shrugged and looked around.

"Oh shush, child. You're doing just fine. I'm just curious about the inside of this here house. You see, I haven't seen it since they carried Miss Rose out that night," Zipporah said with a hint of sadness in her voice.

"Did she die here?" Zoey asked, slightly on edge as she remembered what the waitress had said about ghosts and people dying or disappearing around the strange house in the woods.

"Oh, no! Miss Rose had been right sickly for some time. Moses and I cared for her for three years but then her relatives from her late husband's side decided to put her in a home. They said she would get better care than we could give," the older black woman said with a sad shake of her head. "That was the biggest lie as was ever told since the devil tempted Eve with that there apple," Zipporah said in a sorrowful tone before she continued. "My Moses would have done anything for Miss Rose and so would I. She was as fine a lady as there ever was!"

"Is she still alive?" Hannah asked.

"No, she passed over just three months after she was taken from her home," Zipporah sighed heavily. "I suppose it was like ripping a flower out of the ground by its roots and expecting it to live. You see, Miss Rose was the last of the Durants that had lived on these grounds since the slavery days." Zipporah shook her head sadly again and added, "'Twas a sad day. Now there is no one to carry their story on."

Zoey and her mom stood there stunned, listening to the old black woman. "This house surely can't be that old," Hannah said doubtfully

"No, this here house was built around 1970 just after Miss Rose's husband was killed," the old black woman said, again shaking her head with sadness as she recalled a life filled with tragedy. "Miss Rose said that the big house was getting too hard to maintain after Mr. Jonathan died. That was Miss Rose's husband. I think that she didn't like staying in that there house since that was where she found him dead like that."

"How did he die?" Zoey asked after her curiosity overcame her hesitation.

Zipporah looked closely at the thirteen-year-old girl and then at Hannah before she continued. "The sheriff said that it was suicide but Miss Rose always insisted that it was murder. Moses doesn't believe it was suicide either. He was just a boy at the time but his Daddy worked at the house and Moses helped him out when he wasn't in school," she said and looked away. "He saw the body that night and he still has nightmares about it."

"Is that the house in the woods?" Zoey asked as her curiosity demanded to be answered.

"Yes, child," she said with a sigh. "Now, I have imposed on you for too long and I'd best be getting done with my own chores. But if y'all need anything, you just come across the road and find Moses or my own self," Zipporah said as she walked out the door.

CHAPTER 3 • OAK HARBOR

The next day, Zoey continued to help her mom with getting the house organized. It was amazing that her mother could accomplish so much in such a short amount of time. By early afternoon most of the boxes had been emptied and closets and drawers were filled with the essentials of the single mom and her teenage daughter.

"Honey, I need to go into town and do some grocery shopping," Hannah said. "Would you like to come along?"

"Would it be all right if I stayed here and went for a bike ride? I'd like to do a little exploring!" Zoey asked, expecting her mom to readily agree since she would rather go to the grocery without her daughter's distractions.

"I think that will be all right as long as you promise not to go off too far," her mom replied.

Zoey was thrilled! She loved to ride her bike and looked forward to seeing what was down the country road they now lived on. Of course, there was one other thing on her curious mind and that was just what was on the other side of those woods and would she be able to see any more of the mysterious house next door from further down the road?

A short time later she watched her mom drive away with a wave as she put her bicycle helmet on her head. She pedaled her bike down the drive and made a right onto Durant Road. She noticed the house that Moses and Zipporah lived in across the road. It was a small house but it was neatly kept with a barn behind it. She could see a tractor and other farm equipment stored there. There were a vegetable garden and what looked like a chicken coop nearby. There were fields in every direction from their home.

What really held her attention, however, were the woods on the other side of the road. Zoey knew that these were the same woods that held the old house that she had glimpsed from her bedroom during the storm. Her eyes were glued to the woods and then she saw the familiar fence. She rode slowly so that she could examine it closely. It was not long before she came to a gate.

It was an enormous gateway that had to be over sixteen feet tall with a metal arch across the top with iron letters that spelled out words, some of which made no sense to Zoey. At the top in the largest letters was spelled out "Oak Harbor" and below that name were smaller letters that spelled out "Perfide Aurum Liberat." She stopped her bicycle and stared at the scrolled metal letters and could not help but wonder what those strange words meant.

There were two tall wrought iron panels that were chained closed with a large padlock barring entry onto the property and a "No Trespassing" sign was secured to the gate. Zoey got off of her bike and walked up to the gates. She gripped the metal bars and looked up the brush-covered drive that led into the property. She could tell that at one time it had been a cobblestone drive that formed a loop around what was probably a manicured lawn. The cobblestone lane had been shaded by live oaks of which a number remained with Spanish moss hanging from their branches, while others lay rotting on the ground. Several hundred yards into the property she could see the columns that held up the portico that sheltered what had been a magnificent entry way into the house.

The house was made of brick with limestone added as trim work on each comer as well as around the windows and doors. It had three floors, and Zoey could clearly see dormers in the slate roof above the first two floors. On the left side of the house was a porch made of stone that had arches that supported a flat roof. There was a broad staircase of the same stone that descended from the porch into what had been a formal garden, as evidenced by the remains of a large fountain. On the left side of the house was a separate wing that had only a single floor.

While the house was clearly run down and the grounds had obviously been neglected for many years, there was still something beautiful about it. It captivated her, which is why she did not hear that someone had come up behind her.

"Don't think about going in there, it's cursed," said a boy's voice behind her. "If you go in there you may not come back out,"

Zoey quickly turned around to find two boys standing there. The one that had spoken was about her height and had copper red hair and freckles. He was sitting on his bike. A second boy who had black hair and dark eyes stood beside his own bike.

"What did you say?" Zoey asked.

"That place is cursed," he repeated.

"How do you know that?" Zoey asked.

"My dad told me. He said that the house was built on a Tuscarora burial ground. Whoever walks across their sacred ground will be cursed and slowly go mad," the boy explained with conviction.

"What's a Tuscarora?" she asked as she had never heard that word before.

"The Tuscarora were fierce tribe of Indians that lived in these parts back a long time ago. They got tired of white people taking their land so they made war on them. They killed over a hundred people in New Bern," said the red haired boy.

"Is that true?" Zoey asked as she suspiciously looked back over her shoulder at the house.

Then the other boy joined in and said, "Sure enough! That

there is the Durant house and there have been all kinds of evil things that have happened there!"

"Like what?" asked Zoey as she stepped back, closer to the road.

"Been all kinds of people going in there and never coming back out again," said the dark-haired boy.

"Not just disappearances either," added the boy with red-hair. "There have been people killed in there. My daddy said they found a grave behind the house that had four men buried in it. He told me that it looked like they had been hacked up with an ax or something!"

"They also say that back in the slavery days that old Marse Durant would buy up every slave he could but once they went into Oak Harbor they were never seen again!" added his companion with fear in his voice.

"All them there Durant folk were crazy as a loon!" the first boy said.

"And they all died young because of the curse put on them by those Indians," said the dark-haired boy as he sadly shook his head.

Zoey turned back toward the house and shivered at what the two boys had told her.

"We never seen you around here before. Are you one of the folks that moved into Miss Rose's old house?" asked boy with red hair.

She nodded her head.

"I'm Rufus Johnson and this here is Billy Thornton," he said as he pointed to his friend.

"I'm Zoey Morganton. How old are you guys?" Zoey asked as her curiosity changed from the house to her two new acquaintances.

Billy spoke first and said, "I just turned fourteen but Rufus here is only thirteen."

Zoey could see that Billy was trying to impress her with his seniority. Zoey did not want any part of that. At least not right away.

"What's wrong with being thirteen?" Zoey replied as she stared at Billy with defiance.

"Uh, nothing wrong with it," replied Billy as he seemed to get suddenly nervous that he had said the wrong thing.

Zoey could not help but smile to herself as she watched Billy squirm.

"He always does that when he tries to impress a girl. Billy wants to be a ladies' man," said Rufus as he laughed at his friend while Billy turned red with embarrassment.

"Boys!" Zoey said with exacerbation as she rolled her eyes. "How about we show you around?" Rufus asked.

"Okay," Zoey replied as she got on her bike.

The three of them began to pedal their bikes on past the land that contained the old house. Again, Zoey could not help but look at the overgrown landscape that at one time would have been a showplace. She found it sad, as if she were looking at a corpse. Just after they passed the boundary on the other side of the property from her house, she noticed a dirt road that went through the field on that side and she could see an old cemetery in the distance.

Billy noticed her looking up the dirt road, stopped his bike and pointed, "That's the Durant family cemetery. You can find all their graves up there."

"Do you know how many graves there are?" she asked.

"Not that many in their family plot. There another section that has graves for their black servants. They say there are hundreds of other graves for the slaves old Marse Dupree killed but they're not marked. As for the Durants you can go count them off because all the men were named Dupree. The only difference was their numbers," Rufus said quietly.

"What do you mean, their numbers?" Zoey asked not understanding.

"As I said, they had the same name so you had Dupree Durant, Dupree Durant II, Dupree Durant III and on and on. And their wives are buried by their sides. In all there are five Duprees up there," Rufus said as he shook his head.

"You're forgetting about the one non-Dupree, Rufus. You know, that Jonathan Wilson guy that killed himself," Billy said in a hushed tone.

"Was that Miss Rose's husband?" Zoey asked.

Both boys stared at her for a moment before Rufus asked, "How did you know about him?"

"Miss Zipporah told my mom and me about Miss Rose and how she moved out of the big house after they found her husband dead," Zoey explained.

"It's a good thing she moved out of there or she would have died violently like the rest of them," Rufus said as he shook his head. "The story goes that each of the Durants died by suicide, murder, or accident. Like I said, that house was cursed for sure,"

"Is Miss Rose buried up there too?" she asked.

"I don't rightly know. Haven't been up there since she died and the truth is, I don't want to!" said Billy, with Rufus nodding in agreement.

The two boys began to pedal on down the road. Zoey took another look at the old graveyard before she tried to chase them down.

For the next hour Zoey was shown around the area. The boys lived about a mile from her on the other side of the Oak Harbor plantation house as she now thought of it. She met Rufus's parents and they seemed really nice.

They told her to let her mom know that they would come by and introduce themselves soon. Next they went to Billy's house and she was introduced to his two older brothers whom she quickly took a dislike to! They started to pick on Billy as only a couple of bullies would do.

"Have you kissed your new girlfriend yet?" the older one asked as the younger chuckled.

"I'm not his girlfriend!" Zoey said defiantly but quickly regretted saying anything as they began to tease him about how she must find him repulsive like every other girl around. She was glad when they were able to ride away.

Billy led the way but Zoey could tell that he was upset by the entire scene with his brothers.

"That's what he always gets from those two. They're just as mean as two snakes chasing the same mouse," Rufus said once Billy had ridden far enough ahead to be out of hearing.

"At least he has a good friend in you," she replied.

They rode together back to Zoey's house and as they pulled into the drive her mom came out to greet them. "Looks like you've managed meet some of the neighbors," she said with a smile.

"Mama, this is Billy and this is Rufus," Zoey said as she pointed to each of the boys. "They live over on the other side of the woods."

"It's nice to meet you Billy and Rufus! My name is Hannah. Would you like to come in and have some sweet tea?" her mom asked.

"That's very kind of you, ma'am," said Billy.

"Thank you, Miss Hannah, we sure would!" added Rufus.

The three of them moved to the screened porch as Zoey's mom brought out four tall glasses of iced tea on a tray.

"I'm glad that you were able to meet some other kids your own age, Zoey," she said before sipping her tea, then turned to the boys. "I'm guessing the three of you will be in the same grade at school. Maybe you'll have some of your classes together. It will be such comfort to know that Zoey will have at least two familiar faces at school tomorrow."

"The school is not that big so I'm thinking that we will be together some," Rufus said.

They continued to make small talk while they sipped their tea on that pleasant Sunday evening until the boys said that they must get home for supper.

"We'll see you on the bus tomorrow, Zoey," Billy said as they rode away.

CHAPTER 4 • MISS ROSE

The next five days flew by for Zoey and her mom. She was introduced to her new school. At first, she was intimidated by the new environment and trying to figure out where she was supposed to be. Rufus and Billy were a big help to her as they made sure she knew how to get around the school and what the personalities of the various teachers were like. Zoey began to meet new friends by spending as much time as she could with Billy and Rufus.

The school had the normal type of cliques that seemed to always exist. There were the really smart kids, the goof-offs who were always finding trouble, the athletes, and the misfits. Most of the kids never really fit neatly into any one of these groups, so there always seemed to be an ebb and flow through the various social circles. The two boys made sure she got off on the right foot with the good people and that she avoided the bad ones. All of this along with trying to get acclimated to her classwork made time fly by.

Hannah was also trying to get used to her new work environment. She was learning new procedures and processes, being introduced to her co-workers, and most of all meeting her patients. Every night mother and daughter came home, had dinner together, and then got to work on their respective homework. Finally, Friday came and both mother and daughter breathed a deep sigh of relief.

"What do you plan on doing tomorrow?" Hannah asked Zoey as they relaxed on the screened porch, which was quickly becoming their favorite part of the house.

"I'm not sure," Zoey replied. "Rufus and Billy are going fishing but that's not really something I like. Maybe I'll take another bike ride."

"I'm thinking of going to have a look around the downtown area," said her mom. "There looks to be a lot of interesting shops down there and tomorrow is supposed to be a really nice day. Would you like to come along?" she asked. Zoey sensed that she wanted a little mother-daughter time after their busy week.

"That sounds like fun. I can always take a ride on a different day," she replied but regretted that she would have to delay her real agenda, which was to find out more about the house next door.

The next day Zoey was glad that she did go with her mom. There were many small shops with all kinds of unique things. Her mom bought her a new purse to take to school and they shared a piece of delicious fudge from a small shop. Next they visited the farmer's market where they found a large assortment of local produce, meats, cheeses, and baked goods. By two in the afternoon they agreed that they were shopped out!

After they arrived home, Zoey noticed that Moses was working in the backyard. She had not seen him since that first day, so she decided to go out and talk with him. Maybe he would tell her more about the house in the woods.

"Hi there, Mr. Moses!" she said pleasantly.

The old man looked up at her and smiled his warm smile and said, "It's nice to see you again, Miss Zoey! Is there something I can do for you?"

Zoey suddenly felt self-conscious and wondered if the old black man would think she was being nosy. After all, she barely knew Moses but her curiosity gave her the courage to attempt to find out more about Miss Rose and Oak Harbor.

"Miss Zipporah told us you were really close to Miss Rose. She said that both of you cared for her when she became sick," she began and watched as the old black man went back to pulling weeds. Zoey sensed that he did not want her to see the emotion on his face. "That was nice of you to do that. I think you and Zipporah are real good folks."

"We try to do as the Bible says and love our neighbors but we would have cared for Miss Rose no matter what. She was a good woman! She was always kind to everyone, even to those that didn't deserve it," Moses said, looking into Zoey's eyes. "She also loved this land. In some ways it was like she was a part of it and it was a part of her."

"Did she grow up in the house over there in the woods?" Zoey asked. "Yes, ma'am," he said, looking at the house through the trees with the thinning fall foliage.

"You must know a lot about the house there in the woods. I think the name might have been Oak Harbor," Zoey said, almost like a question.

Moses went back to pulling weeds from the flowers and Zoey wondered if he were going to answer her. "Yes, ma'am, that's the name of it," he finally replied. "It's a pure shame how it's become so run down. It was one of the grandest houses in all of North Carolina. My Pa and I use to help take care of it. We were always working on one thing or another. That there house was built in the 1850's. All this land as far as you can see belonged to it as well. It was one of the largest plantations in this part of North Carolina.

Like Miss Rose, my family has always been a part of Oak Harbor." He looked up at Zoey and grinned, adding, "First as slaves but then as employees. The Durant family was always high-class. Always treated my family like they were real people. Most of the black folk never had it as good as we did," he said with emotion choking the final words.

"I heard that the house was cursed because it was built on an old Indian burial ground. I think they were known as the Tuscarora," Zoey said and watched the old man look back up at her with amusement in his eyes.

"I suspect you been talking with that Rufus Johnson and Billy Thornton," he guessed correctly. "Don't get me wrong. They're fine boys as far as boys go but they've been told too many ghost stories sitting by the bonfire while their daddies drank too much 'shine. If you want to know the truth you just come and ask ole Moses."

"Is it true that Miss Rose's husband was murdered?" Zoey asked nervously.

Moses shook his head sadly and then said, "The sheriff said he killed himself. Said he had squandered all of Miss Rose's money and couldn't face what he'd done."

"But you don't believe that?" Zoey asked, more like a statement than a question.

"I was twelve years old when it happened," Moses replied. "Miss Rose found him first but she called Pa right away. I went with him. It was a scary sight to see. Mister Jonathan laying there on the floor with a gun by his hand. There was so much blood everywhere. Miss Rose was wailing in the hallway like a tortured soul in Hades. Never heard a more mournful sound in my life! Pa kept looking at everything like he was seeing the murder actually happening. He turned to me and asked me what side of body the gun was on. I looked and Mr. Jonathan was face down and the gun was on his right side. Pa told me to always remember that and I asked him why. He said that Mr. Jonathan was left-handed." Moses shook his head again. "That poor man was murdered in cold blood and it don't matter what the sheriff had to say about it!"

"Didn't you try to tell the sheriff what you and your pa had seen? I mean that it was murder and not suicide?" Zoey asked as she tried to grasp what had happened all those many years ago.

Moses looked up at the young white girl and sadly shook his head. "I know that times they've changed since I was a boy, so perhaps you don't understand that back then black folk didn't back-talk no white people and for sure not some lawman. All we could do was try to see to Miss Rose."

"She must have been really sad!" Zoey said.

"She could hardly talk. My mama and meme came and cared for her. They helped her to plan Mr. Jonathan's funeral. 'Twas a sad day watching Miss Rose standing alone at the grave, what with her only being twenty-four years old. Mr. Jonathan's family stood off by their own selves like they didn't want nothin' to do with his widow," Moses continued as he looked off at something only he could see.

"It sounds like they really loved each other," Zoey said, feeling the pain from that tragedy of long ago.

"O yes!" said Moses. "I have never seen two people more in love with each other! Oak Harbor had not seen that kind of happiness in many a long year. It seemed like the old house had finally shaken off all those years of heartbreak." In his mind Moses could see the vibrant social life that only two young lovers could experience.

"What do you mean by years of heartbreak?" Zoey asked.

"Well, over the years there has been a right fair number of tragedies in the Durant family and Oak Harbor itself. Take for instance Miss Rose's daddy. He was Dupree Durant the Fifth. He was killed in a car crash back in 1960. From what Pa and Papaw said it was extra sad since he had drowned when his car ran off the bridge just down the road about a mile from Oak Harbor. They said he must have been drinking. Miss Rose was but fourteen years old," the old black man said. "That was when old man Smithers started running Oak Harbor. Lordy, Pa hated dealing with that old grifter but with him being the family lawyer and all there was nothin' else to do. He was named to be guardian of Miss Rose until she reached the age of twenty-five. Smithers was always telling my Pa to do everything on the cheap. It was a sad time for Oak Harbor," he said as he shook his head with sorrow.

"Didn't Miss Rose notice what was going on?" Zoey asked.

"She was just a girl, not much older than you. Besides, she wasn't around much. Old man Smithers done packed her off to a boarding school till she finished high school and then he sent her off to one of them fancy universities. When she was out of school, he had her sent off to foreign countries so she could get cultured," he said. "I think he was trying to keep her away from Oak Harbor so she wouldn't see what he was doing to it."

"He doesn't sound like a very nice man," Zoey said.

"Oh, no, ma'am," Moses agreed. "He liked being in charge and bossing folks around, being all full of himself. Then along comes Mr. Jonathan and the shoe was on the other foot. Mr. Jonathan was a proper gentleman! He met Miss Rose when she was away at that there university. My Mama told me that Miss Rose said it was love at first sight. They decided to get married after she graduated. Old man Smithers threw a true hissy fit right out there in front of the house when Mr. Jonathan told him they were getting married. Pa said that Smithers about had a stroke when Mr. Jonathan told him that he would be taking over the management of Oak Harbor as soon as they were married. Mr. Jonathan was a lawyer too, you see. He told the old scoundrel that when Miss Rose gets married, the husband would be entitled take over as her guardian and as trustee for Oak Harbor." Moses smiled at the memory.

"It seemed like all was going to be made right again," Moses sighed. "They had a big wedding down in the formal garden. Pa and me was busy for weeks making sure everything was just perfect. I do believe that half the county turned out for the ceremony and the big party afterwards. Then they settled into living in the big house. Mr. Jonathan was always in his study going over papers and such. Miss Rose stayed busy keeping the house and gardens up. That was when I first got to really know her. She had a passion for anything that grew," he said with a smile that turned into a frown as he went on. "Then that horrible night came and everything changed."

Moses gazed through the woods at the house that had once been so alive with love and happiness. He sighed with regret before he continued on. "Then really bad news came out about the trust fund that paid to maintain the property. All the money had been lost or, more likely, stolen. There was a big to-do about what had happened. There was all kinds of lawmen, judges, accountants, and lawyers looking at everything and asking questions. In the end they blamed Mr. Jonathan for the money disappearing. They said the only thing that could be done was to file bankruptcy and they sold off most of the farmland to pay the debts. Miss Rose was left with the big house, the family cemetery, five hundred acres of fields on this side of the property, and a little bit of money to support her. That's when Miss Rose built this house to live in," Moses said as he continued the sad story of Miss Rose.

"Did she ever remarry?" Zoey asked.

"No, she said that her Johnathan was the only man she would ever love," he replied.

"So she just lived here and never did anything else?" Zoey asked, thinking about what a lonely life it must have been.

"Oh no! Not Miss Rose!" he exclaimed with a smile. "She was a right busy woman. She was real active in her church and always was volunteering to help kids that were having trouble with their lessons. Later she started a nursery and landscaping business. Miss Rose surely did love her plants, flowers, trees, and such. She did right well at it too. I worked for her at the business and she let me farm the fields here that she owned. She was right fair with me in her dealing. After about twenty years she comes to me and says she wanted to sell me the land outright. I told her that I'm just a poor black man and I don't have no money. She just laughed and said I could pay it by giving her a quarter of whatever I netted each year. That was only a little more than I was paying in royalties each year. I asked her why she would do such a thing and she told me that she wanted to make sure the land stayed in the Oak Harbor family," Moses said as he wiped a tear from his eye.

"Wow, I wish I could have known her," Zoey said with admiration.

Moses looked at her and then smiled and nodded his head. "She would have liked you and your mama. She purely loved young'uns. Now I'd best be getting on home for supper or Zipporah will get ill with me. I sure don't want that to happen and that's for dang sure!" he laughed as he gathered his tools and strolled towards his house.

CHAPTER 5 • LIGHTS IN THE NIGHT

That night Zoey went to bed and she could not help but to think of all that she had heard from Moses about Miss Rose. Rose's life was both inspiring and tragic. She had overcome tragedy and built a new life. She thought about what a change it would be to go from being a rich girl that had everything to a woman who had to create a business to make a living. Zoey realized that Miss Rose had lost more than her lifestyle. She had also lost the two people she loved the most! It must have been terrible with first the tragic death of her father and then her husband's murder.

Zoey was convinced that it was a murder. It made her wonder who might have killed Jonathan Wilson. No doubt the missing money was the reason for the murder. There was also no doubt that the lawyer that ran the estate would be high on anybody's list of suspects. On the other hand, it might not have been him since Mr. Jonathan had been running Oak Harbor for over a year and he surely would have noticed if Smithers had been stealing.

"Maybe not," Zoey said softly to herself, wondering if Smithers might have been able to hide the missing money.

If the money had not been stolen by Smithers or by Rose's husband, then who else might have done it? This was a mystery like those she had read in some of the books that Meema, her grandmother, had given her. She decided right then and there that she was going to solve this mystery!

Zoey got out of bed and found her tablet on the small desk in her room. She connected to the internet and found the site for the local library. She started searching for old news articles about Jonathan Wilson's death. She was amazed at the number of stories that appeared.

The first story was written the day after his death. It said that he had died from an apparent suicide and that the sheriff was investigating. The next article was several days later and had a big headline that read:

"Suicide Victim Gambled Away Fortune!" Under that headline there was a second one that read: "Durant Family Bankrupt."

Zoey read the lengthy article that said that Jonathan Wilson had made some highly questionable investments that had wiped out much of the sizable Durant family trust fund that went back to the 1850's. Out of apparent desperation he placed a large wager on a football game with an organized crime family and lost the remaining money. The reporter wrote that obviously the young man was overcome with guilt and took his own life rather than face his wife. The article said that over $2,000,000 had been squandered away by the young man.

On the same day as that article there was another one that attempted to document the Durant family history, which Zoey read with great interest:

The Durant Family history goes back to 1853 when Dupree Durant purchased a run down plantation in Craven County. Mr. Durant had previously been a captain of a sailing vessel out of Wilmington called the Audacia. No one knows for sure how he came by his great wealth but accounts from those days said he had vast amounts of gold when he first arrived in Craven County. Rumors circulated for decades that Dupree Durant was involved in either smuggling or outright piracy during his sailing career. Public records indicate that Durant spent over $67,000 to acquire the plantation and build the new house that we now know as Oak Harbor. That would be the equivalent of $710,000 of today's dollars.

Beyond his investment in Oak Harbor, it is now known that Durant and his descendants amassed investments of over $2 million until the late Jonathan Wilson lost the fortune by making bad investments and gambling.

This was not the first time the Durant family has been caught up in controversy. In the 1850's Dupree Durant spent much of his time buying slaves to add to his existing plantation but then most of these slaves were reported as dying soon after they arrived at Oak Harbor. Rumors swirled that Durant was a madman and often killed his indentured servants for the smallest infraction of his strict rules.

In 1862 the Union Army occupied the area and Durant voluntarily freed his remaining forty slaves and actively supported the Union forces. There were other rumors that Durant was a Confederate spy who only appeared to support the Union. This controversy continued until his death in 1881. A second controversy erupted after his death when a mass grave was discovered on the grounds of Oak Harbor. At first it was thought that the bodies were some of his unfortunate slaves but it was later determined that the four men were white and that they had all been hacked to death.

Tragedy has also followed the rest of the Durant family over their time here in Craven County. The suicide of Jonathan Wilson is just the latest in controversial deaths over the last hundred years. Dupree Durant II was found dead from a gunshot wound on the road from New Bern back to Oak Harbor in 1905. His murderer was never caught but for years it was rumored that he had been an assassination target of the Klan. In 1925 Dupree Durant III was crushed to death while working on a tractor in his barn. Dupree Durant IV drowned while fishing on the Neuse River in 1944. This happened just after receiving word that his son was missing in action in Europe and had likely been killed in the Battle of the Bulge. A week after his funeral word was received that his son was still alive. In an ironic twist of fate, the son, Dupree Durant V, was also a drowning victim when he drove his car off a bridge in 1960 while he was drunk.

Zoey set her tablet down, overwhelmed by all the information she had discovered. Some of those things confirmed what Rufus and Billy had told her and others validated what Moses had said. So many things had happened to the family that lived in the house in the woods. There were many more mysteries than just what happened to Jonathan Wilson and the missing money. Where did the original Mr. Durant come by his money? Was he a pirate, a smuggler, or something else? What happened to the slaves he bought? Who were the men whose hacked up bodies were found at Oak Harbor? Why did violent death stalk the Durant family? So many mysteries were wrapped one inside of another.

She turned and looked out the window toward the house that was at the center of these mysteries, even though she knew it could not be seen in the pitch-black dark of the night. She was beginning to feel tired and had just turned off her tablet when she saw something, or thought she had seen something, in the woods. She walked to her window and continued to gaze on the black woods that appeared even darker than the night sky on this moonless night. She gasped in surprise when she saw a faint reddish glow through the thinning leaves. Then it was just gone. She continued to watch and a few minutes later she saw the reddish light again. She wondered if she were seeing ghosts moving about the old mansion.

Zoey's curiosity was now fully engaged. Despite her fear, she put on her robe and slippers and quietly moved down the hall. Her heart was racing as she stepped onto the screened porch. Then she saw the dim red-tinged light again. Her heart was pounding like a drum as she silently slipped out the back door and down onto the patio. She stood there and watched for several minutes as the light moved and then disappeared only to reappear a short time later.

Zoey found herself being drawn towards the woods. She hardly noticed her own steps as she focused on the light that was definitely red in nature. She came to the back edge of the yard and the old iron fence was just in front of her. She was much closer now. The red light was coming through a window in the old house. Zoey could see that the light would move from room to room as if it were searching the old house.

Then the outside light from the patio snapped on, illuminating her standing in the yard.

Her mom's concerned voice called, "Zoey, are you out there?"

At the sound of Hannah's shout, the reddish light was extinguished like a switch had been thrown. She could hear her mom's footsteps hurrying across the lawn towards her.

"What are you doing out here in the middle of the night?" her mom asked with concern and just a little anger.

"I thought I saw something going on in the old house in the woods." Zoey replied.

"You shouldn't be wandering around out here in the dark! There might be wild animals that could hurt you! Now you come back in the house right this minute, young lady!" her mom commanded.

They turned and were walking back toward the house when Zoey heard the sound of leaves crunching behind her in the woods.

"Did you hear that?" she asked her mom in a whisper as she stopped.

Her mom turned back towards the woods. Then they heard the sound again and they both felt as if there were something moving towards them in the woods. Her mom gripped her hand in a vise-like way and pulled her back toward the house as quickly as she could. Soon they started to run.

"Hurry, get in the house!" her mom said with fear as she pulled Zoey up the steps to the porch and through the back door.

Hannah slammed the door behind them and quickly turned the deadbolt as she looked into the lit-up patio. A moment later, a large dog sniffing their trail appeared out of the darkness. The dog seemed to study the patio and the door but then became alert to something behind it. The dog bounded off back into the darkness.

Zoey's mom laughed and said with some relief, "I thought we were being chased by a bear or wild hog. Instead, someone's hunting dog trailed us back to the house."

Zoey was at the window continuing to look into the blackness of the yard towards the woods that were once again hidden by the darkness. She was not convinced that the dog was there by coincidence. What if someone had sent that dog after them?

"We need to get to bed," said Hannah. "Tomorrow will be our first day at church and we'll need to be up by seven. I don't want you up and wandering around anymore!" she added as she gently pushed Zoey toward her bedroom.

It was difficult for Zoey to fall asleep after the night's events. She was looking at the window and noticed that the moon was now visible. The skies must have cleared to allow its appearance. It did not seem as dark outside. She felt her gaze drawn again to the woods. She studied the woods for a long time but did not see any lights or dogs so she returned to bed. She lay there trying to sleep but kept feeling that something was not right. She rolled on her side and looked to the window and for just a millisecond she thought she saw the silhouette of a person's head. She sat up in fright and rushed to the window but could see nothing. Fear overwhelmed her and she ran to her mother's room.

"What's wrong, baby?" her mom asked in a sleepy voice as she was awakened by her daughter's presence.

"I'm scared. Can I sleep with you?" Zoey asked as her heart continued to beat hard.

"Why are you scared?" her mom asked as she pulled back the covers and patted the bed signaling Zoey to join her.

"I thought I saw someone looking in my window," Zoey said as her mom pulled the covers over her.

Then Hannah got out of bed and said, "Let me take a look."

She heard her mother moving around the house before coming back in the bedroom and slipping back into the bed saying, "I looked out of all the windows and didn't see anyone. It must have been a bad dream. That doesn't surprise me after all the excitement tonight! Just snuggle up close and go to sleep."

Zoey lay there with her mom and felt a sense of safety replace the fear that had coursed through her body when she had seen that shadow through her window. Sleep finally over took her and the next thing she knew, Hannah was telling her it was time to get up.

Zoey wondered about all that had happened the night before. The ghostly light, the dog, and most of all the face she thought she had seen at her window. She knew that the first two were very real but perhaps the last was just a figment of her imagination. She decided she would go out and see if there were any evidence that would prove that someone had been looking into her room. She hurried to get dressed for church and then rushed out the back door while her mom was getting ready in the bathroom.

She walked along the back of the house until she came to her bedroom window. She looked at the ground and she saw one of the flowers below her window was crushed into the mulch as if it had been stepped on. She felt the hairs on the back of her head stand up with fear.

"Great, one more mystery to be solved. Who is snooping around Oak Harbor? And our house?" she asked herself, quickly heading back inside.

CHAPTER 6 • INTRUDER

Much to Zoey's delight the first person she saw at church was Rufus Johnson. It was nice to see a familiar face. Rufus's parents came over and introduced themselves to her mom.

"We're so happy to meet you, Hannah! I'm Vivian and this is my husband Butch," Rufus's mother said.

"It's nice to meet you, both. I can't tell how much Zoey appreciates having Rufus for friend!" Hannah replied.

"We do hope that you and Zoey will stay for the pitch-in after service today," Butch said as he shook Hannah's hand.

Zoey enjoyed the service and really liked the mixture of old hymns and new praise songs. The sermon was good as well but her mind kept wandering back to the events of the night before. She was convinced that someone had been snooping around Oak Harbor. They had to know that they had been spotted when they saw her near the fence after her mom had turned on the light. Zoey suspected that they must have sent the dog to track them to make sure they were actually from the house. She decided to confide in Rufus as to what she had seen.

The congregation gathered in the community hall to eat together and socialize. Zoey and her mom were the center of attention as people stopped by to introduce themselves and welcome them to the community. She didn't think she would ever get to talk with Rufus about what had happened the night before but then the blessing was given and people began to converse with the others at their table. Zoey managed to sit down next to Rufus. At first they sampled all the various foods but then Zoey finally had an opportunity to speak to him.

"Something strange happened last night at Oak Harbor," she said almost in a whisper.

"I told you that place is cursed. There are strange things going on there all the time," he replied but she noted that he also kept his voice low.

"I saw a light in the house. It was not a normal light because it was red. It seemed to move from window to window. Then when my mom turned on the patio light it went out in the blink of an eye!" she told him.

"Maybe it was a ghost. Been a passel of bad things that have happened in that house," he said with a hint of fear.

"I don't think so," Zoey replied. "Whoever was there seemed to be searching for something. I just don't understand why they would be using a red flashlight."

"The only red flashlights I ever seen was for people that fish or hunt at night. My daddy told me that it helps them to see in the dark," Rufus offered.

"That doesn't make sense. If you're using a flashlight you don't have to see in the dark," Zoey replied with a confused look on her face.

"Think about what happens when you turn off your light in the bedroom late at night. When you first turn off the light it is hard to see anything but then after a while your eyes adjust and you can see better. The red colored light keeps your eyes adjusted to the dark but lets you look at things like maps and such," Rufus explained. "Also, the red light is harder to be seen by others so it helps to keep you hidden."

Zoey thought about it some more and then asked, "You said that hunters use these red lights?"

"I suppose some of the coon hunters do," he replied.

"Do they use dogs to hunt raccoons?" she asked as she thought of the dog from the night before.

"Yeah, they turn the dog loose and then wait for him to chase a coon up a tree"

"We saw a dog last night right after we saw the red light," Zoey said more to herself than to Rufus.

"Must have been a coon hunter," said Rufus. "The hunter must have followed his dog into that old run down house. He was probably trying to stay out of sight since he was trespassing. If ole Moses saw him moving around Oak Harbor, he would have set the law on him. Ole Moses don't cotton to strangers nosing around that old house."

"Does Moses own the house?" she asked with surprise.

"No, he's just the caretaker. At least he is until some judge determines who will own it," he said casually.

"Why is that?" she asked.

"It was big news after Miss Rose passed away. They couldn't find her will. My daddy said that if a person doesn't have a proper will when they die, the judge has to decide who will get their property. Right now, Mr. Jonathan's kinfolk want it and Nathaniel Smithers says he should take control because it's in the Durant trust," Rufus explained.

"Did you say Nathaniel Smithers? Moses mentioned a lawyer from way back by the name of Smithers but that was over fifty years ago. It can't possibly be the same person!" she said with disbelief.

"From the pictures in the paper of Smithers he looked to be about sixty years old but he didn't look old enough to have been involved that far back. Maybe he's that other guy's son or something," Rufus said as he thought about it.

"Why do you suppose they're making such a fuss about that old run down house and overgrown woods?" Zoey asked herself but did it out loud.

"May I answer that?" said a deep male voice behind her.

Zoey looked over her shoulder and saw Pastor Blain looking at her. "I couldn't help but hear part of your conversation. Miss Rose was a member of this church her entire life. She was a dear woman," the pastor said with smile at her memory. "The reason they both want that house has to do with the treasure."

"Treasure? What treasure?" Zoey and Rufus asked at the same time.

"There's a very old tale that the original Mister Durant had been a pirate or smuggler in the early 1800's. Legend has it that he hid most of his ill gotten gold up there when he was building Oak Harbor. Ever since Miss Rose moved out, there have been a number of people caught trespassing looking for the gold," he explained but then shook his head. "I don't understand why people believe that old tale. If there had ever been a treasure up there, Miss Rose would have surely known about it."

Just then a person across the room waived for Pastor Blain to come over, so he left the two youngsters by themselves.

"I'll bet that treasure story is nothing but a big fat lie," Rufus said with a dismissive tone.

"Actually, I read a story from back when Jonathan Wilson was killed that said something about the first Dupree Durant being rich when he got here. It also said he had been a captain of a ship out of Wilmington and that he might have been a pirate or smuggler. They said it was where all the Durant family money had come from," Zoey replied as she remembered the article about the history of the Durant family.

"Are you ready to go home, Sunshine?" asked the voice of Zoey's mother. "I'll talk with you later, Rufus," Zoey said, getting up to leave.

On the car ride home Hannah talked about the church and how friendly the people seemed to be there. Zoey, on the other hand, was thinking of all the mysteries that surrounded the old house called Oak Harbor. Just today two more mysteries had been discovered. What happened to Miss Rose's will and was there a hidden pirate treasure on the property? These were added to the questions of who murdered Jonathan Wilson, what happened to the money that disappeared back in 1969, what happened to the missing slaves, who were the men found hacked up in the grave, and why did all the Durant men at Oak Harbor die under such tragic circumstances?

At least one mystery seemed to be answered and that was a reasonable explanation for the dog and the red lights the previous night. It made sense that there might have been a hunter looking for a lost dog on property that he should not have been on. Then she thought about the flower that had been stepped on under her bedroom window. Why would a hunter be looking into her room if he were searching for a lost dog?

"Maybe the mystery from last night is not quite solved," she thought to herself. She decided that she needed to tell Moses about what had happened.

A short time later they arrived at home and quickly changed out of their church clothes.

"Would it be all right if I go out on my bike?" she asked her mother.

"That'll be fine. I need some time to get caught up on my patient charting," Hannah replied as she logged onto her laptop.

Zoey knew what she was going to do—go see Moses! In just a few minutes she was riding up the driveway across the road where she could see Moses and Zipporah sitting on their front porch drinking sweet tea.

"Well, look there, it's Miss Zoey!" Moses said pleasantly as he tapped his wife on the arm to get her attention.

"Good afternoon, Mr. Moses and Miss Zipporah!" Zoey replied as she got off the bike.

"It's a right nice day for riding a bicycle. If I was thirty years younger, I might just join you. Come on up here on the porch and visit for a while," Moses said with a big smile.

"Can I get you a glass of tea, child?" Zipporah asked.

"Why thank you, Miss Zipporah. That would be very kind of you," Zoey replied as she sat down in a comfortable chair.

Zipporah slipped into the house while Moses looked at the girl with a gentle smile. Zoey was trying to figure out a way to start asking questions but feared that he might become annoyed by her asking more questions as soon as she arrived. Still, she could not help but think of all the mysteries that were begging to be answered.

"You look like you have a problem, child," Moses said in his deep baritone voice, sensing correctly that something was on the young girl's mind.

"I don't want to be a pest," Zoey began as she heard the screen door open with Zipporah returning with the glass of iced tea.

"Shush child, what trouble could you be?" Zipporah said as she handed the glass to her.

"Well," she started and then hesitated but then quickly added, "I have more questions about the old house."

"You have enough curiosity over that there house to kill a whole heard of cats," Moses said with a chuckle.

"Yes, sir," Zoey replied and then related the events of the previous night.

Moses's amusement slowly changed to serious concern. Zipporah just sat there with her mouth open, shocked that someone had been peeking into a young girl's bedroom.

"Do you think Rufus was right about it being a hunter looking for a lost dog that was flashing the light around the house?" Zoey asked after relating the story.

Moses sat back and pondered her question and then said, "It most likely was but I think I'd better go have a look around."

"Can I go with you? I would love to see the place up close," Zoey asked with a pleading voice.

Moses thought about her request for a few seconds but then said, "I don't see why not. Keep in mind that the house has not been taken care of since 1969, so you mind where you're walking."

Zoey was excited as she set her iced tea down and followed Moses off the porch, walking towards the road. After a few minutes they came to the big gate. Moses reached into his pocket and pulled out a key ring. He looked at the keys and then grunted happily when he found the right one. He opened the lock on the chain that held the gates closed, then pushed on the metal gate. It slowly opened with a loud groan as the rusty hinges complained about being moved after so little use over the years. Zoey stepped onto the actual grounds of Oak Harbor for the first time. She felt a thrill to actually visit the source of so much mystery!

"'Twas a grand old place back in its day," Moses said sadly as they followed the old cobblestone drive toward the main entrance.

Zoey noticed statues placed along the drive that now were so covered with vines that from a distance they looked like bushes. As they got closer to the front of the house, she could see that the front porch had a roof that looked like an ancient Roman temple that was supported by six enormous columns. She could see many closed windows looking out of the building like the eyes of a shark, alive but without any emotion. They arrived at the limestone steps that led to the once opulent front door. There were six steps up to the porch. When they reached the top step, it felt as if the temperature dropped several degrees. Zoey felt a chill and wondered if the house were truly haunted.

"Don't let the house scare you. The house is not evil and the only evil that has ever been here was carried in by outsiders," Moses said quietly as he again searched his keys for the right one to the door.

The lock clicked as the key turned the tumbler and the bolt slid back. The door's hinges creaked as the left door of the double doors opened. When Zoey stepped into the dark foyer she was greeted by the musty smell of a closed-up space. There was a grand staircase that went up halfway to the second floor before splitting to the left and the right, taking a person on to one or the other of the two separate wings of the old mansion.

"We'll go back and check out the kitchen first. There's a back door there and I want to see if it's still locked," Moses said as he moved toward the room to the right.

The room was a reception hall. There was a large mirror on the back wall and a few chairs and tables along the opposite side of the room. Moses walked to the far side of the room where he opened two large pocket doors that moaned as they parted enough to allow Moses and Zoey to enter the next room.

That room was large with an enormous chandelier hanging over a long dining table with twelve chairs around it. The once magnificent formal dining room was covered with dust and cobwebs. Zoey could tell that the room had once been a grand space for dinner parties. She could almost see the ladies in their fancy gowns and the men in their tuxedos bowing and curtsying. There was a gigantic fireplace at the far end of the room with the portrait of a man who must have been around forty years old dressed in an off-white suit with a black bow tie hanging above the mantle. He had piercing blue eyes and his hair was gray at the temples. He exemplified an antebellum southern gentleman.

"Who was that?" she asked as she was entranced by the man's blue eyes.

"That was the first Dupree Durant. He's the one that built Oak Harbor. Come this way," Moses said and his voice broke the spell that held Zoey's gaze upon the portrait.

She turned to Moses and saw him at a door by the fireplace. This door was one of those that could open in either direction by swinging on its hinges.

When they stepped through that door, they entered what appeared to be a hallway but with shelves and cupboards on both sides all the way to the sixteen-foot-high ceiling.

Moses saw that the girl was trying to figure out what this room had been used for. "This here was the butler's pantry," he said, anticipating the question. "They used to keep all the dishes, cups, glasses, and silverware in here. The kitchen staff would prepare the plates and set them on these counters. Then the servers would take them into the dining room when it was time for that course to be served."

He turned and continued into the kitchen with Zoey following behind trying to take everything into her mind, which by this time was spinning with sensory overload. As Moses entered the kitchen he came to a sudden stop. Zoey bumped into his back before she realized that he had stopped.

"Someone has been here," he said as his eyes grew wide.

She tried to determine what he had seen that had made him stop so suddenly but did not see anything that seemed out of place.

"Why do you say that?" she asked in a hushed tone.

Moses pointed to the kitchen floor where she saw fresh footprints on top of the years of accumulated dust. She looked behind her and could see similar steps of their own where they had just been but otherwise there was no other disturbance in the years of dust and cobwebs.

Moses cautiously stepped into the kitchen and continued

to carefully evaluate their surroundings. He walked until he reached the far wall. He followed the trail of footprints into a mudroom. Zoey noted that there were three doors. Two were solid wood doors but the other had once had glass in the upper half of the door, now broken with shattered glass lying on the floor.

"This is where they broke in. We have a real problem here," Moses said quietly as if the intruders might hear him. Zoey looked at first one door and then the other as if she expected the intruder to appear at any second.

CHAPTER 7 • DISCOVERIES IN THE HOUSE

Moses studied the floor of the mudroom and even Zoey could tell that the intruder had moved back and forth many times in the room. It was impossible to tell in which direction they had gone first.

Moses pointed to the door on the right and said, "That door goes down into the cellar and the other goes to the family dining room. I think we should go to the dining room first."

Zoey followed him into a much more intimate room where there was a small round table with comfortable wooden chairs. The room had a much smaller fireplace. A built-in hutch stood directly across from the door they had entered. Her first impression was that it was a space where a family could gather informally.

Moses pointed to the footprints that went across the room to yet another door. She followed along behind him, hoping they would find evidence of who had entered the house. They opened the door to find a staircase going to the second floor and a hallway that continued in the direction of the opposite side of the house. Both had been clearly used by someone recently. Moses chose to go up the stairs.

Zoey listened as each step made the stairs groan and creak. The stairs were so seldom used that Moses had to constantly sweep the cobwebs aside and even walking behind him Zoey felt the webs of countless generations of spiders clinging to her face and arms. When they arrived at the top landing, they again could see many footprints up and down the hall. Often, they could see at each doorway that the intruder had entered the room.

"Somebody's been doing a lot of snooping," Moses said quietly.

"Do you think they've been looking for the treasure?" she asked.

Moses looked at the girl and then asked, "Just how did you hear about the Oak Harbor treasure?"

"I was looking at some newspaper stories back when Mr. Jonathan was murdered," she replied. "There was an article that gave the history of the first Dupree Durant. It said there was a legend that he had been a pirate or a smuggler and that he had a large amount of gold when he built Oak Harbor. I was also told by Pastor Blain that some people still believe that there's gold hidden here."

"That old yarn has done brought nothin' but trouble!" the black man said with disgust. "Some people are too damned foolish for their own good. Back when I helped Pa at this here house after Mr. Jonathan died, we had to chase off people carrying shovels all the time. The only good thing Smithers ever did was to call the sheriff to have a few of them trespassers arrested. It kind of discouraged the worst of them from intruding again."

They walked down the hall that was probably over the dining areas on the first floor. Again there was constant creaking and groaning of the old wood floor as they walked around. Moses opened the first door that they came to and the room was nearly empty of furniture. Then he groaned and shook his head as he pointed at one of the walls that had dozens of holes knocked into the old plaster and lath.

"Now look at that wall! Why would someone just tear it up like that? I know that this place is run down but this is just vandalism for the sake of being mean," he said as he shook his head.

"I bet they were looking for the treasure," Zoey said.

"I guess that I'm going to have to call the sheriff and Nathaniel Smithers," Mosses sighed, clearly not looking forward to that task.

They continued their investigation of the second floor. Each room had varying degrees of damage to it, almost as if it had been randomly done.

Zoey did wonder why there were so many rooms, so she asked Moses, "Why are there so many bedrooms?"

"Most of these here rooms were bedrooms for overnight guests. Down at the other end is where the family quarters are. I surely hope the scallywags that did this haven't destroyed them," he said as he strode purposely toward the other end of the hall.

Near the end of the hall he opened a door to a room that looked over the front lawn. This room was twice as big as the ones down the hall. Again, the room was nearly devoid of furnishings or personal items. This room did have a large walk-in closet and a full bathroom. Zoey looked into the bath and saw what at one time had been a magnificent claw-foot tub that was larger than any she had ever seen before. Again, the impression of the tub was diminished by the years of neglect. All of the plumbing fixtures that were once polished brass were tarnished green and pitted.

"This here was Miss Rose's room when she was growing up. She took most of the furniture from this room with her since it fit in the house you live in now," Moses said quietly as if he was in a visiting room at a funeral parlor and looking on a dearly departed friend lying in state.

"It doesn't look like they got in here yet," Zoey said as studied the room. "True enough," he said with relief as they returned to the main hall.

Zoey followed on his heels as he entered the bedroom at the end of the hall. The room was truly enormous. It took up the entire width of the house on the end opposite the kitchen area. Zoey looked out the window and could see that the roof of the stone porch was just below. She looked off in the distance and could just make out the family cemetery. She was getting a much better view of its layout and noticed that in addition to some headstones there was a mausoleum.

This room had a colossal old bed that had been hand-carved out of wood. It had massive posts on each corner that went up over eight feet into the air. Zoey could see the old ivory bed-curtain rings hanging on what had been a canopy. Beside the bed was a sitting area by a fireplace with two old wing back chairs and a card table between them. The "en-suite" bath was a wonder to see even in its dilapidated state. Included in the bathroom was the largest closet Zoey had ever seen. Moses explained that the room was actually a dressing room where the master and lady of the house would dress for the activities of the day.

"I wonder why our unwelcome guest hasn't bothered with this room. If I were looking for a treasure I would have started where the owners kept their private things," Zoey said as the mystery of the undisturbed master bedroom gnawed on her curiosity.

"I don't rightly know, child," He replied as he rubbed his chin.

Zoey noticed a third doorway on the opposite side of the door that they had used to enter the bedroom from the hallway.

"What was this room?" she asked as she turned the doorknob to enter.

"That there was the nursery," he said with great sadness. "Miss Rose was getting it ready because she wanted to have a baby right away. That was just before her husband was murdered!"

Zoey stepped into the room and saw the empty crib covered

with dust and cobwebs. There were still the remains of newborn-size clothes on the shelves. There was an old rocking-chair by the window that looked over the front lawn.

"What a sad room," Zoey said softly.

"Yes, ma'am. It was like the promise of a life full of joy was snuffed out in an instant on that sad night."

They left the nursery and closed the door as quietly as they could. They walked back past the grand staircase until they came to the back stairway they had come up. Moses opened a door across the landing to reveal another stairway that went up to the third floor. There was no sign of recent use on this one.

"What's up there?' she asked.

"In the old days that was the servants' quarters," Moses replied. "Nobody's been up there for a while."

They turned and descended the stairs back to the landing at the bottom. Instead of going back into the family dining room they turned down the hall. It appeared to Zoey that the tracks in the dust indicated that it had not been visited as much as the other places they had been. She could see that there was a door going out onto the stone porch on the side of the house.

The trail did not go to the porch but to a double pocket doors that were closed.

"This is the study that Mr. Wilson was found in," Moses said he opened the doors that again moaned with unused rollers hidden inside the walls.

Zoey wondered if she would be able to still make out the bloodstains from that long-ago tragedy as she stepped into the room. To her relief as well as her disappointment, all signs of the murder had been cleaned up over fifty years before. The room was filled with empty bookshelves built into the walls and a large desk in front of them. The only other thing in the room was a pedestal that held what had been a set of scales. Zoey could see one of the bowls from the scale lying on the floor but there was no sign of the other. For some reason the device fascinated her.

She walked over and could see that there was a tarnished plaque below the scale. She had to rub some of the tarnish off the plaque to see what it said.

Then some strange words could be seen: "Perfide Aurum Liberat." For some reason those strange words seemed to be familiar. Her brow furled as she tried to remember where she had seen them before. Then it came to her. Those same words were on the gate under the name Oak Harbor.

"Moses, do you know what these words mean?" she asked.

He came over and looked at the tarnished plaque and shook his head that he did not. "I know that I have seen them around Oak Harbor. They're on the gate out front and they're carved into the vault that the first Mr. Dupree is in over yonder in the cemetery."

At just that moment there was a noise back in the direction of the kitchen.

"You stay here, Miss Zoey. If I don't come back in a few minutes, you get out the side door and go fetch Zipporah," Moses said as he moved toward the sound.

She was watching the way that he had gone when she put her fingers on the balance arm of the scale. She was not paying any attention to what her hands were doing when there was a soft click as if a door lock was being opened. She looked around trying figure out what she had heard. She took her hand back off the scale and the click happened again. She slowly pressed down on scale arm and when she was down about three quarters of the way the click happened and this time she could tell that it came from the bookshelf next to the scale. She reached out with her hand and the shelf moved sideways.

Zoey was stunned. She had discovered a hidden door! She walked over and opened it the rest of the way. Inside was a dark room about the size of a small closet. She took a deep breath and

59

stepped into the darkness. As her eyes adjusted, she noticed the room also had a shelf and there were books on it. She reached for the first book and walked back into the study. She looked at a title pressed into the leather binder that said "Personal Journal." She opened the cover and gazed at the first page, which said "Dupree Durant" in neat cursive writing. It was then that she heard Moses returning and what sounded like someone struggling to get away from him.

Zoey put the journal back on the shelf and closed the secret room. She worked the scale arm until she heard the click of the locking mechanism. She had just finished in time to turn and see Moses with a hand over Rufus's mouth dragging him into the room.

"I think I found our unwelcome guest," he said with a surly tone. "I caught him sneaking in the back door and headed down to the cellar.

"What are you doing here?" she asked.

"I came to see if I could prove that the person you saw last night was a hunter looking for his dog," he answered as his eyes glowed with anger as he looked up at Moses.

"Now why would you do that?" Moses asked with suspicion that he was being told a lie.

Zoey could not help but wonder the same thing. She knew that Rufus was terrified of Oak Harbor.

It was then that both Zoey and Moses watched as the boy looked down at his feet before he said, "I was worried about you!" then he turned red as he continued to avoid their eyes.

It was then that Moses began to laugh with deep rolling laugh that grew until Zoey started laughing as well but she had no idea why she was laughing.

Moses finally managed to stop his laughter and with a slight chuckle he said, "Well I'll be! This young feller is sweet on you, girl!"

Now it was Zoey's turn to change skin color as her blush colored her face from her neck to her hairline. Moses howled with laughter again.

"Just you young'uns wait a couple of years and see how you feel about being sweet on someone," he said as he wiped the tears of laughter from his face.

"I found something that I think you both should see," Rufus said hoping to change the conversation.

"What is it?" Zoey asked, hoping to move past the awkward situation as well.

"I'll have to show you," he replied. "All right, lead the way," Moses said.

Rufus led them out the back door and into what had been a garden of some type with a couple of old buildings on the verge of falling down. He cut between the two buildings. At first it looked as if there were nothing but impenetrable brambles in front of them but Rufus lifted up a low hanging tree branch to reveal a narrow path.

"I thought this was a game trail at first but look at this," he said as he knelt down and pointed to a soft patch of ground that had a boot print, "I picked these tracks up over yonder by the gate going to the cemetery. That's where I got in."

Rufus then continued to follow the path until he came to a split. Again, he squatted down and pointed at the tracks. The boot print was there but there were also paw prints of a good-sized dog.

"I think this is the guy with the dog that came to your place last night," Rufus said and then pointed to the left split. "That takes you back toward the cemetery but I need to show you where the trail on the right goes."

He started down the trail with Zoey and Moses following and it took a few minutes to work their way through the woods. Suddenly he stopped and again lifted some low growing branches up to reveal the fence in front of them. On the other side was Zoey's back yard.

"This guy has been watching you. Look over here," he said as he pointed to a hunter's blind.

On the inside of the blind there were a lot of boot and paw prints.

"Whoever it is they've spent a fair amount of time watching your house," the boy said.

Moses studied the prints and then pointed to one. "This one here is different from the others. You see this here cut mark in the sole? This one over here doesn't have it. The boots are two different sizes as well," he rubbed his chin and looked around the blind again and said, "We got at least two people prowling around here at night."

"I think one of them is the lookout while the other is up at the house searching for the treasure." Rufus said and Moses nodded his agreement.

"Let me show you something else," the boy said.

Rufus then pushed through the tree branches in front of him to the fence by one of the vine-covered brick posts. He pulled back and suddenly there was an opening that could be walked through. When he released the iron fence it snapped back in place. Moses walked up and looked at the fence and then frowned.

"It's been cut!" he said and was clearly concerned.

"There's another cut section of fence over by the little gate going to the cemetery," Rufus said. "Whoever's been doing this has been here a lot!"

"I guess I'd better call the sheriff," Moses said as he stood up. "And Mr. Smithers."

"I have another idea," said Rufus. "My dad has some trail

cameras. If we set a couple of them up around here, maybe we could see who they are."

Moses smiled and nodded his agreement to the plan.

"You go get your cameras and make sure your daddy doesn't mind them being used," the old black man said.

"Zoey, we'd best go lock up the front gate," said Moses. "Then you and I'd better go have talk with your mama," he said.

"We can't do that!" Zoey said with a panic.

"We have to tell her," he said as he looked her in the eyes. "You might be in danger."

"She'll call the sheriff and if she does that the bad guys will just disappear until no one is paying attention. We have to give time for Rufus's plan to work," she pleaded. "Please! I promise to stay in the house with the doors locked and the curtains closed."

Moses started to shake his head but then Rufus said, "I don't think they're interested in Zoey or her mom. They're only keeping watch over here because it's the only house that might see them sneaking around at night. I think what happened last night was that when Zoey came out here to investigate and her mom turned on the lights, the lookout was caught sleeping. He probably panicked and let the dog go to figure out who had caught them snooping around."

Moses thought about it some more and then nodded his agreement and said, "We'll try it for a while but when I say its time, I'll call the law and let them handle it."

CHAPTER 8 • CAMERAS & BOOKS

Zoey was thrilled that they were going to trap the bad people who had been trying to find the treasure. She was absolutely certain that this was about the treasure. Just the thought of a trove of real pirate gold fueled her imagination with pictures of sailing ships flying the Jolly Roger with their cannons blazing. It reminded her of one of the old movies that her Pap would watch when she stayed with her Meema.

Zoey was glad that she had talked Moses out of telling her mother about the person who had been watching them from the woods. She had been terribly frightened last night and no doubt her mother had been, too. Today she had gotten to see what the intruders had been up to at Oak Harbor. They had been systematically searching the house. All of the rooms that had been disturbed were either at the back of the house or on the side toward where she lived. Until recently their presence could not have been easily observed since no one had lived in Miss Rose's house. They had obviously stayed away from the front rooms and the side with the stone porch since either could be seen from the road or by Moses from across it. They must have become alarmed when she and her mother moved in next door just as the trees and undergrowth were shedding their foliage. That had to be when they decided to start watching her house. When she had gone outside to investigate their lights, they must have panicked. She felt certain that Rufus was correct about the lookout being caught off-guard last night.

The question that she now struggled with was why did the

lookout send the dog? Rufus thought he had done it to track her mother and herself to make sure they were from the house. The more Zoey thought about it, the more she did not think that was the case. Whoever was watching from the woods would have been able to see her and her mother in the light from the patio.

"He didn't need that dog to track us. He could have just stayed hidden and let the lights be a mystery," Zoey thought to herself.

It then occurred to her that perhaps the lookout was trying to frighten them. Maybe even make them move out. Perhaps he had even wanted to be seen looking into her bedroom to scare her. As much as it terrified her to think of it, she knew intuitively that last night was the intruders' best opportunity to murder her mother and herself if that were what they intended to do. If they harmed her mom and herself the law would be crawling all over the area, including Oak Harbor. More than ever, she was convinced the camera trap was the best way to catch the intruders before they became truly desperate.

If the intruders were not stopped, they would continue to tear apart the old plantation home and if they did that, they would eventually discover the hidden space with the books in it. That book that she had briefly held in her hand was very old. She remembered seeing the name Dupree Durant written in flowing cursive script like she had seen on a wedding invitation her mother had once received. She desperately wanted to get back into that secret room to get a look at those books. Perhaps it would be even better if she took the books out of the house before the intruders could find them.

Maybe they had the answers to some of the mysteries that surrounded Oak Harbor. Perhaps they would even tell her where the treasure was hidden!

Zoey returned to Moses' house so that she could get her bicycle. She then sped off to accompany Rufus back to his place to get the trail cameras.

Moses decided he'd better check out the intruders' trail to see if he could learn anything else while he awaited the two teens to return.

She met up with Rufus at the road that went up to the Durant family cemetery. She knew that she needed to go see it for herself. She remembered Moses' saying that the inscription of "Perfide Aurum Liberat" was on the first Dupree Durant's tomb.

"I must find out what those words mean! It has to be a clue," she thought to herself as she pulled her bike up next to Rufus.

"You're sure that your dad won't mind you using the cameras?" she asked as she waited for him to get on his bike.

"I think so," he said sounding less positive than he had in the woods a little while earlier.

They rode off together side by side. Her mind drifted to the teasing that Moses had given Rufus back at the house. She liked him as a friend but to suddenly be confronted by his really liking her as a girl was terrifying. She was not sure that she was ready for that part of her life to begin. All of the changes her body had been going through were challenging enough. On the other hand, there was something different about Rufus. Billy Thornton had also attempted to get her attention that first day but she had quickly stopped his thinking of her like that, or she hoped that he had. Why did she not shut Rufus down like she had Billy?

"Is this what being a teenage girl is going to be like from now on?" she wondered as she pedaled on toward the Johnson house.

They rode their bikes past the house that Rufus's family lived in to a building located behind it. She could see a pickup truck parked under a metal carport next to it. The door to the building was open. Mr. Johnson stepped outside as they were getting off their bikes.

"There you are!" Mr. Johnson said as he looked at Rufus and then at her. "Your mama's been wondering where you got off to!" he said with a slight rebuke in his voice but then smiled at Zoey and said, "It's nice to see you again, Miss Zoey. I do hope that Rufus here has been staying out of trouble!" The last part was a slight tease of his adolescent son but also a gentle probe to find out what they had been up to.

"We've been trying to figure out if that dog they saw last night was just a lost hunting dog or was somebody snooping on them," Rufus said nervously.

"I heard about that at church earlier," recalled Mr. Johnson. "I'd have to admit that someone snooping around like that would make me nervous, too."

"We did some stomping around in the woods over there at Oak Harbor...," Rufus started to say but his father held up his hand to stop him right there.

"You know ole Moses Jones don't allow anyone on that property, so you'd best stay off of it before I have to come get you back from the sheriff," he said. "You and I would be spending some time back here in woodshed teaching you some manners if that happens!"

"It's not like that all, Mr. Johnson," Zoey intervened. "Mr. Moses was with us when we were there. He's just as concerned as the rest of us," she said, trying to defend Rufus from his dad's wrath.

Mr. Johnson looked at her and back to his son and sort of a grunted. "I suppose that makes it all right but you make sure ole Moses is okay with you being on that property if you go on it again, okay?"

"Yes, sir!" Rufus said.

"Did you find anything when y'all looked around the woods over there?" Mr. Johnson asked with more than a little curiosity.

Rufus seemed to hesitate and Zoey was concerned that he was losing his nerve to ask for the use of the cameras so she jumped in. "Yes, sir, we did. That's why we came to talk with you," she said.

Zoey's speaking up gave Rufus renewed confidence in talking with his father, so he added, "We're pretty sure that there's been someone doing some poking around in the woods where they shouldn't be."

Zoey wanted to keep from getting Rufus's father overly concerned, so she stepped back into the conversation. "I think my mom is much more concerned about what happened than she's let on. She doesn't want to make a bad impression on the neighbors by calling the law over nothing. What if some innocent hunter that was just looking for a lost dog should get arrested?"

"That's right," Rufus continued. "You know Moses doesn't want to be dragged into that fight going on over Oak Harbor. That's why I suggested that we put up a couple trail cameras to see if someone is poking around at night. If we knew who they were for sure, then Moses could put the law on them."

"Exactly," Zoey affirmed. "We're hoping that you would let us use a couple of your trail cameras. If we don't see anybody on them, that would tell us that it was just an innocent hunter looking for his dog. If we do see someone, we would know who to put the sheriff on."

Rufus's father looked thoughtful for moment and then asked, "Moses is okay with this?"

They both answered right away, "Yes, sir!"

"I suppose it would be all right," he said and then looked at Rufus. "You know where they are, so go get 'em, boy."

Rufus was off like a shot. Zoey couldn't help but notice the grin on Mr. Johnson's face.

"Mr. Johnson?" she asked. "Yes, ma'am," he replied.

"My mom would rather not have any of this being talked about, so I was wondering if we could keep this just between us for the time being?" she asked. carefully studying the man's face.

He looked at her again, shook his head, and said, "Women-folk have always amazed me with their wanting to protect their image. I suppose your mama does have a good reason, being new and all. The good Lord knows that all the other women love to talk about each other. It's like they got nothing better to do!" He nodded. "Okay, just between us but if you have even a hint of trouble over there you call 911 right away, then Moses and myself. We can probably be there quicker than the law."

"Thank you, sir!" she said gratefully as Rufus came back out with a canvas bag with the cameras in it.

"Did you check them there batteries like I showed you?" his father asked him.

"Yes, sir. They're all fresh and ready to go," Rufus replied.

Mr. Johnson pulled a note pad out of his pocket and quickly wrote his number on it and handed it to Zoey.

"You tell your mama to call me if she needs someone to come and look around," he said seriously. "Tell her it would be no trouble at all because that's what us neighbors do for each other."

Zoey and Rufus got on their bikes and started towards Oak Harbor. When they approached the gravel road to the cemetery, Zoey followed Rufus up the lane. She was looking at the graveyard as second by second they drew closer to it. She could see a fence similar to the one around the plantation and inside were a number of large tombstones marking off various graves that held the Durant men and their wives. That was as she had expected it to be but what dominated the scene was a massive mausoleum that, if anything, reminded her of a Roman or Greek temple. She guessed that it was ten feet wide by twelve deep and at least twelve feet tall.

Suddenly she became aware that Rufus had stopped his bike and she was about to ride into the back of him. Zoey hit the brakes on her bike hard and immediately knew she was about to crash. The back tire on the bike slid out from under her and she found herself on the ground.

"Are you alright?" was the next thing she heard as she opened her eyes to see Rufus looking down on her with concern.

She quickly tried to assess if she were injured in any way. Thankfully she had been wearing her helmet so she did not strike her head on the hard ground. Other than some minor scratches and a pain on her backside there was nothing injured other than her bruised ego.

"I'm all right," she moaned. "I didn't see you stopping until it was too late. I was too busy looking at the cemetery!"

Rufus took her hand to help her up and she felt better as she got back on her feet. She then noticed that he continued to hold her hand as his eyes became glassy as he looked at her. Zoey was surprised that she, too, was captivated by the sensory experience of their holding hands and looking into each other's eyes. In an instant it was all over and they both pulled their hands back while they looked at anything besides each other. That was when she noticed that she had torn the knee of her jeans and could see a scrape on her shin.

"If you're okay we'd best be getting started on setting up the cameras," Rufus said as he turned towards the gate leading to the plantation.

Zoey walked behind him but continued to think about her feelings as she followed Rufus. He seemed so much different to her now than he had earlier at church. She was so lost in her thoughts that she failed to notice Moses standing about a dozen feet to the left of the gate holding the severed section of fence back to allow them to enter.

"I've been waiting on you two. Did you get your daddy's cameras?" he asked Rufus but he had a grin on face that made the two teens blush.

Rufus nodded as he stepped through the opening.

"I've walked the trail a couple of times and I have a few spots picked out. Do you know how to set them up and get them pointed at the right places?" Moses asked.

"I've set them up for my daddy before and during deer season," the boy replied as they made their way down the path.

"How many do we have?" Moses asked.

"I got three of 'em," Rufus replied as he pointed at the canvas bag on his back.

"Okay, our first spot is going to be right here," Moses said as he stopped.

Rufus looked around at the area that was one of the more open spots on the trail. Most of the growth was only ankle high and there were only a few sparse trees. Frankly, it was a perfect spot since there was no cover for someone to be obscured by.

"We just need a good spot to hide the camera," he said after he had looked around.

"What about that tree back there about fifteen yards? Would a camera there pick up motion down here on the trail?" the old black man asked.

Rufus studied the tree branch of an ancient live oak and slowly nodded that it would.

"I should be able to put it on that dead branch and then put some Spanish Moss around it to distort the shape," Rufus said with confidence. "If we're getting pictures, they should be good profile shots of anybody on the trail,"

Rufus pulled the canvas bag off his back and handed it to Zoey. He removed the first camera and smiled at her as he pulled a tablet from the bag and handed it to her.

"The camera uses cellular service to link to this tablet. When I get the camera set up, you'll need to move around on the trail," he said looking at Moses who nodded that he understood. He then looked at Zoey and said, "You should see a picture appear of Moses. When you see his face, let me know."

Zoey nodded her head that she understood what she was to do.

Rufus quickly moved through the ankle-high brush in a direction away from the tree before moving parallel to the trail back to the tree so that he would to not leave an obvious path to where the camera would be. Soon he was at the low-hanging branch he had pointed out. He tested the strength of the dead branch and became satisfied that it would hold his weight. He pulled himself up on the branch and shimmied his way out to a V formed where the branch split in two. He quickly secured the camera to the branch using the straps on the camera.

"Take a few steps up and down the trail," Rufus called back to Moses who immediately began to pace back and forth.

Zoey was a little surprised when the tablet in her hands suddenly vibrated but there was absolutely no sound. She looked down and could see Moses and herself clearly in the picture that had popped up.

"I got the picture and I can see us both clearly!" she shouted so that Rufus could hear her.

Zoey watched as the boy collected some nearby Spanish moss to hang it around the camera without obstructing the lens. In a few seconds it was hard to pick out the camera even though she had watched it being placed on the branch a few minutes before.

Zoey watched as Rufus lowered himself from the tree and again moved parallel to the trail away from the tree in the opposite direction that he had approached it from. After some distance he moved back toward the trail they were on. After he rejoined them on the trail he looked back to where he had just passed and nodded to himself, satisfied that he had left no obvious trail that might be noticed.

"Looks like your daddy has been teaching you how to move in the woods," Moses said with a smile.

"I do like being outside," Rufus replied with a grin.

They then continued up the trail until they came to the spot where it split towards the plantation house or continued on towards Zoey's house.

"I think we need one here," Moses said.

Rufus began to scan the area trying to think as his father had taught him about hunting in the woods. He realized that if they could find a spot closer to the house facing back to where they were standing, they would have a great head shot of anyone moving toward the house. Then his eyes focused on the dilapidated outbuildings. He noticed that there was a gap between some of the siding boards.

"I just spotted the perfect place," Rufus announced. "You see that gap in the siding on that building over yonder?" he asked Moses, who looked at the building and then nodded. "I'll get the camera placed and let you know when to move around," Rufus said enthusiastically.

In just a few minutes they heard him say, "Go ahead!"

Moses took a few steps on the trail as Zoey held the tablet and felt the vibration in her hands. She looked at the screen and there was a clear picture of Moses and her looking at the camera. That amazed her since she could not even see where Rufus had placed it.

She was showing Moses the picture that had been taken of them when she began to wonder where Rufus was. Moses must have been wondering the same thing, as he was also looking down the trail toward the run down buildings where Rufus had said he would place the camera.

"Now where did that boy get to?" Moses said to himself.

"Right behind you!" Rufus's voice suddenly said from behind them. Zoey jumped, startled at the sudden appearance of her friend behind her.

"How did you get there?" she asked.

"My daddy always told me to never come and go the same way from a place where you're trying to catch your target. What you're hunting might pick up on the path you made," he said with a big smile.

"Yeah, you're a country boy all right and that's for dang sure!" Moses said, grinning with admiration. "We'd best be getting on to that look-out's spot."

They returned to the trail that would take them to Zoey's house. The woods were much denser here and difficult to move through. Eventually they approached the hunting blind.

"What do you think, Rufus?" Moses asked. Zoey could tell that the old man had become extremely impressed with the young boy's skills in the woods.

Rufus sat back and studied the woods for some time, then seemed to grow interested in a spot on the opposite side of the hunting-blind.

"Stand here while I work my way around over yonder, Rufus said. "I think I can put the camera up in that sweetgum tree. We should be able to get a shot of anyone sitting here in the blind. The camera can be made to go into video mode that can actually video them. We can be watching them while they're watching us," he said with a chuckle. "It runs the battery down pretty quickly but it might be useful in short bursts," he said and then he slipped silently into the brush.

Zoey looked in the direction of the tree Rufus had pointed to and tried to catch him moving towards it. Several minutes had passed when much to her surprise she noticed that he was already in the tree looking back at her.

"How does he do that?" she whispered under her breath in amazement.

Moses had seen him as well and waved his hand at him. When he did, Zoey felt the now familiar vibration in her hand as a picture of the two of them standing in the blind materialized.

She looked up and gave a thumbs up to Rufus that all was working as it should.

"I'll meet you back up the trail!" Rufus called out as he shimmied down the tree.

Zoey and Moses started up the trail and soon were joined by Rufus. They all walked silently as the day began to segue into evening.

When they got to the split in the trail, Moses said, "I'd best be getting back home. Zipporah will be plumb worn out with worrying by now. You let me know if you get anything on those cameras."

They watched him walk off towards the old plantation house before they continued to their bikes. Zoey started to think of all that had happened that day and then she remembered the books.

"I have to go back into the house," she said quietly.

"Why?" Rufus replied.

"I found something today and I think it's really important that no one else finds it," she said.

Rufus looked at her and she could tell he was debating whether or not entering the house was such a good idea but then he just nodded and pointed back to where they had parted with Moses.

It did not take long before they were back in the study. Zoey walked over to the old scales and Rufus watched as she pressed down on the arm. There was the soft click and she smiled in triumph as she slid open the bookcase that concealed the room.

"That's pretty cool!" Rufus said with some admiration as he peered into the dark interior.

"I wish I had a flashlight," Zoey said.

Rufus reached into the canvas bag and pulled out the tablet out. He quickly looked at the apps on the screen and turned on the flashlight function. It was not the best light but it was better than the dark. He held it up and they noticed that there were three books on the shelf.

Zoey picked up the first book and she was confident that it was the one she had seen earlier that day. She gently opened the cover and sure enough there was the elegant signature of Dupree Durant. She carefully turned the page and read a title with some difficulty: "The Confession of Dupree Durant." Below that was the subtitle: "Pirate, Killer, Prevaricator!"

"What's a prevaricator?" Rufus asked.

"I have no idea but I need to read this and I think we'd better take the others as well," Zoey replied.

"Put them in the bag," Rufus suggested, opening the canvas bag that he had taken back from her after placing the cameras.

Zoey only glanced at the covers of the other two books but she could see no words on the outside as she slipped all three into the bag. They then closed up the bookshelf. It was only as they stepped outside that they noticed how late in the day it had become. They rushed back to the bicycles and quickly rode back to the main road, where they stopped.

Rufus got off his bike and removed the bag from his back and said, "I think you should take this."

"What about the tablet?" Zoey asked.

"I think you should keep it with you." He looked at her and she could see concern on his face. "You'll get an alert at your house if any pictures are taken. Promise me that you'll call Moses at the first sign that those guys are back! He'll know what to do," he said as he helped her put the bag on her shoulders. "I'll see you on the bus in the morning," he said with a smile. "I had fun helping you today."

"I had fun too! I'm glad you were here to help," Zoey said and suddenly felt sad that the day was over.

They pedaled away from each other towards their respective

homes as quickly as they could before the fading light turned to night.

CHAPTER 9 • CONFESSIONS & OATHS

Zoey arrived home just as the last of the light faded from the eastern North Carolina sky. She put her bike away along with her helmet. She cringed a little as she went into the house and expected her mother to chastise her for being gone so long. She found her mom in the kitchen making supper and, thankfully, not overly concerned about her late arrival.

"Did you have fun exploring the area on your bike today?" she asked pleasantly as she continued to concentrate on what she was cooking.

This surprised Zoey as she was expecting at least some concern from her mother about her tardiness, especially after the previous night's events. She figured her mom would be worried to death about her since it was after sundown. Zoey dreaded what was likely to come from her mom's concern, since she had that innate ability of a mother to put a guilt trip on her whenever she had been bending the rules. Being out late was bad enough but Zoey had an even deeper reason to feel guilty. Zoey had never made the decision before to deliberately mislead her mother. Deep down she knew she was about to step across that line so she cringed as she answered her mother.

"Yes, I stopped by to visit with Moses and Zipporah for a while and then I ended up running into Rufus. We did some exploring," Zoey said and that was the truth with just a little bit of other information withheld.

Zoey tried to convince herself that what she said was mostly the truth but another deeper voice in her soul called her a liar.

"That sounds like fun," her mom said as she turned to see her for the first time. Zoey watched as her mother's smile turned to a slight frown before she said, "You look like you've been rolling around in the dirt and you've torn your pants! Did you have an accident on your bike?"

It was only then that Zoey saw herself in a mirror in the living room. Her hair was tangled, there were dirt and brambles on her clothes and hair, and her pants had a hole in the right leg from when she had fallen off her bike. Hannah walked over and took a closer look at the scrapes and scratches that were mostly from the bicycle incident, while the others were acquired from her time walking through the brush of Oak Harbor.

"I think you'd better go take a bath and afterwards I'll put some Neosporin on those scrapes," her mom said. "Don't bother putting those pants in the hamper, just throw them in the trash. It's a good thing that you chose to wear an old pair today." Then she noticed the canvas bag in her daughter's hand. "What's that?"

"Just some old books we found," Zoey replied. "I wanted to bring them home to take a look at them."

She could see the wheels spinning in her mom's head, so Zoey decided she needed to change the subject. "I talked with Mr. Moses and Mr. Johnson about what happened last night. They agreed that it was most likely a hunter just like Rufus thought but they both said that if you need to have someone stop by and check things out, they would be happy to."

"That's mighty kind of them to offer to do that!" Hannah said right away. She was quiet for a few seconds before she continued. "It was a terribly frightening event last night. Frankly, I was beginning to believe that it would be best for us to find someplace else to live. I mean, it's just the two of us here in this house all by ourselves."

Hannah looked into her daughter's eyes before continuing what she wanted to say. "The more I thought about it, I realized that this was a critical moment for me and for you." She paused again as her words became more difficult to say. "I know you don't remember your father. You were just a baby when he died." Her mom's eyes glistened as tears wanted to form. "He was my rock. He always made me feel safe and loved. Then he was gone. After that I was afraid of everything because I was all alone. I tried to shut off the world so that I wouldn't be afraid but the more I stepped away from life, the more frightened I became. That was when your Meema came to me and told me that I either needed to learn to control my fears or my fears would always control me." Again her mom looked Zoey straight in the eyes and smiled. "She was right then and now. You and I need to control our fears no matter what, even if there is real danger!"

Zoey was surprised-and moved—by the conversation. Her guilt intensified about hiding things from her mom. No matter the reason. Would her mom feel the same way if she knew how she was trying to mislead her? Guilt began to gnaw on the thirteen-year-old girl.

"Mama, I need to tell you something," Zoey said quietly.

"You can tell me anything you want to, sweetie," her mom replied with an encouraging smile.

For the next hour Zoey told her mother all about the adventures she had experienced that day. Hannah listened carefully, only asking questions to clarify what she was being told. Zoey held nothing back, including finding the secret room with the books as well as her confused feelings for Rufus and his for her. Finally, she had nothing left to share and waited for her mother to say something.

"First," Hannah said, "I agree with you that those intruders, as you called them, were just trying to scare us last night. I'm glad that you got Moses to investigate what they've been doing over there. I think that the plan to identify them is a great idea." She paused for a moment with a smile. "I don't know what to make of the books you retrieved from the house but I agree they're safer out of the house than in it. I'm sure you will turn them over to the rightful owner when you know who that is," she said and then giggled. "Most of all, I appreciate your taking me into your confidence about Rufus! Boys are confusing but they can be fun as well. I hope we can always talk about what you are going through. No matter what!"

Zoey hugged her mom tightly and felt so much better now that she was no longer keeping any secrets from her.

"Now, go get cleaned up and we'll see if dinner is edible," her mom said with a smile.

Later that night Zoey sat at the desk in her bedroom. She pulled out the tablet that was linked to the cameras. She checked and there was no new activity at any of the cameras. She set it aside and pulled out the books to take a closer look at them in the much better light of her room.

She looked at the one she had first picked up in the house again. The cover only said that it was a personal journal. On the first page in a calligraphic style of writing was the signature of Dupree Durant. Zoey wondered at how disciplined a person had to be to create such artistic script just to sign their name.

She then turned the page to see the title of the book in the same script: "The Confession of Dupree Durant" with a subtitle of "Pirate, Killer, Prevaricator!" The next line read: "Set by my own hand on May 17th in the year of our Lord, 1854."

Zoey was amazed that she was holding a book that had been written 168 years ago in the author's own hand. It sent her mind into a tailspin to think of what she held in her hand.

She looked at the subtitle again. She knew what a pirate and a killer were but she had no idea as to what a prevaricator was.

She got her tablet out and quickly did a search for "prevaricator." The result said it was "a person who intends to deceive or speaks falsely." Zoey puzzled over why any person would admit to being a thief, a murderer, and a liar.

She began turning pages that were filled with the flowing script of Dupree Durant.

Zoey closed the first book and looked at a second book. It also had "Personal Journal" impressed into the leather cover but the book was obviously from a different source than the first one since they didn't look like each other. She opened the cover and on the inside it did have the flowing script of Dupree Durant but somehow it looked different. Perhaps the hand was less steady or written with less confidence. She turned to the second page and there was a simple title: "The Secret History of Oak Harbor." Like the first book, there was written a date: "December 12th in the year of our Lord 1880."

When Zoey turned the page she found a different handwriting. It was also a flowing cursive script but clearly different from the writing in the first book. She wondered why.

She decided to read the first few lines:

This is the final accounting of the life of Dupree Durant upon this temporal world that has been my home for the last sixty-two years. My dearest wife, Moriah, is transcribing my final confession as to what happened since the birth of our beloved son Uriah. She is doing this out of love so that my descendants will have an account of how they came to be and the terrible price that was paid for their position in this world. I do this to first inspire them to act boldly in their lives to confront and give battle to the forces of ignorance and injustice. Secondly, I desire that they each come to know that who and what they are were bestowed upon them by grace and not merit and that they, too, should extend grace to all they encounter, with a heart of mercy."

That first paragraph made Zoey want to continue to read but she also understood that it would be best to read the first so-called "confession" before the latter.

She turned her attention to the third book. The cover on this one was also made of leather but on the cover was written those strange words again: "Perfide Aurum Liberat." Zoey hoped that perhaps the meaning of those words would be made clear on the first page of this book.

She opened the cover and on the next page in yet a different cursive script was the title, "The Duties of Marse Durant," and under that was the signature of Dupree Durant II and then the now familiar date reference: "Documented by myself on February 12th in the year of our Lord 1881."

Zoey turned the page and was disappointed to see a single page that read:

The Oath

I hereby swear to administer the duties of the position of Marse Durant to the best of my abilities. To see to the upkeep of Oak Harbor and the preservation of the entire family. To do so with a spirit of love, joy, peace, forbearance, kindness, goodness, faithfulness, gentleness, and self-control. Further, I swear to extend mercy and grace so that others may know hope and peace. So help me, God!

Under this oath were four different signatures, one by each Dupree Durant followed by a date, which Zoey assumed to be the date the oath was taken. She wondered why Miss Rose had never signed the oath. Maybe it was intended for only the men of the Durant family. Before she could investigate any further, however, the tablet monitoring the trail cameras lit up briefly and she knew that a new picture had been taken. Her body stiffened with the fear that she was about to see the intruders.

She quickly opened the app to the most recent picture and was greeted by a raccoon looking up at the camera from the hunting blind.

"You may be an uninvited guest but you're not the one we're looking for!" she said with a laugh as her tension faded.

To make sure she had not missed anything else she looked for other pictures and quickly became amazed at how many animals were wandering around the woods next door. In all she counted three raccoons, a opossum, and a deer.

She had just closed down the tablet when her mom stuck her head in the room. "Time for bed. You have school in the morning and I have a lot to learn at my new job," she said as she walked over to where Zoey was sitting.

"Okay, Mama," she replied and as she did, she yawned so hard it felt like her jaws would pop as her body decided it had been deprived of enough sleep in the last twenty-four hours.

"I love you, sweetie! Sleep tight," her mom said as she turned to leave but Zoey stood up and hugged her mom tightly.

"Thank you, Mama, for all you do," Zoey said softly as her mom stroked her hair.

In just a few minutes she was sound asleep and stayed that way until morning.

CHAPTER 10 • YOUNG DUPREE

The next week seemed to fly by for Zoey. Her workload from school kept her busy late into the night but no matter how busy her evenings were, she always took time to review any new pictures taken by the cameras. By Friday all she had seen were pictures of the local wildlife. Raccoons seemed the most common but there were numerous others. On Wednesday she looked at a photo and was surprised to find a mama black bear with two cubs on the trail closest to the cemetery.

When she got on the bus the next morning she quickly went and sat across from the boys and said, "I have a picture of bears over at Oak Harbor!"

Rufus sort of nodded at her like it was no big deal.

"You didn't tell me there were bears around here!" she said, wondering what she would do if she saw a bear while she was just walking around her yard.

"Actually, there are a lot of black bears around here," he replied.

"That's the God's honest truth!" Billy added.

"You might have told a girl about that. What if I just stumbled into one in my back yard?" Zoey said as she pictured herself being attacked by an angry bear.

"They usually run away if they see you first or, more likely, hear or smell you first," Billy said with a smirk on his face.

"Why would a bear run away from a person?" she asked, expecting a sarcastic response.

"Because a bear only has one predator that hunts them and that is people. More bears are killed by people than the other way around," Rufus replied with a serious tone as he looked into her eyes.

When he did that, Zoey found herself suddenly flustered as all kinds of other thoughts blotted out her concerns about bears.

"The most dangerous thing about bears is getting between a mama and her cubs," Billy said which snapped Zoey out of her thoughts of her growing feelings for Rufus.

The rest of the week passed without any other notable events.

On Friday she arrived home and again checked the camera only to find nothing of note. It occurred to her that this evening would be the first opportunity to read some more pages of the books from Oak Harbor. Zoey went to her room and retrieved the first book. She sat down in the living room, turned on a light, and opened the cover. Again, she was amazed that she was reading the actual writing of man from 1854. She began to read the neat cursive script and was immediately captivated by the words.

On May 17th in the year of our Lord 1854 at the age of thirty-six I became the father of Uriah by my beloved wife Moriah. Upon the recognition of this event, I have seen that it is time that I confess to my activities of the last two years. I do not find it merely a coincidence that the date of the birth of my second son is the anniversary of the beginning of my descent into a life of piracy, murder, and deceit.

But let me not get ahead of myself!

I want this confession to be a record of the true events that brought me into a new life. A new life that is now filled with danger and intrigue of my own making. I want my sons to know who their father truly was for better or worse. I will begin with my early life as it is essential to understanding how I came to be here.

Zoey was filled with the wonder of what she was reading. Dupree Durant had two sons? The second one was named Uriah so he was definitely not Dupree the Second! The original Dupree was freely admitting that he was a pirate but what was this about a new life that was filled with danger and intrigue?

She had to read on!

I was born to a Quaker family in eastern Pennsylvania. My father was a farmer who instilled in me a diligent work ethic. He and my mother both hoped that I would accept their faith but I was a rebellious youth. When I was twelve, I ran away from home to the big city of Philadelphia. I tried many times to apprentice to various tradesmen as a way to put food into my belly and secure a place to sleep but employment was hard to come by. I went hungry many a night those first few weeks on my own.

The city could be a hazardous place. I learned to watch my back as there was violence and crime all around me. Shortly after my arrival in the city, I was accosted by a group of toughs who were about my age. I was lucky that I only lost my shoes and not my life in that encounter.

Zoey's mind was filled with wonder that Dupree Durant was even younger than she was when he left home and set off on his own. Zoey thought of herself as a self-confident person but to leave and go away to live on your own at twelve! She could not even imagine doing such a thing. Things must have been very different in those long-ago days. She put those thoughts away and returned to the words of Dupree Durant.

I eventually made my way to the docks on the Delaware River. A kindly old merchant by the name of Witherspoon took mercy on me and gave me a job as a stevedore moving goods off the ships and into his warehouse. It was hard work but he fed me three meals a day, gave me a place to sleep in the warehouse, and paid me four bits in cash per day.

Her mind tried to conceive of a time when a person would be given food to work and then sleep in a warehouse. She could not get her mind around such an arrangement. She also could not help but wonder what four bits in cash was. She read on and tried not to be distracted by her own curiosity.

It was while I worked on the docks that I discovered my infatuation with the sea. I would work in the holds of ships and could not help but to imagine the foreign places that they had been. I had been taught to read and write by my mother and I could see the labels on the crates, boxes, and barrels that were offloaded daily. They were from England, France, and other lands that I had never heard of. At night I dreamed of visiting those faraway lands and the adventures I might have. Such are the dreams of youth!

Six months after I had become a stevedore, I was working near a ship that was being made ready to sail to Liverpool, England. I overheard a conversation between the captain and his chief mate. The captain was being informed that their cabin boy had been diagnosed with a fever and would be unfit to sail on the tide. I saw my opportunity and stepped forward to offer my services to the ship.

The captain looked at me and said, "You are already employed, laddie. Now if you were able to call upon your Master and convince him to give you a letter of introduction with his endorsement as to your good character and that he has consented to your termination of employment without notice, I would look favorably toward signing you on."

I stood there taken aback for a moment before I ran off to the warehouse. Mr. Witherspoon listened to my excited babble and smiled warmly before he said, "Always knew you were meant for the sea and far-off lands filled with mystery and adventure. I will have your letter in a half-hour. Now you should go gather your belongings and settle whatever matters that will need to be finalized before you depart," he said as he pulled his pen from the holder on the desk.

Not only did he write the letter, he accompanied me back to the ship, which was named the Courageous. I watched in awe as the captain and Mister Witherspoon shook hands at the bottom of the gangplank as if they were old acquaintances.

"I see you are still up to your old games," the captain said with a chuckle.

"'Tis no game to see that a boy has the chance to become a good man through honest work. Too many like him would otherwise end up in one of those gangs and probably at the end of a rope before he could grow whiskers. You take good care of him and I will go pull another out the jaws of hell," Mr. Witherspoon said as he turned and handed me five silver dollars.

I asked what the money was for and he said, "Your future."

He shook my hand and walked off towards his business.

"You're fortunate to have crossed paths with that man, laddie," the captain said. "Witherspoon had a twin brother who was hanged for murder after he became a tough in a gang. Now he seeks out and saves as many boys as he can to make up for the one that he could not save."

Zoey was astonished at the world she was being introduced to. Children her age working and sailing away on ships while others became criminals that could be executed. It boggled her mind so much that she failed to hear her mother come in the house.

"Did you have a good day, baby?" her mom asked. Zoey jerked with surprise that her mom was in the room.

"Oh, hi, Mama. I was so caught up in what I was reading that I didn't hear you come in," Zoey said as Hannah leaned down to give her a hug.

"What are you reading?" she asked as she looked over Zoey's shoulder.

"It's one of those books I found over at Oak Harbor that I told you about," Zoey replied.

"Wow, that is a really old book! And handwritten in such beautiful script. What's it about?" her mom asked.

"The title said it is a confession of being a pirate, killer, and prevaricator but so far it seems to be about the man that built the house next door and was the ancestor of Miss Rose. His name was Dupree Durant," Zoey replied.

"What in the world is a prevaricator?" her mom asked and sounded just as puzzled as she had been before looking it up.

"I didn't know either, so I looked it up on the internet. It turns out it's fancy word for someone who deceives or lies," she replied.

"That doesn't sound like a very nice person," her mom said with a frown.

"I don't know what to think yet," Zoey said. "He's writing this as an account of what happened in 1852 through 1854 but the part I'm reading now talks about his early life when he was just a boy. He wrote that he ran away from home when he was twelve. He worked on the docks loading and unloading ships but the part I just read was about him going to work on a ship bound for England." She paused for a moment and then added, "Just think about it. He was younger than me and was going to sail across an ocean to another country!"

"That is quite a story. You'll have to tell me more about it or maybe I can read it, too," she said and then sighed. "But right now, I'd better get some food going for us!"

Zoey turned back to the book and began to read again.

That was the beginning of my life at sea. I spent the next eight years on the Courageous. First as a cabin boy, then as an ordinary sailor. The captain and chief mate took a liking to me and after a couple of years I was being taught how to navigate and con the ship. I began to learn all the jobs that I could.

When I was twenty, the captain called me to his cabin while we were awaiting to unload in Boston. He told me that I had progressed as far I could on his ship and that it was time for me to take a new berth. He went on to tell me that he had an acquaintance that was the captain of a whaler named the Ceto and was looking for a third mate.

"'Tis time for you to make that next big leap, laddie. I have given Captain Rogers my letter of recommendation for you for the position

of third mate. I would wager that in another eight years you will be captain of your own ship!" he said with pleasure.

He then explained that if I signed on, I would be looking at a four-year voyage that would take me to the Pacific. I was thrilled with the opportunity but also sad to be leaving the ship that had become my home for so many years and my shipmates who had become my family.

I knew that my captain was right and that I had learned all that I could from my time on the Courageous, so I made the arrangements to accept my new position aboard the Ceto.

My new position as third mate was challenging. First, I had to become familiar with being on a whaler. The vessel was built for the express purpose of hunting the largest animal on earth. It staggered my mind as I thought of boarding one of the small boats and pursuing a creature that could smash our fragile craft with a flick of its tail. It would be my job to command one of the boats and with the assistance of the harpooner to sneak up on the whale, put a harpoon in the beast, tire the whale out by allowing it to drag us through the ocean, and to lance the leviathan until it was dead. If we were successful at that we would tow the fifty-ton carcass back to the ship, where the full crew would butcher it and refine the oil from the blubber. This would continue until we filled every available barrel with the valuable commodities gathered from the whales that included baleen and ambergris in addition to the oil.

My second role as third mate was to manage my division for each of their four-hour watches. This role was somewhat familiar to me from my time on the Courageous but the bigger challenge was to learn my men and for them to become familiar with my standards.

The final role that I had to learn quickly was to become a member of the Officers Mess. As a new officer I was under the magnifying glass.

I am pleased to say that I overcame all of these challenges.

The life of any sailor on a whaling ship is long periods of boredom and mundane tasks that are briefly interrupted by moments of terror and exhilaration. My first success as a whaler was off of Brazil as the Ceto was sailing south. We came across a pod of humpback whales. The captain ordered us to man the boats. I was fortunate enough to have an experienced crew and we approached our prey with stealth and cunning. My harpooner directed us to the perfect position. I watched in awe from the tiller as he hefted the harpoon and in the blink of an eye thrust it deep into the monstrous beast.

I was mesmerized as our spool of rope began to shoot away with astonishing speed. The harpooner poured water onto the rope as it began to smoke from the friction as it passed over the gunwale. I ordered all hands to pull for all they were worth, to put on as much speed as humanly possible before our line went taught. I was nearly thrown over the transom when the line snapped tight and our whale took us on what they called a "Nantucket sleigh-ride."

It took all the courage I had to not order the line cut but instead to allow the beast to drag us around like an angry child would a pull-toy. I have no idea how long it took but eventually the beast tired and sat on the surface. It was at this time that I gave the order to move in for the kill. Again, my seasoned harpooner showed his skill as he plunged the lance deep into our stricken target. The experienced crew had tried to tell me about making a kill but none of it could have prepared me for the fountains of blood that we were bathed in.

That was when I felt both the satisfaction of a successful hunt but also the somber regret of taking the life of such a magnificent creature. We next had to tow the massive carcass back to the ship. After we had returned to the ship my next new experience was to endure the processing of our catch for the first time. They say that sailors on other ships can smell a whaler before they see it. I can attest that there is more than a little truth to that observation.

As time progressed, I became accustomed to life aboard a whaler and the Ceto in particular.

Five months after we had left Boston, we made the arduous passage to round Cape Horn and entered the Pacific Ocean. I have never seen such enormous seas! Some of the waves were the size of mountains. It was only after we had made the transit that the captain mentioned that he was glad that the weather was "rather temperate" this time. I did not look forward to the return passage!

Our time in the Pacific was productive and in only a little over a year we were approaching our capacity, which was a record for the Ceto. Our spirits were high as we plied the waters near the Sandwich Islands. The entire crew enjoyed this part of our voyage as we found the natives of the islands to be friendly and we were able to routinely acquire ample fresh water and foodstuffs. It was difficult for me to reconcile the accounts I had read of Captain Cooks death at the hands of these same natives just some sixty years before.

It was in these times that I became good friends with the fourth mate of the Ceto. His name was Meredith Williams. This was his first cruise as a mate but he had been on four previous voyages. He was a wealth of information to me as I tried to learn all I could about my new profession.

The other subject that we spent considerable time on was the speculation of what our lays would be worth upon our return to Boston. There were so many factors that would determine our shares. First, there was how much cargo there would be, as well as what the market price would be for the oils and the bone. Next would be the expenses of the ship that included everything from food to sails. The longer the voyage took, the more those expenses added up against the value of the cargo. We were both enthused that this was turning out to be an extremely profitable voyage as we had only been at sea for sixteen months. If we got just one more whale, we would be making the dash back to Boston. Even the captain agreed that we would likely complete our voyage in half the time he had expected.

Much to our delight we did indeed catch our final whale within a week of our speculation. We began our return voyage, which would be considerably shorter than our outbound since we were full up on cargo and would not be hunting.

Then tragedy struck the Ceto! One morning I was preparing to take my next watch when Meredith burst into my stateroom and solemnly announced that the captain had died in his sleep. This was a shock to all of the crew since Captain Rogers had been a well-liked and respected commanding officer for many years. It was a hard sight to see his body slide off the board and into the depths of the Pacific. There is nothing lonelier to witness than a burial at sea but such is the lot of many a sailor to not lie near their kith and kin until the day of resurrection.

Unfortunately, this was not the last of the misfortunes to befall the Ceto on her voyage home.

As I had feared, the return passage around Cape Horn was much worse than the outbound. The words of the late Captain Rogers haunted me as I stood my watch through the worst of it. The chief mate, who was our acting captain, was assisting the helmsman at the wheel during the height of the storm. I had just looked upon them as they struggled to keep the bow into the oncoming waves when my attention was called away by one of my deckhands. The ship was hit by a rogue wave that knocked every man off their feet and washed to the rail. I regained my feet on the pitching deck trying to account for the men of my watch when I felt the ship being pushed by the gale-force wind sideways into the oncoming waves. I turned back to see if there were damage at the helm and could only see the ships wheel spinning out of control! The chief mate and helmsman were nowhere to be seen and it was obvious that the wave had swept them to their deaths in frigid waters.

I could feel the ship being turned on its side and I knew that we would soon be capsized if I did not act. It was only by God's grace that I reached the wheel to try to regain control before we floundered in the turbulent sea. I was struggling mightily to right the position of ship when two other hands joined mine at the wheel. I looked up to see my friend Meredith smiling at me as he said, "This will be a night to remember!"

Indeed, it was a night to remember as we corrected the direction of the ship and managed to ride out the storm. With the coming of *dawn, the wind began to drop and we were able to gain headway to complete the transit into the Atlantic. It was at that time a bond was formed between the two us, as can only be formed between men who have stared death in the face and survived to tell the tale.*

Regrettably, that was not the last of the troubles to come from that night. As Meredith and I relinquished the helm to a replacement helmsman we began to wonder what had become of the second mate. I instructed one of the crew to go find him. It was only a few minutes later that the crewmen returned and said that I should accompany him. We went to the second mate's stateroom where we found him curled in a ball on his bed. We could get nothing but terrified whimpers from him. At that point I realized that I was in command of the Ceto.

I met with Meredith a short while later and informed him of our situation. He nodded thoughtfully and then told me that I should gather the crew and inform them. I had my hands full as Meredith and I worked out a new watch structure for our reduced crew. I also made the decision that we would make our best speed to return to Boston and to not call on any ports before then. My fear was that our ship and valuable cargo might be confiscated and that our crew would lose their lays.

The crew took the news quietly but I do believe they supported the remaining officers. We also hoped that the second mate would recover with some time. Unfortunately, this did not happen. No matter how we tried, the man would not take any sustenance. Two weeks after our passage around the Cape he was found dead in his berth. It was likely his death was caused by dehydration but in my heart, I was certain he had died of fear!

We arrived in Boston one day after our departure date of two years before. The news of our ships journey traveled like wildfire, not just in Boston Harbor but it quickly spread up and down the east coast of the American continent. Meredith and I met with the ship's owners and then with authorities to review the logs of the Ceto and our actions. In the end we were commended for our actions that saved the ship and returned it to port. We were both handsomely rewarded for what we had done. I was awarded half of the captains lay as well as my third mate lay. Meredith was awarded half of the chief mates lay as well as his fourth mate lay. I was also offered a position on a different whaling ship as chief mate but I turned it down. I decided that I did not want to be a whaler anymore. Instead, I took my compensation and bought a partial ownership in a new schooner that was to be based at Wilmington, North Carolina. I lost track of my friend Meredith but I always suspected that the two of us would meet again. We had shared a moment that few men ever experience. We had faced death and did not blink. We had become brothers that had been forged in the fires of battle against the wrath of nature. I did not believe that any two men who had been through such a trial could be anything but devoted to each other throughout their lives.

I would live to regret those beliefs!

Zoey was stunned with the account of the young Dupree's life and she knew there would be so much more.

"Time for supper!" Hannah's cheerful voice called out from the kitchen.

With great reluctance she set the book down before going to eat supper with her mom.

CHAPTER 11 • A NEW BEGINNING IN WILMINGTON

Later that night Zoey lay in her bed and again picked up the confession of Dupree Durant. The book was not what she had expected from reading the title. Instead of a simple confession it was an account of his life, which he wanted to make sure his sons could read. He seemed compelled to document how his life had unfolded before coming to a new one at Oak harbor.

Some of the things he had written were hard to put into a context that Zoey could understand. Just one example was how he had said that the Ceto had spent time near the Sandwich Islands. Zoey had never heard of such a place and had to research the name on the internet. She found that Hawaii had been called the Sandwich Islands by many people in the early nineteenth century. This was just one of the many things that she had to try to find the modem meaning of as she read the account of his life.

She also had at first struggled to read the cursive letters used in the book but it did not take long before she began to get the hang of it. In fact, she was so impressed with the style that she had begun to practice imitating the letters with her own hand. She could see that if she mastered the skill, she would be able to write much more quickly than she could print. She also liked it because it was like writing in a secret code.

She quickly found the spot where she had stopped reading before supper.

So it was that I came to North Carolina to take command of my new ship the Audacia. I purchased a one-third ownership in the vessel with two thirds owned by a tobacco exporter named Julius Noble. Julius was an enterprising man who had immigrated to Wilmington from Plymouth, England sometime around 1810. He had prospered purchasing tobacco in areas around Wilmington and shipping it off to his old acquaintances back in England. With the opening of the Wilmington & Raleigh Railroad, Julius knew he would be able to greatly expand the area he could buy tobacco from. He decided that he wanted to assure the ability to ship his tobacco to wherever the best market prices could be achieved. Thus it was that he decided to become a ship-owner.

Julius had read of my exploits on the Ceto and decided that I would be an excellent candidate to be the captain of his new schooner. He wrote to me and offered me the position of captain. While that was an intriguing offer, I decided to make a counter-offer. I proposed that I would accept the position as captain if he would sell me a portion of the ownership of the ship. I awaited his reply anxiously for the next month. When his response arrived, he invited me to come to Wilmington so that we might meet to see if a partnership could be arranged. Thus it was that I arrived in North Carolina in October of the year of our Lord, 1843.

From our first meeting we took a liking to each other. It was clear that he had the contacts in many places to ship tobacco for profit. In me he found a partner that he could trust, since I would be responsible to secure profitable cargo for the return voyage. This would allow us to maximize our profits.

We quickly negotiated my purchase of a one-third interest in the Audacia. He then invited me to come to his home for dinner that evening.

When I arrived that evening, I was introduced immediately to Julius's two sons. The older of the two boys was called Junior, since his Christian name was also Julius. The younger son was named Caleb. Julius explained that both of his sons would eventually join him in the tobacco business. Junior had just received his degree from the University of North Carolina while his younger brother would be starting at Chapel Hill the following year.

"You have Junior to thank for naming your ship," Julius explained as we enjoyed a drink before dinner was served.

I had wondered about the name of Audacia and was pleased to learn that it meant "boldness" in Latin. I liked that name, as it reminded me of my first ship the Courageous.

A servant announced that dinner was about to be served and that the ladies were awaiting our arrival in the dining room. I accompanied my host and his sons and entered a room with a magnificently set table. I was immediately introduced to Julius's charming wife, Maud. Then, to my eternal delight, his fifteen-year-old daughter, Bernadette.

I must admit that I had never been educated in the etiquette of my social betters. I had always been a sailor and other than the Captains Mess I had no real table manners. I confessed as much to my hostess and prayed that she would have mercy on me. It was then that Bernadette proudly announced that she would be honored to instruct me in the proper actions at the table.

It was a special night for me and I became instant friends with the entire family but I could not help but feel a special connection to the young Bernadette.

After that evening I became a regular dinner guest at the Noble estate. My days were consumed with fitting out my new schooner and in finding and hiring the best crew available. The day finally came when the ship was ready to depart on the high tide. The entire Noble family came to wish us Godspeed and bon voyage. I was touched when I noticed a tear welling in the eye of the young Bernadette at our parting.

Thus it was that I began my first voyage as a captain of my own ship. Our first port of call was Plymouth, England. There I oversaw the sale of our cargo and the purchase of a cargo of tools for shipment to Philadelphia.

When we arrived in Philadelphia, I called upon my old benefactor Mr. Witherspoon. It was a joyous reunion and also fortuitous, as he was able to introduce me to another wholesaler that had a shipment of textiles destined for North Carolina.

Julius was thrilled with the profits from our venture and we celebrated with a feast at his home. It was on this occasion that I was reunited with Bernadette. She had celebrated her sixteenth birthday while I was on the maiden voyage of the Audacia and she was visibly changing from a girl into a woman.

At the end of the evening, Julius requested a private word with me. It was then that I noted some concern on the face of the young Bernadette as her mother whisked her away.

Julius seemed to have difficulty finding words at first, which was quite unlike him. He finally spoke up, saying that he and his wife were concerned about Bernadette's growing infatuation with me. He asked me frankly if I had any feelings for her. I had to take several minutes to collect my thoughts. There was no doubt that I found the girl most intriguing. I also had to admit to myself that she was a most becoming young woman who was not just beautiful but witty and graceful. I shared these thoughts with her father and watched his face for a clue as to how he would react.

Finally, nodding more to himself than to me, he said, "You are fine young man but you are also a sailor. I know that you are much more experienced in the ways of the world than my dear Bernadette. As your partner and friend, I have become fond of you but as a young girl's father I have concerns about the inequity of your knowledge of women compared to my daughter's lack of knowledge of men. Bernadette is still a child in many ways but she is drawn to you like a moth to a flame. Her mother and I are concerned that she will act in haste to capture your affections. We could tell her to no longer see you but undoubtedly, she would choose to ignore us. We fear for a girl in her mindset and doubly so when the object of her desire is so much more worldly and could decide to take advantage of her."

I was taken aback by this conversation but as I thought about it,

I could understand their concerns. They had always treated me with the utmost hospitality and respect. I pledged to Julius that I would not take advantage of the situation and I would inform Bernadette that we could only be friends.

Julius smiled and shook my hand in thanks for my handling of the delicate situation. Before I released his hand, I added that when Bernadette turned eighteen that I would be asking for his permission to court her.

He nodded and smiled and said, "I suspect that we will all rejoice on that day!"

So it was that I told Bernadette that we needed to stay as friends until her eighteenth birthday. She replied that her feelings for me would not change but she agreed to the arrangement. We remained friends but I thrilled every time I was in her presence and I knew she felt the same.

I was glad to be at sea as it made the inner turmoil more bearable when I was removed from her intoxicating presence. Between 1844 and 1846 I made a dozen profitable voyages on the Audacia. When I returned in the fall of 1846, I was met by Bernadette as I stepped off the dock. She was stunningly beautiful in her blue dress when she greeted me in the company of her mother. She took my hand in greeting and then with excitement announced that she was now eighteen. Maud then smiled and said that Julius would be expecting my call that evening.

So it was that my courtship of Bernadette began. Our ardent feelings grew like the intensity of a hurricane with each of our meetings. The long separations while I was at sea did nothing to assuage our passions and so it was that in the spring of 1848 we were married. The joy of that time still makes my blood run hot.

In 1849 I returned from a voyage and was informed by my dear wife that she was with child! To know that I was to become a father was the second greatest joy of my life that had only been eclipsed by knowing the love of Bernadette.

Julius and I attempted to arrange my next voyage to allow me to be back in port before the expected birth of my child, which should have been in June of 1850. Unfortunately, the happiness of my life disappeared before I could return. Unexpectedly, Bernadette went into labor just as her eighth month began. A doctor was called. She struggled for nearly two days before a boy was delivered. He was small but appeared to be healthy. However, the same was not true for my dearest Bernadette. She died four hours after my son's birth.

Zoey was deeply moved at reading the tragic love story from over 170 years before, and knew there was more to come. She had known something was going to become of Bernadette since Dupree Durant had said that the mother of his second son was named Moriah back the beginning of the account of his life. She had to read on even though her eyelids were growing heavy.

I was taken to her grave and wept bitterly at the misfortunes of life. I pledged on her tombstone that our son would know of her and her gentle ways. He would also know that she would have loved him. I also pledged that I would do all I could to see that he grew into a man that she would be proud to call her son.

I returned to the home of Julius Nobel and was introduced to my son. I was informed by my father-in-law that Bernadette's dying wish was for the boy to be named Dupree Durant the Second. She insisted on the formal name so that the family would not have two Juniors. Maud informed me that they had hired the services of a wet nurse to assist in the care of the child. She was a Negress who was owned by a personal friend of my mother-in-law and answered to the name Hattie. The first time I laid eyes on her she was holding my son gently and rocking him while humming a soulful tune that spoke comfort for all the sorrows of this mortal existence to anyone in hearing distance. My own tortured soul felt soothed by her comforting tune which brought a tear to my eye.

I believe that this was the first time I had even thought about the slavery that went on around me every day in North Carolina. I was raised a Quaker, a faith that did not hold with slavery, but I had never accepted the faith as such. Now I was suddenly confronted with my son being cared for by a woman who was considered a possession to be leased out! At that moment the institution of slavery felt reprehensible to me.

Bernadette's family was very kind while I mourned her passing but sooner or later I would have to figure out how my son and I would move forward. My primary concern was trying to raise my son while being at sea for months at a time. I decided that it was time to end my career as a sailor.

Julius offered to make me a partner in his tobacco export business but I could not do that as it smacked of charity and it would have been unfair to Junior and Caleb. In the end I determined that I needed more time to work out my future. I told them that I would return to sea for another year or two while my son would be cared for under their watchful eyes. I pledged that by the beginning of the new year of 1853 I would find new employment that would keep me on land. Unknown to them, I approached Hattie and arranged to pay her a salary for caring for little Dupree. The silver paid to her would serve to salve my guilt at using a slave to care for my son. Deep down, I hoped that she would secure her freedom from what I gave her.

So it was that I returned to my life at sea but the joy I had always known at being on a fine ship in the vast expanse of the ocean was greatly diminished. As time progressed, the pressure to find another way to make a living increased but no answer would come. My desperation began to grow with each return to Wilmington.

Zoey wanted to continue to read but her eyes would not stay open. She looked at the clock by her bed and saw that it was after 1:00 in the morning. She set the book on her nightstand with care and turned off the light.

CHAPTER 12 • CAMERAS & BEARS

Zoey awoke the next morning to sunlight shining through her bedroom window. She got up and opened her curtains to see that it was a glorious fall day. The sky was that unmistakable Carolina blue that the quickly diminishing fall leaves looked even more colorful against.

She and her mom had just finished breakfast when there was a knock on the door. When Zoey looked outside, she saw that both Rufus and Billy were standing there.

She opened the door and asked, "What are the two of you up to?"

"It's a nice day to be outside. We're going to ride the bikes around but first we need to go change out the batteries in the cameras," Rufus replied. "We thought you might want to come along."

"Is it all right, Mama?" she asked as her mother stood nearby.

"I would like you back before noon," Hannah said. "I have a surprise for you this afternoon. In fact, maybe your friends would like to have lunch with us," her mother replied.

Zoey wondered what sort of a surprise her mother might have for her but did not press the issue.

"Okay, we'll be back in time for lunch but you'd better make a lot of food. I've watched these two eat at school!" she said in a teasing way for the boys to hear.

"Thank you kindly, Miss Hannah," the boys said in unison.

Zoey quickly put on her helmet and pulled her bike out of the carport.

"Maybe we should tell Moses that we're going to go onto Oak Harbor property? You know he doesn't like people wandering around over there," Zoey said as they prepared to leave.

"We saw him out in his yard on our way over to see you. He told us to go ahead but not to go in the house," Rufus said before they started down the drive.

They pedaled in silence as they went by the front entrance to Oak Harbor. Zoey noticed that Billy gave the old house a nervous look. She was certain that he was hesitant about going onto the mysterious property.

Moments later they arrived at the road that went up to the cemetery. This time Zoey paid attention to what she was doing but she also felt a sense of connection to Dupree Durant whose remains were so close-by. He had been a complete mystery to her but now that she was reading his words she felt as if she were beginning to know him. He was a man who had loved, experienced tragedies, and made his own way by hard work and taking risks. She still could not reconcile why he claimed to be a pirate, killer, and liar by what she had read so far. She was certain she would understand everything once she finished the book.

They stopped near where the fence had been cut by the intruders.

"We need to be careful to not leave a trail. Nobody has been here since we were last Sunday. I think I can find a different way to the cameras without taking the trail, so follow me," Rufus said as he held the fence open for the two of them.

Zoey was once again impressed by the way Rufus could move without leaving an obvious trail. Billy followed right behind him and while he was certainly better in the woods than Zoey, he was no match for Rufus.

"Am I really comparing the two of them like everything they

do is a competition?" she thought to herself. She was glad that she was behind them so they would not see her blush when she thought of her growing feelings for Rufus.

She could not help but recall reading the words of Dupree Durant about how he had fallen in love with the young Bernadette. The attraction he had felt for her and the certainty that she was in love with him as well came through powerfully in his narrative.

"Is that what I'm feeling for Rufus and he for me?" she asked herself and again felt her heart beat a little faster. "That's ridiculous!" she thought to herself. "They were so much older than Rufus and me!"

That thought had no more than crossed her mind when she remembered that Bernadette was fifteen at the time she was falling in love with Dupree.

Zoey was startled to realize that she would be fifteen in just over a year!

Rufus stopped and held up his hand before he bent down to examine the ground. He then motioned for Zoey to come up and join him.

"I think the intruders were here last night. Look at this boot print. It has the same cut-mark we saw last week. I think they changed how they're coming and going," he said quietly.

"Do you think they know about our cameras?" she asked.

"Hard to say. They may have changed because they nearly got caught or maybe they noticed signs that someone had been looking around. The one thing we know for sure is that this is a fresh trail and they were here last night," Rufus said.

"I think we'd better move one of the cameras to cover this trail," Billy said.

Zoey and Rufus nodded that they agreed.

"I'll go get the one we had on the old trail and set it up here,"

Rufus said as he slipped off into the brush to get to the camera.

"I think I should back-track this trail and see where they're getting past the fence now. You wait here and tell Rufus what I'm doing," Billy said as he began to go off through the undergrowth away from the trail.

Zoey stood there looking around and suddenly felt very alone. She began to think of the bears she had seen on the cameras. Now every small sound seemed to be amplified as she wondered if the bears were watching her.

What if she had inadvertently gotten between the mama bear and her cubs?

She began to scan the woods carefully looking for a black shape hiding in the brush. She turned to look behind her and nearly jumped out of her shoes when she saw Rufus was standing there!

"Oh my God! You nearly scared me into next week!" she said as the initial shock began to wear off.

"I'm sorry! I didn't mean to scare you. Where did Billy get off to?" he asked but then they both heard Billy approaching.

"I found how they've been getting in," Billy said." There's a big tree back by the creek that fell over on the fence. It smashed it as flat as a pancake. I can see where they've been riding four-wheelers up to the opening. It would probably be a good place to put a camera," Billy said.

"Lead the way!" Rufus said excitedly.

It was not a long walk to get to the back of the fenced property. Rufus suddenly stopped as they approached the enormous tree that had smashed the fence flat. Zoey watched as he bent down and examined something on the ground.

"Looks like the bears have been coming and going this way as well," he said as he looked back up at Zoey.

"How do you know that?" she asked.

"This here is a fresh pile of bear scat," he said with a grin. "Poop," he added when he noticed Zoey looking puzzled.

Then Rufus looked around and found a new place to mount the camera. He quickly got it in position and did his best to obscure it with twigs and Spanish moss.

"I think we should take a look around the rest of the woods back here. We should be able to find a way to the hunting blind over by your house," Billy said and Rufus nodded his agreement.

It took the two of them only a few minutes to find a game trail that took them in the direction they wanted to go. Occasionally either Rufus or Billy would stop and look at the trail. Zoey had no idea what they were seeing but after a short time they would cautiously move on again.

After the third time they did that, she had to ask, "What are you guys looking at?"

"There are a lot of animal tracks but no humans. It looks like our intruders have not come to this part of the property," Rufus said as Billy nodded his agreement.

They had continued on for some distance when they came across a collapsed structure that at one time had been quite ornate. There was a fountain nearby and they could tell there had once been a well-maintained formal garden surrounding it.

"Looks like it was a gazebo at one time," Billy said as he walked around the ruins before they continued.

Zoey quickly became disoriented and knew she would never be able to find her way back out of the woods if she were separated from the boys. Then Rufus stopped and pointed to a tree in front of them. He signaled for them to stay put. Zoey wondered why they were being so quiet as they moved through the woods but trusted that Rufus had good reason for whatever he did. She watched as he quickly went to the tree, slithering up it as if he were a forest animal himself. It was only then that she saw it was the tree where they had hidden the camera looking down into the blind.

A few minutes later he returned and said, "I don't think they've been in the blind since we put the camera up. They may have abandoned it."

"I'll bet they spotted something and now they must be avoiding all their old trails. Either that or there's something else that got them spooked about coming to the blind," Billy said.

"I don't know what to make of it but I think we should leave the camera here for now," Rufus said thoughtfully as he continued to scan the woods around them. "I think we should make our way between the fence and the woods until we get on the other side of their trail and then cut back to the house and check on the last camera," he said.

Zoey followed along as they walked by the fence that was between her yard and the woods. She was starting to daydream when the boys froze in their tracks and squatted down. Rufus looked at her and held his finger to his lips for her to be quiet and for her to squat down like he had. Then he pointed up into a tree just a dozen steps in front of them. Zoey looked up but couldn't see anything but the tree at first, then she saw movement.

There in the tree were the two bear cubs she had seen in the photos. She was thrilled to see them in real life. They seemed so cute and cuddly but then she heard one of them make a sound like it was calling out a warning. Now she understood why the boys were staying so quiet; they had no idea where the mama bear was.

All of the background noise of the woods, like the chirping of birds and buzzing of insects, stopped when the cub called out. It was as if every creature in the woods knew that trouble was coming. Then there was the sound of leaves and twigs being trod upon by something big! Zoey watched as the mama bear appeared at the base of the tree only steps from where the three of them were attempting to be invisible. She watched as the bear stood up on its back legs and looked directly at her and the two boys. She was certain they were about to be mauled.

To her shock she watched as Rufus stood up slowly and looked at the bear and said calmly, "Hey, bear, we're just passing by." He then signaled for Billy and Zoey to also stand up and whispered, "Just turn and walk calmly away from the tree like you have no interest in it."

They did as Rufus directed but Zoey could not help looking over her shoulder at the mama bear. She saw the bear lower herself back down onto all four paws while keeping a careful watch on the humans as they moved away.

"That cub must have spotted us and got scared. It called for its mama to come for protection," Rufus said as they continued walking along the fence.

A few moments later the two boys stopped again.

Rufus turned and looked at Zoey and said, "I think I know why the intruders stopped coming to the blind! You see all the acorns on the ground and those bushes with the berries on them? That's like an all-you-can-eat bear buffet!"

"I bet that made them think twice before they went wandering around in the dark over on this here side of the house," Billy said with a laugh.

"We need to move back towards the plantation house now," Rufus said as he pointed towards another game trail that headed in that general direction.

Rufus let Billy take the lead as they moved toward the house, now visible through the thinning leaves.

"Did it scare you when that bear came out of the woods?" he asked and Zoey noted that his voice was filled with concern rather than taunting.

Zoey nodded her head that she had been scared. "I was glad that you were with me, though," she said. "You make me feel safe." Zoey felt her cheeks redden with embarrassment but then felt glad that she had said those words to Rufus.

Rufus looked at her for a second and then grinned with pride. He nodded his head and said, "We'd best catch up with Billy."

Rufus stopped them when they came to the dilapidated structure with the camera in it. He cautiously went into the building. A few minutes later he returned with the camera.

"That building is on its last legs. A piece of the roof had fallen in and blocked the lens from taking any pictures. They could have put a marching band through here and we would never have gotten a picture of it! I'm going to have to put it somewhere else," he said, looking around.

Zoey looked around as well and then she noticed that there was ivy growing on the back wall of the house. "What about there in the ivy by the back door? We know that's how they've been getting in the house," she said.

"That's a great spot!" Rufus said with enthusiasm, which gave Zoey a warm feeling.

It only took a minute for him to hide the camera.

"Time to get back out of here. I think we should go over to the other side of the house and move straight towards the fence," Billy said as he started in that direction.

It didn't take them long before they found the opening they had come through earlier. Five minutes later they were approaching Zoey's driveway when she spotted her Meema's car parked near the carport.

Both Rufus and Billy watched as she jumped off her bike and raced through the door with a happy scream, "Meema!"

CHAPTER 13 • MEEMA

Billy and Rufus came in the door behind Zoey to find her hugging Meema. What neither of them could possibly have known was just how special the bond was between Zoey and her grandmother.

Meema had always been there for her from her earliest memories. Her mother had told her that they had lived with her grandmother for over a year after Zoey's father had died in the accident. Zoey had no living memories of those times, as she had only been an infant. Nonetheless, that is where the bond had been forged between them. Zoey listened to everything Meema had ever told her. She had introduced Zoey to so many new experiences, like the time they went to New York together for a girls' weekend. She would never forget the sights they had seen or the many strange foods they had tried.

Zoey knew there was more to it than just her grandmother's indulgent nature that made their relationship so special. Meema encouraged her to master different skills from her earliest age, such as sleeping in her own bed and being polite in public. She had given Zoey so many interesting books to read that made her imagination grow and her curiosity to become so insatiable. Meema had fostered her innate empathy for others that made Zoey such a caring child. She had encouraged Zoey to try different forms of art, which helped her to see the beauty in the world around her. She had reinforced a strong work ethic that always drove Zoey to complete whatever she had started. Meema was the positive reinforcement to her mother's discipline. Meema was her beloved mentor!

"Meema, this is Rufus Johnson and back there is Billy Thornton. They're my friends," Zoey said.

"Pleased to meet you, ma'am," Rufus said politely.

"The same here, Mrs. Morganton," Billy said trying his best to be formal to impress the ladies.

"Meema's name isn't Morganton. Her name is Connie Thompson," Zoey said as Billy started to turn red at his social error. "She's my mom's mom."

"Now, don't you fret about calling me by the wrong name," Zoey's grandmother said in a way that put Billy immediately at ease. "There is no way that you could have known my name until I introduced myself. You boys just go ahead and call me Miss Connie."

"We're ready to eat so please go and get washed up," said Hannah. "Meema and I will be waiting at the table."

It was only then that all three of them realized just how dirty they had gotten stomping around the grounds of Oak Harbor.

A few minutes later three freshly scrubbed teens took their seats at the table. Zoey's mother had placed a platter of fried bologna, bread, sliced tomatoes, lettuce, and their choice of condiments in the center of the table. Each of them had a bowl of homemade mac-n-cheese at their seat along with a plate for the sandwich they would assemble for themselves. Once they had said grace, they all dug into the delicious lunch.

As Zoey had warned, the two boys seemed to be bottomless pits when it came to food but her mom had taken the warning seriously and prepared extra helpings of the mac-n-cheese.

"The three of you seemed to have gotten pretty dirty this morning. Just what exactly we're you doing?" Hannah asked between bites.

"We went to check on the cameras over at Oak Harbor," Zoey replied. "I didn't want the batteries to get run down," Rufus explained.

"We ran into a mama bear and her cubs while we were doing it!" Billy blurted out.

"Y'all ran into some bears?" Meema asked with astonishment. "Just where is this Oak Harbor?"

"Oak Harbor is the property next door," replied Rufus pointing to the woods behind the house. "The bears were no big thing. We showed the mama that we meant no harm and just gave her a wide berth."

"Sounds like it was a good thing that Zoey had a couple of country boys along," Meema said with praise as she looked the two boys over again.

Zoey noticed both of her friends bursting with pride at Meema's kind words. Part of what made her so special was that she always seemed to make people feel good.

They ate in silence for a while until Zoey's grandmother asked, "Why are you putting cameras up over there?"

To everyone's surprise it was Hannah that answered. "There have been some trespassers over there and these kids have been helping the groundskeeper by putting up some cameras to identify who they are."

"And just what are these trespassers doing over there?" Meema asked with some concern in her voice. "Have you spoken to the police?"

"There's a rumor that there's a treasure over there. Mr. Moses, that's the caretaker, says that it's not true but people still come around looking for it and tearing things up," Zoey answered.

"Mr. Moses is afraid that if the police get involved that it will just make other people come to look for it as well. He says it has happened before, back when he was just a boy," Rufus added.

Zoey watched as Meema shook her head and allowed the subject to drop for the time being. She was certain that her

Meema would have more questions about what was going on when they were alone.

After lunch, Billy and Rufus said their goodbyes and headed off on their bikes. Hannah needed to do some grocery shopping, which left Zoey alone with her grandmother.

"It sounds as if you and those boys have been having quite the adventure, what with trying to catch trespassers, running into bears, and looking for a treasure. I suspect there is a much longer story to be told," Meema said as they sat alone on the back porch.

Zoey could not help but share all of the things she had learned and the many mysteries that begged to be solved. She told Meema about the murder of Jonathan Wilson, the missing funds that were intended to maintain Oak Harbor, and the legal battle for control of Oak Harbor caused by Miss Rose's missing will. Zoey also shared the many older rumors about Oak Harbor such as murdered slaves and the mass grave of bodies that was discovered on the grounds. As she was finishing up her account of Oak Harbor, she mentioned the books she had found hidden in a secret closet and what she had read so far.

At the end of the account Meema could only shake her head in amazement at what her granddaughter had been up to.

"Now that we've talked about the mysteries of Oak Harbor, we should have a nice chat about these two boys. It would appear to me that you're rather sweet on that Rufus boy," her Meema said with a smile and a twinkle in her eye.

Zoey blushed but she knew Meema could read her like an open book in the broad daylight of a summer afternoon. It was another long conversation but it felt so good to talk with someone with whom she knew she could share anything. Zoey spoke of her confusion about the growing feelings she had for Rufus and the way he had made her feel safe when they had confronted the bear. How his concern for her safety drove him to overcome his own fears and sneak into Oak Harbor, alone, to investigate what the intruders had been up to. His concern for her when he had learned that someone had been looking through her bedroom window. Finally, they had a long talk about why Zoey felt something different for Rufus than Billy.

"That is one of the mysteries of life!" Meema exclaimed. "Why a person is attracted to one person and not to another. However, from what you've told me, I think I can see some of the reasons you feel differently about Rufus. He seems to be a leader while Billy is a follower. He's also someone who can be resourceful, such as his abilities in the woods. He listens to you and that is saying something for any man! He also cares for others and does what he can to help them. That shows loyalty. Most of all, I can see that he really does care about you in a special way," she said with that all knowing smile.

"What am I supposed to do about it? I don't think I'm ready to be anybody's girlfriend," Zoey said.

"Everything will come in its own time, Zoey! Just take each day as it comes and let tomorrow take care of itself. For now, just be his friend," she replied as she squeezed Zoey's hand.

Zoey reached over and hugged Meema tightly. She felt so thankful to have such a knowledgeable and loving woman to guide her through life.

"Now I'm ready to take a little walk. How about showing me this Oak Harbor?" her grandmother suggested.

The two of them walked across the back yard so that Meema could get a better look at the old plantation house. Zoey explained the basic layout of the house and that the end with kitchen is what they could see from the backyard. Zoey hoped that they might spot the bears but she saw no sign of them. Next they walked to the road and proceeded to the main gate with its iron scrollwork. Her grandmother studied the lettering.

"Oak Harbor, Perfide Aurum Liberat," Meema said, enunciating each word as if she knew them by heart and then she added a translation. "Treacherous Gold Makes Free."

"You know what those words mean?" Zoey asked in surprise.

"It's Latin. It was the language of ancient Rome," Meema explained." I learned to read it as part of my history studies when I was in college a lifetime ago. It was not unusual for the old plantation families to adopt a family motto expressed in Latin. I think it made them feel rather superior to the common folk. What they were really doing was just being uppity!" Meema tilted her head, pondering the motto. "It is a rather strange motto, though. I could understand Aurum Liberat which would translate as 'gold makes free' but why would it be treacherous? I suppose that's just another mystery for my granddaughter to solve!" Meema said with a chuckle.

CHAPTER 14 • A PIRATE'S TALE

That evening Zoey went to her bedroom and pulled out the confession of Dupree Durant again. She was anxious to see what the next part of the account would tell her about the founder of Oak Harbor. She opened the old book to where she had stopped the night before and began to read.

There were only eight months remaining before the deadline would expire on my pledge to end my career as a sailor. I had no idea of how I could replace my employment as a sea captain with one on shore where I could provide for my son. On each of my returns after a voyage, I could not help but to notice how much little Dupree had grown. This only added to my desperation to fulfill my vow. I had just returned from a long voyage and noticed that little Dupree seemed to have no idea who I was but he knew everyone else around him! As for myself, I was but a random stranger to my son. My anguish increased to the point that I was uncertain if I could carry such a ponderous burden upon my back!

It was then that an old acquaintance reappeared in my life. One day, my chief mate knocked on my cabin door and informed me that I had a visitor waiting on the dock. He handed me a calling card that said Meredith Williams, Chief Mate of the Seahorse.

I hurried down the gangway and indeed, there stood my old friend from the Ceto. We greeted each other as only brothers who had not seen each other for many a long year would. We agreed to have supper together that evening to catch up with one another.

That evening was a fine time to be with my old shipmate. Admittedly we had too much rum before our meal but the liquor helped to loosen our tongues and ease our conversation. I told him of my life and the tragedy of my wife's death along with my determination to change my career to be home with my son.

He smiled as I told the last part and then he said, "'Tis the curse of the sailor's life. We go to sea to see the wonders of the world and in the end, we wonder why there is no place for us in it but to wander the seas. In the end they simply commit our mortal remains to the watery depths to await the Judgment Day."

I responded that he had the crux of the issue. I said that I had tried to think of anything that would allow me to raise my son and not miss two thirds of his life while I was at sea.

He seemed to study me again as if he were considering something. After several minutes of silence, I asked him what was on his mind.

"'Tis hard for a man to change course once he has begun his journey in life. The years seem to add their weight in a way that pins a man to his position. 'Tis not easy for men such as ourselves to try to start over at the bottom," he mused.

I thought of my thirty-four years and did not feel old but I did understand that I would never be able to compete against younger men for the opportunity to learn a new trade.

"But what if you had a fortune that would give you the capital to try anything you wanted or perhaps to do nothing at all, and live a life of leisure?" he said with that all knowing smirk on his face.

"Well, I have no such fortune and I have no idea how that could be done," I replied with laugh at what I thought was his attempt at levity.

"A little piracy could," he replied quietly.

Zoey was excited as she read this part. Clearly Dupree Durant was about to document his time as a pirate.

I was taken aback at the suggestion. I had always been an honest man in my dealings.

"You're daft, man," I said. "They would hunt us down and hang us from the highest yardarm!"

"Not if it was only the one time and the haul was good enough," he said as he studied my face.

"You would still have to know which ship, where it will be, and when. Then you would need to board and seize it from the crew. Sounds like a good way to die!" I replied.

"What if the crew of the ship were willing to mutiny for a share of the cargo?"

I was surprised by his words but I was intrigued by them as well.

"It sounds as if you have been working on something," I said and waited for a reply but he just sat there with that all-knowing grin still on his face. "Out with it, man!" I said as my patience was wearing thin.

"My ship the Seahorse sails from Philadelphia to Panama and back again. Our cargo is mostly bananas but a few months ago our captain was contracted to take on shipments of gold to be brought back to Philadelphia. Panama has become a shortcut for the gold being shipped from California to Philadelphia where it can be minted into coins. My crew would gladly take the ship, tie the captain up in his cabin, and abandon ship with the gold. They would just need passage to a friendly port where the proceeds may be divided and they could all go their own way," he said as he lifted his cup of rum to his lips.

My mind was racing at the thought of this audacious project.

"Maybe there really is a pirate treasure!" Zoey thought with excitement as she continued to eagerly read the account of the meeting between Dupree and Meredith.

"How much gold?" I asked.

He simply held up two fingers. My mind raced again as I did the math on the value of 200 pounds of gold and came to a number of over $66,000.

"You 're saying that the cargo includes 200 pounds of gold?" I asked. He shook his head no and said, "No. Tons!"

My mind reeled at the thought of that much gold! 4,000 pounds!

"What will be the split?" I asked as I recovered my composure and my greed took control. In retrospect, I am certain that it was at that moment that I made a deal with the Devil.

"As the leaders of this enterprise, you and I would take 1,500 pounds each. My crew will split 500 pounds among them and the same for your crew. 'Tis a King's ransom for everyone!" he said with an evil laugh.

I believe that I became blinded by the phenomenal wealth that I would have! With 1,500 pounds of gold, I could acquire a business or even a plantation that would provide for my family down through the generations. I could create a dynasty!

Meredith and I worked out the details of the plan. He assured me that no one would be harmed and no one would know of my ship's involvement. I would rendezvous with the Seahorse off Ocracoke Island, where the treasure would be shifted onto my ship. The captain of the Seahorse would be left tied up in his cabin with the ship at anchor. It would take hours or perhaps days before the theft was discovered. By then we would have sailed to New Bern, where the gold would be divided and all would go their separate ways.

I liked the plan and felt good that no one would be harmed. What I did not know was that I was being lied to.

On the night of the rendezvous, the two ships indeed met, although the arrival of the Seahorse was later than planned. I set my men to transferring the gold onto my ship. I had hoped that Meredith's men would launch their boat to speed the work along, but there was no sign of them. It was then that Meredith called across the water telling me that he had taken casualties and that there were only two sailors besides himself to offload the cargo. I did not like this news as there was not supposed to be any opposition except by the captain.

"What had gone wrong?" was the question I kept asking myself over and over.

I decided that it was too late to back out of this bargain and we would get past whatever had happened. After all, there was all that gold.

When we had finished the transfer of the gold, my launch made one last trip, returning with Meredith and his two remaining men. As soon as he was aboard, Meredith became most insistent that we make sail and get away from the Seahorse quickly before we were discovered.

I felt ill at ease but I gave the order to get underway and to make our course for New Bern. We had only sailed about a half-mile from the Seahorse when there was a massive explosion that obliterated the Seahorse and any poor soul that was still on her.

I turned to see Meredith holding two Navy Colt revolvers, and they were pointed at me.

"Just do as you are told and you and your men will stay alive!" he told me.

I turned to see that Meredith's two compatriots were holding revolvers on

my crew as well.

"Now get us into the Neuse River!" he ordered. I had no choice but to comply with his demands.

Zoey sat there shaken as she read about how Dupree had been lured into an act of piracy and then betrayed by a man he thought of as his brother. She felt compelled to read on!

I had my chief mate take the helm and steer a course for New Bern. I reminded him to keep a weather eye on the shoals near Brant Island.

Meredith stood near me looking at the charts and our compass heading. I could tell that he was watching for any sign of deception on our part.

I tried to discern what Meredith's true intent was. Would he really release my crew if we did as he told us? My conclusion was that he intended to kill us all once the Audacia had served its purpose. I determined this based on what had become of the Seahorse and the poor souls that had manned her. Clearly, he did not intend to leave witnesses behind.

It was my good fortune that the seas began to grow in the Pamlico Sound once we left the lee of Ocracoke Island. The deck began to pitch and it took every experienced man on board to trim the sails and helm the ship. I used this activity to move among my crew and told them of my fears. I implored them that they should be prepared to retake the ship on my signal. Meredith and his two henchmen had the guns but we outnumbered them seven to three. I watched as my men began to arm themselves with makeshift weapons such as unused belaying pins.

While the weather allowed me to pass the word it also made it impossible to pick a moment to act without putting the ship in danger. I decided we would wait until we entered the calmer waters of Neuse River. I moved back to be near Meredith where I became aware that he had begun to watch my crew more closely. I did not want him to catch any of my men arming themselves so I decide to start a conversation with him.

I asked him directly if this had always been his true purpose, to betray an old friend. He just gave me that all knowing look and told me that I had betrayed him back on the Ceto so now it was my turn to reap what I had sown. I was truly staggered by this reply, for to my knowledge I had done him no wrong those many years before. I asked him just how I had betrayed him. I watched as the anger was plain on his face. He replied that we should have split the bonus for saving the Ceto. I tried to explain to him that the payout was determined by the owners and not myself.

"You did nothing to influence them on my behalf! You got your money and purchased your interests in this ship and became captain! You married into a family that has money and only your foolish pride keeps you from living off of them! You worry about raising your son while I have never been married due to myself being *a poor prospect for any woman of quality! Upon our reunion, I heard you complaining of your situation but you have never asked what had become of me! While you were being captain, I was taking guff from whatever captain as would pay me enough to buy my drinks while in port. Now I will use you to gain my fortune just as you used me those many years ago!"*

The bitterness of my former friend overwhelmed me.

I asked him if he were really going to let us go. His only response was to stare into the darkness.

As we entered the mouth of the Neuse River the chop quickly diminished. It was then that I decided to give the order. It became apparent that my plan had been observed, for as soon as my men moved to attack there were three shots fired and three of my men were down. Two of my deck crew were killed instantly and my chief mate laid on the deck by the helm writhing in agony with a shattered left arm.

"That was very foolish, Dupree!" Meredith hissed as he reached down and pulled my chief mate up by the back of his shirt.

I could tell by the look on his face that he was quite insane. His eyes looked like burning coals as he said, "Now we will have a trial."

He called everyone but me to the rail. He told me to stay at the helm. His two men took Chief Mate Brown by the arms, which made him scream in agony. They pulled him to the rail facing the water.

"This man is accused of attempted mutiny. How do you find him?" Meredith asked his two thugs.

"Guilty!" they said.

"The penalty for mutiny is death!" Meredith said and he then put a bullet into my poor Chief Mates head.

I watched in horror as his body fell into the river below.

Meredith then turned to me and said, "Do everything I tell you, when I tell you, and I will pardon you and your remaining men. If not, you will all be summarily executed!"

I nodded that I understood. He then instructed me to make for Alligator Gut, which flowed into the river near Cherry Point. When we approached, he told me to get the ship into it where it could be hidden. I knew my time was growing short. Meredith was clearly a lunatic and would leave none of us alive. I needed to create another opportunity to overpower him and the other two. I could see that my three remaining men understood our desperate circumstances. I spotted a place where there was a submerged tree just under the surface. I hoped to hang the ship up on it which might buy us more time. What I did not know was the tree was more like a pike and when I hit it the ship became impaled on it. The hold began to fill with water.

Meredith ordered my men and myself to haul the gold to the deck. We worked through the rest of night and into the morning. The ship settled on the bottom of the small river leaving only the deck dry.

I could see that Meredith was at a loss as to what to do next. His anger was quickly growing with his frustration and fear that we might be discovered. I suggested that it would be wise to move the gold off of the ship and to conceal it on dry land. We could abandon the Audacia and set fire to the upper deck. When discovered it would be assumed that it had been another pirate victim.

He grew thoughtful and made up his mind. Meredith decided to have my crew cut down our mast so that our rigging could not be observed from passing traffic on the river. After this was accomplished, he informed me that his two men would oversee my surviving crew as they moved the gold ashore while he held me hostage on the ship. He then called his two men close to him and gave them further instructions, which I was certain included the killing of my crew once the work was done.

So it was that he sent my three men with his two lackeys to move the gold ashore. I lost count of the number of trips they made but by afternoon the last launch began its journey to shore. I knew the hour was nigh that I either overcame Meredith or my life was over.

I had hidden a belaying pin in the small of my back under my coat.

My hand reached back and found it. Meredith had turned his back to me to watch the progress of the launch. It was then that I swung that heavy pin at the back of his head with all of my might. There was a sickening sound of his skull being crushed before he toppled over the railing and into the water below. The last I saw of his body it was floating face up on the current, back toward the Neuse River, and on to the sea.

It was then that I heard a series of pistol shots in the direction of the shore. I hoped that my remaining crew had found the courage and opportunity to overcome their guards. In a few minutes I knew that it was not to be as Meredith's henchmen reappeared and began to row back to the ship. I knew I only had minutes to prepare to meet the two armed killers. I quickly retrieved a fire ax from the companionway. I would have the slimmest of opportunities to kill them before they killed me.

I hid myself below the rail as I heard them securing the launch before they pulled themselves up the rope and onto the deck. I listened to their movements and could hear the first man's feet against the hull. It was then that I jumped up and slammed the ax into his surprised face. It was a scene that will haunt me to my dying day.

To my good fortune the body of my victim dropped onto his compatriot below. I leapt over the side with the ax in my hand. I landed in the boat and raised the ax to slay my final opponent. I slammed the ax down into the other man's chest. As I did there was the report of his revolver and my world went dark.

Zoey was beside herself as she read the account of this horrific violence! The thought of killing another person with an ax sent chills through her body.

It was then that the tablet linked to the cameras buzzed. She picked it up and what she saw made her forget about Dupree Durant's confession!

CHAPTER 15 • THE TRAP IS SPRUNG

Zoey stared at the tablet and could see two men entering the grounds at Oak Harbor. They were hard to see because of their camouflage clothes and hoods. In the same picture she could see two four-wheelers on the other side of the fence.

Zoey quickly went to find her mom.

"They're back, Mama! What should we do?" she asked as she handed the tablet to her.

"I think we'd better let Moses know what's happening. It'll be his decision if he wants to call the law," her mom answered as she handed the tablet to Zoey's grandmother.

Zoey looked over Meema's shoulder at the picture as she heard her mom begin to talk to Moses on the phone.

"Hi, Moses. This is Hannah over across the road," she said and waited for a second. "I'm afraid that the intruders have returned to Oak Harbor," she said, and listening again. "Thank you, Moses! We'll see you shortly," relief flooded her voice. She turned and said, "He'll be right over. He said that we shouldn't be looking out the window and that it would be best for us to ignore them."

In just a few minutes there was a quiet knock on the front door. Hannah went to the door and glanced through the peephole before opening it. Moses stepped into the room with obvious concern. Zoey quickly went over and handed him the tablet. He studied the picture for a few seconds.

"That doesn't look like the place where we had put one of

the cameras," he said softly before looking at Zoey and adding, "That's all way in the back of the property near where the creek is."

"We just moved it today when we were over checking the cameras," Zoey said as she felt guilty for forgetting to update him when she got home. "Rufus found a new trail that they've been using. I guess none of us remembered to tell you about it."

"No harm done, child," he said softly in his deep voice. "As a matter of fact, I'm glad y'all did that. Was there anything else you found over there?"

Zoey nodded that there was. She explained that the camera in the old building had been blocked by debris from the collapsing roof and how they had moved it to the ivy near the back door. She then explained that the hunting blind appeared to have been abandoned, probably due to the bears that had recently taken up residence nearby.

"I could see that," he said with a chuckle. "There are a fair number of oak trees on that part of the property and a whole passel of berries this time of the year. I'll bet it was quite comical when those boys ran into old mama bear over there!"

Just then the tablet signaled another picture. Zoey swiped the screen and they were greeted with a fine picture of a man looking directly at the camera.

"I never seen that boy before," Moses said as he studied the man's face.

Zoey could see that the man must have used something to darken his face so that he could stay hidden in the shadows. She could make out that he was clean-shaven with just a wisp of dark hair sticking out from under a knit cap.

"Looks like he's headed into the house through the back door," Zoey said.

Moses looked up at Hannah and asked, "What time do y'all usually go to bed?"

Her mom glanced at the clock which indicated that it was going on 10:00 and said, "Any time between now and eleven."

"Do y'all leave any lights on after you go to sleep?" he asked.

"Just the kitchen light over the sink. Why?" her mom replied.

Moses seemed to study the house for a minute and then said, "I want to see what they're doing before I call the law. I have a feeling they'll claim they went on the property to look for their lost dog. I suspect that's why they bring it along. The sheriff will likely tell them that they're trespassing and let them go with a warning. If I can say that they broke into the house then they would have to be arrested. I need to be able to say that I saw them inside the house."

"You want to watch for them from here so they won't notice you," Zoey said, understanding what Moses wanted to do.

"That's right, child!" he replied with a nod.

"My bedroom window has the best view," Zoey said with growing excitement at the subterfuge. "We could shut the door and turn off the light like I've gone to sleep. Mama and Meema could continue to move around for a little while before they do the same,"

"Yes, that'll work," Moses replied. "Once I've seen them moving around inside the house over yonder, I'll call the law on them! I suspect the deputy will be able to catch them back at their four-wheelers

Zoey looked at her mother to see if it would be okay and could see concern on her face.

Meema squeezed Hannah's hand and said, "It's going to be all right, baby. It's time to get the law involved."

With that said, Zoey's mom nodded her agreement. Zoey led Moses down the hall and into her bedroom. He stepped out of sight of the window while she moved around to allow any observer to see her going about her normal bedtime rituals.

Then she turned off the overhead light and crawled onto the bed before she turned off the lamp on her nightstand.

The room plunged into darkness. They stayed quiet for ten minutes before she slipped back off the bed and approached the window. Moses came to stand by her but back away from the window to stay in the darkness.

They watched in silence for some time. They heard Hannah and Meema moving around and then the soft sound of each of their bedroom doors being closed. It was only a moment later that they saw a light flash on and off in the woods. Zoey judged that the watcher had moved his position much further towards the back of the property and was signaling that the house was dark. It sent chills down her back as she now knew they must have been there all along, watching.

A moment later she saw the same red light begin move around the house just like she had seen it that night two weeks before. Moses lifted his phone and began to video what he was seeing. Zoey was concerned that the soft glow of light might alert the watcher but nothing happened. Moses closed the camera and dialed 911.

Zoey could hear a voice answer the call, "This is 911. What is the nature of your emergency?"

"This is Moses Jones, the custodian for the Oak Harbor property on Durant Road. Someone has broken into the old plantation house," he said calmly.

"Yes, sir. Are you in danger?" the operator asked. Zoey could hear her typing on a keyboard.

"No, ma'am. I can see them moving around the upstairs from my neighbor's house. They got into the property through the fence in the back of the property by Tuscarora Creek. I saw a couple of four-wheelers back there. I think if you could put a deputy or two back there and have one show up at the front they'll run right to your deputies," Moses said.

"I'll relay that to the deputies in route," said the dispatcher. "Please stay on the line. Whatever you do, please do not leave your location or approach the deputies with any weapon," the operator said.

"Yes, ma'am," Moses said with a grin, putting the phone on speaker and muting the pickup. "Things are fixin' to get real interesting!"

They sat in silence for ten minutes and watched the house as the red light randomly appeared in different locations. Then as if out of nowhere a number of spotlights illuminated the front of the old house. She and Moses became instantly blinded to anything that was not illuminated in the glare. They could hear the sounds of hurried movement at the front gate.

Zoey hoped that the deputies had taken Moses's advice to have men positioned at the back of the property. She felt the tablet vibrate with an indication of new pictures. She looked and could see the back of one of the intruders fleeing down the path from the back door. A moment later another picture showed a smaller man with a dog attempting to get over the fallen tree and off of the property. In the same picture she could just make out several other shadowy figures. Then another photo was displayed of a man on the ground with a sheriff's deputy on his back. The next photo captured a second man being taken into custody.

"Mr. Jones?" inquired the voice of the 911 operator.

Moses quickly unmuted the phone and said, "Yes, ma'am."

"The deputies have two suspects in custody. They are currently searching the house but they are requesting that you join them to verify what might be missing or damaged," the voice said.

"Thank you, ma'am. Please tell them that my neighbor and I will be coming to the front gate, directly," he said as he winked at Zoey.

"I will do that. Please have a safe night, sir," the voice said, ending the call.

They stepped into the hall to find Zoey's mother and grandmother waiting for them.

"The sheriff's men have them in custody. They asked that I come over and meet with the deputies looking through the house. I would like Zoey to come along with me. She saw evidence of them in the house and will be able to corroborate what I saw," Moses explained.

"Maybe we all need to go over there!" Hannah said.

Moses studied the young mother and finally nodded his agreement. All four made their way down the drive and onto Durant Road. Hannah had the inspired foresight to grab a flashlight as they left the house.

"Wouldn't want to surprise a nervous deputy still looking for bad guys!" she said calmly.

It was a short walk and as they stepped onto the road, they could see three different sheriff's vehicles with their noses pointing at the main gate. Their spotlights illuminated the structure as if it were the middle of the day.

As they approached, a deputy saw them and came to see if they were the expected party that had made the call.

"I'm Moses Jones, sir," Moses replied. "These here people are my neighbors right on the other side of Oak Harbor. This here is Mrs. Hannah Morganton, her daughter Miss Zoey, and I'm sorry but I really don't know your name, ma'am," Moses said as he looked at Meema.

"I'm Connie Thompson. I'm Hannah's mom from Raleigh," Zoey's grandmother introduced herself with a smile.

"I'm Deputy Henry Rawlins. I'm the officer in charge. I have a couple of teams clearing the house as we speak and I would like you to take a look and see if anything's missing or any damage done. I also have a couple of other men looking around the grounds but to be honest with you, there could be all kinds of people hiding in those woods. I'll bet those grounds have not been maintained in the last forty years!" he said.

"Been more like fifty years!" Moses admitted.

The deputy looked at Moses and nodded. "Could you take me through what happened tonight?"

"Well, sir, about two weeks ago Miss Zoey noticed lights moving around through the house. She went outside in her backyard to get a better look. When she did, the lights went out and she and her mom were chased back to their house by a dog," Moses started the story of what had happened.

It took some time for the whole account to be given but Deputy Rawlins took careful notes. Zoey and her mother would occasionally add a few extra comments along the way.

"So, why do you think they broke into the house? After all, it is kind of run down," Deputy Rawlins remarked as Moses concluded the tale.

Zoey couldn't resist quickly blurting out, "They're after the treasure, of course!"

The deputy looked at the thirteen-year-old girl with a skeptical eye and asked, "What treasure would that be?"

It was at that point that Zoey realized she had broached a subject that Moses and, for that matter, she herself was not prepared to thoroughly discuss.

"It's just an old legend that goes back to when this house was built," said another voice from nearby.

Everyone turned their heads to see a well dressed man standing just outside of their small circle.

"Good evening, Mr. Smithers," Moses said. Zoey could detect just the slightest bit of surprise in his voice.

Then the name registered that this was the attorney that represented Miss Rose's estate and was fighting for control of

Oak Harbor to keep it out of the hands of the Wilson family, Rose's late husband's relatives.

"Good evening, Moses, and everyone else as well," Smithers said in his refined southern gentleman's voice. He then turned to the deputy and said, "Allow me to introduce myself, officer. I'm Nathaniel Smithers. I am the attorney that is overseeing the Durant family estate, which is primarily comprised of this Oak Harbor property. It also includes the property leased by Mrs. Morganton. The sheriff and I are personal friends. When he heard that something was going on out here at Oak Harbor, he gave me a call." Smithers paused for a moment, then continued. "The young lady is likely correct about the intent of the intruders. It has been rumored since the construction of Oak Harbor in 1853 that a treasure of gold is hidden on the property. Every so often that legend rears its ugly head and a few individuals will attempt to search the house and the grounds for the gold. Isn't that right, Moses?"

"Yes, sir," the old black man affirmed. "My pa and I had to run a bunch of them off back when Mr. Wilson died."

"Ah, yes. I had nearly forgotten about that, but then I was in high school at that time," Smithers said as he seemed to be recalling other issues from that same time. "That was when my great-uncle and grandfather served as the executors for the estate of Dupree Durant the Fifth. This house has vexed my family for over a hundred years," he said quietly as if to himself.

Just then the deputy's radio activated and he talked into his mic before he looked up and reported, "The house has been cleared. If Moses would be so kind as to accompany me?"

"I would like to suggest that Miss Zoey come along," said Moses. "She and I were in the house just two weeks ago," Moses said as he looked towards Hannah, seeking permission. "After all, two memories are better than one."

Zoey's mom nodded her consent.

"What about you, Mr. Smithers? Care to join us?" asked Deputy Rawlins.

"No, I believe I will wait here," the attorney replied.

The deputy led the way to the front door. They entered the same way they had two weeks before. This time the front rooms of the house were illuminated by the spotlights at the front gate. However, wherever the light could not reach appeared to be completely consumed by the dark. Moses borrowed the deputy's flashlight to look into those areas. Moses noticed that there were several sets of fresh tracks going into different parts of the house. They could have been left by the intruders or they may have been from one of the deputies searching the house.

Moses led them on pretty much the same route that he had taken with Zoey two weeks before. Not much appeared to have changed. They went upstairs and walked through the guest rooms and into the family quarters. Like downstairs, there were no noticeable changes. When Moses opened the door to the stairs going to the third floor, they could see that they had been used since their last visit.

"Better go see if they've been doing any mischief up there," Moses said as he climbed the stairs with Zoey and the deputy in tow.

When they came to the top of the stairs, there was a series of small bedrooms with two hall baths. In one of those rooms a wall had been taken down recently and there was still a pry-bar on the floor. Behind the disassembled wall was what appeared to be a hidden staircase that had been sealed off at the floor many years ago. There was evidence that the intruder had been trying to pull up the boards that had been used to cover the opening.

"Looks like this was what he was tearing into tonight," Moses said and Rawlins nodded his agreement.

They returned to the main floor and went to the study. Zoey's heart almost stopped when she saw that the pedestal on which the scale had set had been knocked over on its side and the shelves concealing the secret closet were pushed open. Moses was mystified when he saw the now exposed storage room with the single book shelf.

"Never knew this was here!" Moses said as he stared into the empty space. "I thought Pa knew about all the spaces in this old house."

Deputy Rawlins took his flashlight into the small room and closely examined the bookshelf and said, "Looks like some books that had been on this shelf for a long time have been removed recently."

Zoey cringed at the knowledge that she was the one who took the books. On the other hand, if she had not, they might now be in the wrong hands. She needed to finish reading those books!

They walked back out the front door and down the drive to the others who were waiting at the front gate.

Deputy Rawlins walked up to Mr. Smithers and reported the findings.

Smithers said, "I want to press charges against those two men that were apprehended tonight. They clearly have been doing damage looking for something. It would appear that they might have found it. As you have said, something has been removed from a hidden closet in the study. Those books are likely to be of great value."

Smithers was obviously surprised by the news of a recently opened secret storage space and missing books. Zoey could see concern spread across the lawyer's face.

"I would also ask Mrs. Morganton if she would press charges for their incursion on her property two weeks ago! Especially for looking through the bedroom window of a teenage girl! They need to answer for their behavior!" the old lawyer said with outrage.

CHAPTER 16 • THE BIRTH OF OAK HARBOR

Zoey woke up Sunday morning to the sound of rain beating against her bedroom window. She thought through the previous night's events. The sheriff had the two intruders locked up in the jail. Today she would see Rufus at church where she could catch him up on what had happened. The one thing she was not sure about from last night was the introduction of Mr. Smithers into things.

Zoey had convinced herself that he and no doubt his great-uncle and grandfather before him were evil men. She was sure that the great-uncle had been the one who had stolen the Durant family trust money and was likely the murderer of Jonathan Wilson.

However, last night he did not come across as an evil man, he just seemed concerned for Oak Harbor, which was his job as trustee. Then Zoey felt a shiver that was not caused by the damp cold air on the outside of the house. Dupree Durant had not detected the evil in Meredith Williams until he had been betrayed! Maybe evil people were not so easily identified.

"Leaving for church in thirty minutes!" her mom called from her bathroom.

Zoey had started to get dressed when her eyes landed on the books she had taken from the study at Oak Harbor. Others now knew that there had been books hidden in the secret closet. Those books were now "missing." Zoey felt that soon a search for their whereabouts would begin. Deputy Rawlins, Moses, and

Mr. Smithers assumed that the two men now held in the jail must have them. Soon someone was going to become aware that somebody besides those suspects must have taken the books and she would be on the short list of other people who had recently been in the study.

She looked around her room and decided that she should start hiding them whenever she was not around. Her eyes landed on the small desk in her room. It was built into the wall and had drawers on both sides.

She bent down and pulled the bottom drawer all the way out. There was enough room under the drawer for the books to be stashed. She then put the books in and put the drawer back in place. She closed it and the books were safely out of sight.

Church was fun and she did find time to tell Rufus about the night before. He was glad to hear that the intruders had been arrested.

Zoey had no idea why she did what she did next but she asked, "Would you like to come over to the house after church so I can give you all the details and show you the pictures?" immediately she blushed as she knew in her mind that she was asking him over just so she could spend time with him.

Rufus also turned a light shade of red. "I wish I could," he said. "But it's my aunt's birthday over in Morehead City. Maybe we can get together tomorrow after school? It's Halloween and we could go to Trunk-or-Treat here at the church."

Trunk-or-Treat was a Halloween event in many communities where instead of going house to house, residents brought their cars to a central location and distributed treats from decorated tailgates and trunks.

Zoey was flustered with all sorts of conflicting thoughts and feelings but then she nodded that would be all right with her.

"Oh my God! He just asked for a date and I said yes!" she thought silently as the butterflies began to flutter in her stomach.

On the car ride home Zoey remained quiet as she thought about asking Rufus to spend time with just her and how that suddenly had turned into his asking her to go to Trunk-or-Treat with him. She had not even thought about Halloween until just now. She had no idea what she was going to go as! Maybe she could call him and tell him she couldn't go? Then she felt guilty, knowing she would hurt his feelings if she didn't. That would be worse than not having a costume!

"Oh my God, I have a boyfriend!" she screamed silently to herself with all the mixed feelings that went with it.

It took a few more minutes to build her courage before she said to her mom and grandmother, "I need a Halloween costume. Rufus asked me to go to Trunk-or-Treat with him tomorrow."

The two women giggled in the front seat as her mom turned the car back towards town.

The next several hours were filled with frustration as they searched for any available costumes but there were none to be had anywhere.

"Pull into that Goodwill store over there," Meema said.

"They're not going to have any Halloween stuff," Zoey said sadly as her frustration was building.

"They probably don't have costumes but they have all that we will need to make something from scratch," Meema said.

Zoey had her doubts about how going to the thrift store was going to make any difference.

"Don't underestimate your Meema," her mom said with a chuckle. "Remember, she's the thrift-store-shopping Queen!"

They spent the next hour looking through clothes-racks until Meema pulled out a white tee-shirt and white leggings. She then pulled out a black set of the same.

"You'll wear the white under the black and I'll cut some bone shapes out of the black. A little white and black face paint and you're a skeleton!" Meema said triumphantly.

Zoey had her doubts but she had no better ideas so they quickly made the purchase and then went to a drugstore for makeup. At home Meema and Hannah seemed to work magic, and appeared to be having fun doing it. In less than an hour Zoey was looking at herself in the mirror wearing the best skeleton outfit she had ever seen.

"Tomorrow after school I'll get your face made up and you'll be the prettiest skeleton at the Trunk-or-Treat!" Meema said as Zoey flung herself into her arms.

"Thank you, Meema! I love you!" Zoey said as she hugged her grandmother.

Later that day, with the potential Halloween disaster averted, Zoey excused herself and went to her bedroom to read more of the account of Dupree Durant.

After she retrieved the book from its new hiding place, she curled up on her bed and began to read.

When I next awoke, I thought that I had found myself in heaven. I was lying in a fine featherbed with clean sheets and blankets covering my body. I could see that there were two large windows that were open to the outside and a gentle breeze with a hint of the ocean stirring the lace curtains.

I was absolutely certain that I had passed over the great divide when the most beautiful angel appeared above me and placed a cool damp cloth against my brow. The angel had light ebony skin that had no blemish. Her fingers were long and shapely as they wiped the perspiration from my face. Her dark brown eyes focused on my own and her lips turned into a glorious smile of white teeth.

"So, you have decided to rejoin the world!" the angel said in a musical voice.

"Where am I?" I asked in a voice that was raspy and cracked.

"You are at the Meadows on the Neuse. It is the property of Elvira Hale and she is most anxious to make your acquaintance," the angel said as she disappeared from my view.

It was then that I knew that I was indeed still on the temporal plane I had always known. I felt pain in my right shoulder and could tell that I had a heavy dressing that went from my front to my back. I could also tell that I had been stricken with a fever for some time. My entire body felt weak and I grew dizzy when I tried to lift my head. From the dampness of my bedding, I could tell that my fever had only recently broken.

Then my angel reappeared and lifted a cup to my lips. As the cool water touched my parched tongue, I realized that I had never tasted any nectar as satisfying in my mortal existence.

"Do not give him too much at one time, Moriah, " said another female voice in the room. "He is still very weak and he may not be able to keep it down."

This voice sounded older, educated, and cultured. I tried to turn my head but everything in my body hurt so I laid still and tried to master the pain.

"Just take it easy, young man, " said that same voice as an old woman came into view above me.

I could tell immediately that she was a woman of high station from her fine clothes and the way that she handled herself as she looked me over. Her fingers pulled open my eyelids and then the back of her hand pressed my forehead.

"Your fever has broken," she announced as she pulled down my sheet and pulled back the dressing from my wound. Her fingers poked and prodded the wound causing me to groan with the pain. "Excellent. You have good feeling to the wound area. The infection seems to be clearing," she pronounced as she reached for a bottle and uncorked it before pouring the fluid into my wound which began to burn like it was on fire. "A terrible waste of fine rum but it *does help to cut down on infections in wounds,"* she said as she shook her head. *"Help me to get him into a sitting position, Moriah."*

The two women quickly helped me to sit up in the bed. My head was spinning from the pain but it soon began to recede.

"That's better," said the old woman as the young Negress smiled at me with that intoxicating smile.

The old woman continued to study me, then said, "Moriah, please fetch a bowl of broth for our guest."

I watched as the young servant left the room. She walked with such grace that she appeared to float.

"I suppose that you have a good many questions for me," said the old woman with that aristocratic voice. "I assure you that I have a good number for you as well. Perhaps it would be best for me to tell you what I know of you first. You were found in a launch just off of my dock here at the Meadows. There was a dead man in it with you. He had an ax buried in his chest. You had a fine bullet hole in your shoulder. Fortunately, it was a straight through wound that did not pierce anything of vital importance. The chief threat to your life was infection and fever. That has now passed but whether you live or die now will be determined by your account of how you and the dead man came to be on my property."

"May I ask how long I have been here before I answer your question?" I asked.

"You have been here for ten days," she replied

"My name is Dupree Durant and I was the captain of the ship Audacia out of Wilmington. My ship was taken by pirates and forced to sail into the Neuse River. The pirates wanted to offload our cargo. They had said that they would release us but it soon became apparent that they intended to leave no witnesses to their crime. My crew and I decided it would be better to die fighting than to be slaughtered like sheep. I was the only one to survive. I was trying to decide what I should do next when two of the pirates that had been sent with the final load of cargo returned. The only weapon I could *find on short order was a fire ax. I killed the first man as he came over the rail, his body dropped on the other, and I leapt upon him and buried the ax in his chest. Then all went black, as he must have gotten off the shot that wounded me as I killed him,"* I said. It was what I considered the truth to be with the minor omission of the gold and my part in its theft from the Seahorse.

She studied me for a while and then she said, *"I think you will live for now. I also think that you have not been totally truthful with me."*

For the next two weeks I continued to heal from my wounds. Moriah would tend to me every day and I found myself enthralled with her gentle ways and smoldering beauty. Elvira Hale was the name of the woman who treated my wounds and was the owner of Meadows on the Neuse. We became friends, conversing daily. She was widowed and had been married to her doctor husband for fifty years until his death the previous fall. Her husband had been a notable physician and she had spent most her life assisting him as he treated the grievously ill and injured. That is where she had acquired the skill to heal me.

She and her husband had never been able to have children, which was their greatest disappointment in life. She was now sixty-eight years old. Her world revolved around her small estate on the Neuse just before it emptied into Pamlico Sound. She loved this place and planned to be buried next to her beloved husband on a low ridge overlooking the sound. What saddened her was what would become of her slaves, although she never used that term for them. She always called them her servants or even her people.

It was this line of conversation that kept bringing my thoughts back to Hattie, the wet nurse that cared for little Dupree. I hated the thought of her forced service and wanted so badly to not be involved with that terrible institution.

Thus it was that Elvira and I became of one mind on the institution of slavery. We spent considerable time during my convalescence discussing the issue. She had grown up in southern society, where the role of the Negro in the institution of slavery was their only proper place. This had been drummed into her from the time she was born. She had inherited her slaves from her father, as had her husband from his family. Living with them around her every day refuted the notion that they were an inferior race that needed to be enslaved for their own good. Worse, as she interacted with other slave owners, she discovered that some of them were just cruel by nature, while others oppressed the enslaved out of fear that their chattel would rise up and murder their owners one day.

"For some of the owners, slavery is like a man who has caught a tiger by the tail and the only way to keep from being mauled is to hang on ever tighter!" she said.

I also confessed that I had a growing disgust with the institution. I had seen slaves all around me in my time in North Carolina but mostly I just ignored them as not my concern. It was after the death of my wife and the need for my son's care that I had day-to-day interaction with a slave. I too, had seen that Hattie was a human being with all the values and flaws of any person. There was no innate inferiority in her from her race or any other cause. In fact, whatever her shortcomings, they were likely due to the lack of education and opportunity that was perpetuated by slavery.

Elvira sat back and smiled at me after that particular conversation and said, "Imagine that! Two southern abolitionists discussing their hatred of that peculiar institution."

One day I asked Elvira why she feared for her people when she went to her heavenly reward. It was then that she told me about her nephew, Thaddeus. She explained to me that he was a beast that pleasured in the pain and suffering of others.

"He's a sadist, he only knows pleasure when others are in pain of his making," she said as tears formed in her eyes. "What terrifies me is that when I die, he will inherit my sweet people! When he visits, he walks around looking at my servants as if he were a butcher selecting which of the chickens will die today. I'm particularly afraid for my dear Moriah. He has demon eyes when he looks on her."

I was deeply troubled by the admission about the perversions of her nephew and doubly so for the angel that had cared for me with such tenderness.

I know that what I write next will be considered an abomination in much of the south. I had fallen deeply in love with the ebony goddess that I called Moriah. My mind worked feverishly on the problem of Elvira's human "property" and no legal solution could be found. In my mind, however, I had an illegal one that might work!

The next day I approached my hostess and asked to have a private conversation with her about the problem with her nephew.

"First, my lady, I wish to beg your forgiveness. I left out parts of my story on how I came to the Meadows. It is true that my ship and crew were taken by pirates but we had been their willing accomplices," *I said as I started my confession to her. I described the events that had transpired from the transfer of the gold onto the Audacia until the killing of the final two pirates.*

"I had concluded that much when you told me the tale on your sickbed," *she said with a gentle smile before she continued.* "But what, pray tell, does this have to do with my people?"

"Allow me to ask a question of you first, my lady," *I asked and she nodded for me to proceed.* "Why do you not just free your people now?"

"I would dearly love to do that. However, I am old and I do not have the resources to hire help to care for the Meadows. In some ways, I'm like the man with a tiger by the tail," *she said wistfully. Then in a harsher tone she added,* "Thaddeus watches all that I do. He has already attempted to declare me unfit to handle my own affairs. If I petitioned to emancipate my slaves, he would intervene with the court and take control of them immediately."

I now had a much greater appreciation for the quandary that my hostess found herself in but my proposal would still solve her dilemma and give me the opportunity to be with Moriah.

"What if you were approached by a wealthy person desiring to buy *your slaves?" I asked.*

"I would never agree to their sale! I would have no idea if they would be treated humanely," she replied.

"What if I were the buyer?" I asked as she looked skeptically at me.

I explained that the gold was still likely sitting on the shore not far from the wreck of my ship. If we recovered the gold, I could then purchase her servants and free them.

She shook her head and told me that Thaddeus would protest the sale and would likely question the source of the money putting me in jeopardy.

I thought about it some more and said, "What if I do not give them their freedom? What if I purchase a plantation where they could live as free men and women who were paid for their labor and allowed to control their own lives? If some of them wanted to leave, I could claim that they had died."

I told her that I knew of certain captains that would see that they were transported to friendly shores such as Canada. I even pledge that I would give anyone leaving a sufficient amount of gold to establish a new life. The more I thought of it, the more enthused I became toward the venture. I could see that I could end the tyranny of slavery for so many!

"It is a bold plan!" she said with enthusiasm. Then her smile faded and she said, "I would never be able to manage the Meadows without them. I despise slavery but I'm too old to give up its benefits to me. Also, we are forgetting Thaddeus, he is sure to protest the sale."

"I wonder if he would be so inclined if I paid a top dollar price and then agreed to lease them back to you at an attractive rate. It would be difficult to argue that he would not benefit from such a trade," I replied.

"Yes! That will work!" she said with her own growing enthusiasm. "We will need to have everything drawn up by attorneys with a bill of sale and contracts. I know of some lawyers that we can use,"

It was then that I decided to bring her into my confidence with regard to Moriah.

"I have one final requirement that must be part of our agreement. Moriah will not be leased back to you," I said and dreaded the next phase of our conversation.

I was dumbfounded when I heard her next words. "God bless you!" she said. "You will take her from here and far beyond my odious nephews reach!" She smiled that gentle smile and added, "I know you will always care for her as only a man who truly loves a woman can."

She then embraced me and kissed my cheek. So it was that my new life was to be formed!

Elvira consented to allow me to enlist some of her male servants in the arduous task of recovering the gold. It took us some time to find the remains of the Audacia in Alligator Gut but the gold was located with relative ease from the position of the wreck. It was sad but our search was made easier upon the discovery of the bleached bones of my crewmen on the spot where they had been brutally murdered near the hidden gold. Elvira was kind enough to inter their remains in her family plot and provide them with markers.

While this was going on I had two other tasks that needed to be done. First was to write my in-laws that I was alive and that I would soon be coming for little Dupree. I explained that I had been the victim of piracy and that my ship was lost but that I had come upon good fortune after and was paid a sizable reward for the destruction of the pirates. That reward was sufficient for me to acquire a plantation near New Bern and to pay off Julius's share of the Audacia. I had located land for sale that came from a failed plantation near New Bern. I acquired the land and planned the construction of a grand house that would be called Oak Harbor. I gave it that name as there were many oak trees where I chose to construct the main house and as a sailor the harbor is where one finds refuge from the sea.

The second task was to woo the fair Moriah to become my wife.

I thought she would leap at the prospect as I knew that she was physically attracted to me and a bond had formed between us. She told me that she would willingly be my lover but that no black woman could ever be a proper wife for a white man in the South.

She also told me that my fantasy of making Oak Harbor a place where Negroes could live in peace was a fool's dream. She was quite blunt about how quickly the charade would be discovered. She claimed that the blacks would be punished and sold back into the worst of situations. As for me, I would be flogged in the public square and then lynched as an abolitionist. My son would likely be murdered before my eyes.

I told her that I understood the risks that I would be taking but that I could no longer tolerate the inhumanity that surrounded me. She asked me why I did not leave the south and go to where slavery was not the way of life? I told her that to just turn my back on the misery of the world was condoning it by a sin of omission.

"All a man can do is try to make things better!" I said as I begged her to let me try.

It was then that she began to soften to my plan. She told me that she loved me but that the only way my plan would work was for me to publicly be all the things that I hated. I would have to be a harsh slave owner that openly supported the institution.

We talked about how this image might be portrayed. She told me to allow her to talk with other slaves to see how many of them would willingly join the endeavor by realistically allowing themselves to be worked hard and publicly punished for even minor infractions. I would always be referred to as Marse Dupree by all the Negros at Oak Harbor. As for her personal relationship with me she would only be my willing concubine.

This one instruction from her was unacceptable by me. I told her she would be my son's nanny for public consumption but that in the eyes of God that she would be Missus Dupree Durant and that our children would be the equal of my own son.

So it was that Moriah and I became husband and wife before the eyes of God until we were parted by death. The ceremony was performed by one of the servants that served as their pastor and was witnessed in our family bible by Elvira Hale.

So it was that Oak Harbor was born! Out of treachery, gold makes free the slaves! "Perfide Aurum Liberat!"

Zoey read the account with growing fascination. As a child of the 21st century, the concepts of life in the antebellum south were immensely foreign to her own. Just the concept that a person was defined by skin color seemed inherently flawed but for many people of those days it was just accepted as an irrefutable truth. She thought about how Dupree and Moriah had to hide their interracial marriage from the world or they would be executed or imprisoned! In Zoey's world such relationships were an everyday reality. What a strange, fragile existence they must have lived.

The one thing that became clear to her was why the family motto had become "Treacherous Gold Makes Free!" The gold had been acquired as a result of treachery but it had set the slaves of the Meadows free.

CHAPTER 17 • ESCAPES & SUSPECTS

Zoey was just getting ready to delve into the remaining pages of the book when she heard a knock on the front door. Her curiosity kicked in and she stuck her head in the hall to see who it was. Her mom opened the door with a surprised look on her face.

"Deputy Rawlins!" Hannah said with a little apprehension. "Please come in out of the rain."

"Thank you, ma'am," he replied as he came into the house holding his hat in his hand.

Zoey walked down the hall to see why the deputy had come to see them.

He looked to see her moving to join her mom while at about the same time her grandmother walked in from the kitchen.

"I'm afraid that I have some bad news to share with y'all," he stated and it did sound like he regretted having to bring the news. "The two men we arrested last night were released this morning."

"How could that have happened?" her mother asked with shock.

"Someone made an administrative error and released them on their own recognizance. After they were released, we found out that their driver's licenses were counterfeit. As if that wasn't bad enough, someone lost their fingerprints," he said as his eyes flickered from one of them to another.

At first no one knew what to say but then Meema said in a rather suspicious tone, "It sounds to me like those guys must have friends in high places to arrange that many mistakes to occur within a few hours."

Zoey looked at the deputy and could see the embarrassment on his face. Then he looked carefully at her mom and seemed to make a decision.

"I can't defend what has happened and I would agree that three mistakes in less than twelve hours was either incompetence or criminal," he said. "I have my suspicions."

"Would you care to share your suspicions with us?" Meema asked with a raised eyebrow.

Deputy Rawlins nodded that he would and said "Perhaps we should have a seat."

"Certainly, would you care for a cup of coffee?" her mom asked as they went to the table.

"That would be very kind of you," he said as he took off his jacket, draped it over the back of a chair, and sat down.

Her mom quickly brought a cup of coffee and asked, "Do you want cream or sugar?"

"Black will be fine, ma'am," he replied as he accepted the cup from her and looked into her eyes.

Zoey noticed that they seemed to freeze for an instant before they both looked away quickly after they had exchanged that glance. She noticed that Meema must have found something amusing as her eyes gleamed and her lips formed a subtle smile.

"You said that you have your suspicions, Deputy Rawlins?" Meema asked politely to break the tension between her daughter and the deputy.

"Yes, ma'am. Last night I was surprised to see Mr. Smithers at the scene. He's a pretty big player in the local community, especially in politics. His relationship with the sheriff is not just one of friendship. He was one of the power-brokers that put the sheriff into office," he said nervously.

"Are you saying the sheriff probably had the guys released because Smithers told him to?" her mom asked, looking distressed at the idea.

"I'm not sure, but I don't believe so," the deputy began. "The sheriff has always been a straight arrow as far as I know. However, Smithers has made other friends in the department. I have seen some things that are hard to explain that have been connected to him. For instance, Smithers's grandson got in some trouble a couple of years ago. Nothing real big, he got stopped for reckless driving and the deputy that pulled him over could smell alcohol on his breath. He gave him a sobriety test which he failed. He was arrested and had a blood sample collected that placed him at twice the legal limit.

Since he was still a minor at the time it would mean an automatic loss of his driver's license until he turned eighteen, a fine, and up to thirty days incarceration. When it was time to go to court, the blood test evidence had disappeared, so the charges were dropped."

Zoey could not help but think of the death of Jonathan Wilson all the way back in 1969 and how the conclusion of what happened had been so quickly determined. She blurted out, "Do you know anything about the death of Jonathan Wilson back in 1969?"

He looked at her with a face that said he had never heard about it.

"That was so long ago," her mom said. "Mr. Smithers would have been only a boy."

"His great-uncle was in it up to his neck. Don't you remember what Zipporah told us about that night?" Zoey replied.

"Maybe I should hear about this," Rawlins said. "There was an exchange last night between Moses and Smithers over some old event and his great-uncle."

"Mr. Smithers's great-uncle was the attorney for the estate of Dupree Durant the Fifth who died way back in 1960," Zoey explained. "Uncle Smithers took over running Oak Harbor until Rose Durant would turn twenty-five. From what Moses told me, Smithers was always stingy in keeping up the estate. Then Miss Rose got married to an attorney by the name of Jonathan Wilson, who kicked Smithers out and took over. One night, Miss Rose found him dead in the study with a gunshot to the head. The sheriff said that it was a suicide but Moses said he saw the body. Mr. Wilson was shot in the right side of the head and the gun was by his right hand but Mr. Wilson was left-handed." Zoey looked closely at the deputy to see his reaction.

"I've seen some strange things when a person decides to take their own life but using your weak hand to fire a shot is not one of them," he said thoughtfully.

"There was an investigation that determined that Mr. Wilson had lost the trust fund that supported the estate of Oak Harbor," Zoey continued. "They said that was why he killed himself. They ended up turning the estate back over to Smithers to file a bankruptcy. Most of the farmland was sold off to pay debts. Miss Rose was left with the old house and some land on this side. She built this house and lived in it until she was moved into an assisted living facility by her late husband's family. I have heard that Smithers and the Wilson family are fighting tooth and nail over the house next door." Zoey paused at what seemed to be the end of her narrative, then added, "I think Uncle Smithers stole the money back in the sixties and our Mr. Smithers wants the house since he thinks there's a treasure hidden there!"

Deputy Rawlins thought about what he had just heard. He sipped his coffee thoughtfully and then looked at her and said, "That's quite a story. Perhaps I should look into some of the old files and see what I can find out."

Zoey smiled when she heard the deputy's reply.

"In the meantime, I don't want to worry y'all but there were a few things that caught my attention last night," he said with a concerned look. "The first was that exchange of looks between Smithers and Moses. In my job, I have learned to read people and my conclusion about those two is that Moses doesn't like or trust Nathaniel Smithers. If what Zoey says is true, I might have sensed a family feud that goes back more than a generation. The second was the secret storage closet in the study. It was clear that nearly everyone was surprised about that concealed room and there was clear evidence that some books or documents had been hidden there for a very long time. We don't know who took them but my guess is that neither Moses nor Smithers had any knowledge of them. I do wonder what those items would tell us about a treasure on the Oak Harbor property," he said as his eyes went from one person to the next sitting at the table.

They all sat in silence for a while as they pondered his words. Zoey could not help but think of the books just down the hall. She had not finished reading even the first book yet but she was convinced that she would learn if there really were a treasure hidden at Oak Harbor. Perhaps she would even know where to look for it. She thought about sharing that she had the books but again she thought of how Dupree had not been able to detect the duplicity in Meredith Williams. Perhaps Deputy Rawlins was not all that he seemed to be!

"I have one final worry to share," he said with deep concern. "There is something going on here much bigger than two amateur treasure hunters being arrested. Someone broke them out of jail and I suspect it was done because of the missing books." He stopped to convey the seriousness of what he was saying. "If they do have the books then someone already knows the secret of Oak Harbor," he said with a frown. "If they don't have them, the benefactor that got them out of jail will begin to look at anyone else who might have had the opportunity to come into possession of those books."

They all felt the deadly seriousness of what Deputy Rawlins had to say.

"Zoey would be included on that list. I want you to be very aware of what is going on around you. I don't believe that they would harm you but they will try to determine if you have those books," he said and Zoey felt a chill run down her spine.

The deputy got up and put on his coat and Hannah escorted him to the door. Zoey could hear the normal "thank you" and other pleasantries as she showed him out of the house. Her mom watched carefully as the patrol car left, turned down the road, and disappeared from sight.

Hannah came back to the table and said, "I think we'd better have a talk about those books!"

Zoey spent the next hour talking about the discovery of the books and what she had read so far. Her mom asked who else knew that she had the books. Zoey explained that the only other person aware of the books was Rufus, since he had accompanied her into the house to retrieve them.

"So who do you think we can trust at this point?" Meema asked. Zoey's mom shrugged her shoulders.

"I don't like that Smithers guy," Zoey said quietly.

"I agree with that. He was at Oak Harbor almost as fast as the deputies. He clearly had other reasons to be there than to look over a run down plantation house," Meema said.

"What about Deputy Rawlins?" Zoey asked and wanted to get the take of both her mom and Meema.

"I have mixed feelings about him," her mom said as she looked away.

"I think we'll have to get know him better. He seems to be what he says he is but we really don't know him that well," Meema said with a chuckle. "I do know that he found your mother rather intriguing and I suspect your mama also found the first exchange at the table rather exhilarating."

Zoey looked at her mother with interest as she saw her blushing.

"It's all right, baby," Meema teased. "He's a rather good looking guy and he did come here out of concern for all of us. However, he did only have eyes for you!"

Zoey joined her grandmother in laughing at her mother's discomfort and was happy to see her mom also begin to giggle and then laugh at the situation.

Her mother was trying to stop but then laughed even harder. "When this is all over, maybe I'll go out with him if he's not in prison!" she managed to say as she gasped for air between more giggles.

It took them several minutes to regain their composure.

It was Zoey who managed to get back to the discussion first.

"The next likely suspect would be the Wilson family. Just like Smithers they're trying to get control of a run down mansion. The only reason they could want it is for the treasure," she said as the two older women nodded in agreement.

"That's true and they also took Miss Rose away from the care of Zipporah and Moses. They both have hard feelings about her being moved into the assisted living facility. I even got the impression that they blame the Wilsons for her death," her mom said.

"What about Moses and his wife? He seems pretty possessive of that old property, himself. I know that Zoey has told me that he claims not to believe in the treasure but why does he want to be in control of that old run down property if he's not searching for it himself?" Meema said thoughtfully.

"I don't want to think bad things about them but he didn't want to call the law after he learned of the intruders," her mom added.

"I don't believe that Moses is one of the bad guys," Zoey chimed in. "He was going to call the law until Rufus and I convinced him not to. He was even going to tell Smithers but he sure wasn't looking forward to doing it!" Zoey said, not believing that the old black man was anything other than what he appeared to be.

Then she again remembered how Meredith Williams had deceived Dupree Durant due to simmering feelings of being cheated for many long years.

"Could Moses be holding a grudge that went back to his childhood?" she thought to herself.

"Would you tell him that you have the books?" Meema asked Zoey just after she had finished forming her own new doubts.

She lowered her eyes and shook her head that she would not.

"So, there we have it. There is no one that we can truly trust," Meema said.

"What about Rufus?" Zoey asked as she searched their eyes.

"That boy is absolutely infatuated with you! You're the only treasure he desires!" Meema said.

Zoey went red and was approaching crimson as the other two giggled at her discomfort.

"You should tell him not to talk to anyone about you having the books," her mom said gently after regaining her composure.

CHAPTER 18 • REWARDS & REGRETS

Later that evening, Zoey again picked up the book of Dupree Durant's life. She felt compelled to read the rest of the account. She started to read the flowing script from nearly 170 years in the past.

The year of 1853 was an eventful year. Ground was broken on the Oak Harbor house in January. I contracted with an architect located in New Bern to design the house and the grounds. Unknown to the architect was the fact that Moriah had much to say about the design of the house. She was concerned that the house must present all the right outward appearances that spoke to an arrogant slave owner. There were rooms for social gatherings of all the notables from the area. There would be Galas and Balls where the gentry would gather so that ladies could gossip while the men conducted business and talked about the price of tobacco and cotton.

Moriah lectured me daily about the importance of the image that we would all have to maintain. To thàt end, she also incorporated into the design a number of concealed passageways where the Negroes could move without being observed. The most important of these was the stairway that connected the servants' quarters on the third floor with the master's private suite on the second floor. I blushed from my toes to the top of my head when she said that she intended to see to her master's every need!

Moriah had a great eye for how to make the management of the house easier for the workers who would see to the day-to-day household chores.

I had intended to use only the labor of the staff I acquired from the Meadows in construction of Oak Harbor but Moriah quickly told me that it would take too long and that we should hire a builder to do the work. I was resistant as I knew that no matter whom I chose they would make their profit off the backs of slaves. Moriah explained that was exactly the point of doing so! From the start I must appear to be an avid proponent of slavery. I did not like what had to be done but in the end I agreed.

In addition to designing and beginning construction on the house there was the business of completing the purchase of the slaves of the Meadows. True to her word, Elvira and I began to work with two attorneys to complete the sale of her slaves and for me to agree to lease their services back to her for the rest of her life. One complication that became obvious from the start was the need for me to convert at least part of the gold bullion into minted gold or into readily available funds at a bank.

I had never considered how dangerous this would become! Two tons of gold was worth $1,322,000! That kind of gold would be sure to attract attention and raise all sorts of questions as to where it had come from.

Zoey wondered what $1,322,000 would be worth in current money. She picked up her tablet and divided $1,322,000 by 64,000 ounces and determined that the gold was worth around $20.65 per ounce back then. She then got the current price of gold and was shocked that the same amount of gold today would be worth $122,000,000!

"Oh my God!" she said aloud in total amazement.

If there were a treasure next door it would be of enormous value and that would explain why Smithers and the Wilsons were fighting so hard for control of the house! Zoey continued to read with even more intensity.

It was Elvira that once again came to my rescue when she informed me that there was a banker that her husband had done some business with up in New York. She wrote me a letter of introduction to the man and suggested that I take only a small portion of my gold to him and negotiate a deal for him to buy it from me at a five percent discount from the market.

So it was that I made the trip to New York and began my new banking arrangement that would allow me to sell bullion from time to time and have the proceeds returned to bank accounts that I controlled in North Carolina.

Shortly after my trip to New York I had the distasteful experience of meeting Thaddeus Hale. Just as Elvira had warned, he made an appearance as soon as possible after learning of the proposed sale of the slaves at the Meadows. I could hear him raging at his aunt in the most foul language and threatening violence against her person. I am certain that his intent was to bully her into abandoning the transaction.

I am sure that, to his dismay, she was made of sterner stuff than he had anticipated. The conversation then became much quieter and I could no longer tell where it was going. Then he stepped out of the parlor and set his eyes upon me. There was nothing but unmasked hatred in those eyes and I am sure he found nothing but the same reflected in my own.

"You must be the scoundrel who is trying to defraud my aunt! I shall file suit to overturn this sale!" he said with venom dripping from every word.

"That would be your decision to make but I do not believe that you would prevail," I said as calmly as I could. "The price to be paid is above the market price and the terms of her leasing the slaves back are quite reasonable. In the end your aunt will have gold in hand and her staff secure for the rest of her life. After her death, you will receive her estate and probably a significant amount of money. I doubt that any judge will see where you have been harmed."

I could see that his mind was thinking through my words. Thaddeus may be a sadist but I could see he was also a greedy man. While this was going on, Moriah walked by to enter the parlor. She was likely summoned by Elvira after the confrontation with her odious nephew.

"You may be right about how a judge would see this," he started to say as he followed Moriah's every step. "I might withhold my protest if you would sell me the wench," he said and his voice had moved from greed to lust.

I shook my head that I would not even consider such a deal as my anger began to grow.

"I'll pay you twice what you paid for her," he said quickly.

"Moriah is not for sale at any price," I said as I tried to keep my rage in check.

"Perhaps after you have had her for a year you may grow weary of her. My offer would still stand," he said in a way that was so distasteful that it was all that I could do to not pummel the man where he stood.

"I think you should leave now," I said as I motioned toward the door.

He gave me an evil sneer as he headed out the door. I followed along to make sure he did no harm before he left.

The stable boy stood at the bottom of the steps and Thaddeus yelled at him to fetch his horse while raising his riding crop as if to strike the boy. The boy ran off to get the horse as Thaddeus expressed in the most offensive language just how lazy and ignorant slaves were.

"Aunt Elvira has been too light with the whip!" he said with disgust.

I stepped close to him as I barely controlled my urge to murder the man and said, "You are not welcome here, sir. I heard your threats against your aunt and if you ever talk to her like that again I will demand satisfaction on the field of honor!"

The boy returned with his mount as Thaddeus stood there with his mouth open, knowing full well that my threat was sincere. I could also see that he was a coward. He then dashed to his horse, leapt upon it, and dug his spurs deep into the animal's flanks. The horse reared in pain nearly throwing him off before it bolted through the gate.

I looked down at the stable boy who was smiling from ear to ear after seeing the demon that had threatened every soul at the Meadows for as long as he could remember flee in fear.

With the completion of the sale, things began to change quickly. To this point only Moriah was aware of the entirety of my plan. The conversation with the other slaves was as interesting for me as it was to them. Moriah had prepared me for the meeting. She told me that to be a slave, one had to never let a white person learn what was truly on your mind. You always lowered your eyes and never let your emotions show on your face and under no circumstances should you share your inner thoughts with a white person.

It took some time for them to begin to ask questions and then to make suggestions on how the public image for both myself as Marse Dupree and they as my slaves could be achieved. They did understand the importance of my being perceived as a harsh master, to keep other whites from looking too closely at the inner workings of Oak Harbor. After all, we would all be in mortal danger!

One of the older slaves made an observation that had gone unnoticed by Moriah as well as myself and that was the lack of an overseer. He had been a slave at a large plantation when he was just a teenager. There was always one or more hired white men who would watch the slaves and meet out punishment. If Oak Harbor did not have an overseer or two it would surely draw unwanted attention.

It was out of this conversation that I decided to make another trip north with my next shipment of gold. I had previously discovered that the banker I was working with was an avid abolitionist. When I explained what I was doing he was quite taken with my bold plan, so much so that he cut his fee in half on my transactions. He then introduced me to his circle of antislavery friends who, in turn, introduced me to Robert Smithers.

Zoey froze when she saw the name Smithers mentioned in those long-ago times with Oak Harbor.

"Could that possibly be an ancestor of the Nathaniel Smithers I met last night?" she asked herself before reading on.

Robert, or as he preferred to be called, Bob, had emigrated to New York from England. He detested slavery and had pledged to do whatever he could to help slaves flee to freedom. As we got to know each other a deep friendship developed. He confided in me that he had two others besides himself that would be willing to move to North Carolina. They would pose as my overseers and work with me on shipping any of the slaves north that wished to go.

So it was that I had the infrastructure in place to begin my personal war against slavery!

I returned to North Carolina via Wilmington to pay a call on the Nobles and to collect my now three-year-old son. I received a warm reception and spent several days with my in-laws. Little Dupree had no recollection of me and tended to cling to Hattie s skirt. She encouraged him to become familiar with me, and I admired how much she could alleviate his anxiety. The next day I approached her owner and inquired as to whether they would consider selling Hattie to me. They were hesitant to do so but I continued to insist. It was then that they revealed to me that Hattie had three children of her own and it would break their heart to separate Hattie from her children. I offered to buy them all at a generous price.

The Nobles were somewhat taken aback by my sudden embracing of slavery but then wished me well on my new plantation venture.

Hattie and her children were absolutely silent as we journeyed by land back to the Meadows in the wagon that I had purchased along with a fine team of horses in Wilmington. My Negroes came to greet me but quickly became subdued when they noted the newcomers. I quickly instructed them to find a suitable place for Hattie and her children to be housed.

I then went in the house and greeted Elvira and Moriah. Moriah melted into my arms telling me that she had missed me terribly. I informed them of my purchase of Hattie and her three children. Moriah became thoughtful at the news. This acquisition was a little sooner than she had anticipated but decided that bringing Hattie was my only option due to little Dupree's need for her continued care during the transition.

I brought Hattie and little Dupree in and introduced them to Elvira, who was quite taken with my son. Moriah also greeted both of them warmly before she told Hattie that she would instruct her on what would be expected of her at the Meadows.

I retired to the study to read the correspondence that had accumulated while awaiting my return. Several hours later Moriah stepped into the study and closed the door behind her. She informed me that Hattie was thrilled with her new situation and that she would stay with us until young Dupree no longer needed her. Moriah then informed me that the father of Hattie's children was a runaway and that she wanted to find him to reunite their family.

Once again, I was deeply saddened at the pain and sorrows inflicted by the abhorrent institution of slavery.

Even as I tried to reconcile this news in my mind, Moriah delivered a thunderbolt of her own. "I was so happy to meet your son today. I hope that as he grows up, he will come to accept me as his stepmother and our child as his sibling."

She then sat in my lap and nuzzled against my neck. It took a moment for me to understand the significance of what she had just said!

I was to be a father again!

After that day my life became ever more hectic. Smithers and his two friends, along with their families, arrived in New Bern. I had instructed my builder to erect three cottages on the estate to house my new overseers in anticipation of the arrival of my slaves. He was also to build sufficient cabins to house twenty slaves.

My plan which was developed with Moriah s assistance and with the endorsement of the other Negros, was for me to purchase slaves at various auctions in eastern North Carolina. We determined that it was time to begin. The slave who had started his life as a field hand was named Ezrah. He agreed to accompany me as my man-servant as I attended slave auctions in eastern North Carolina. He would use hand signals to tell me when to bid. My Negroes understood that Oak Harbor must be a successful plantation to serve our purpose. For this to happen we would need sufficient field hands to produce the cash crops of tobacco and cotton. They estimated that for full production I would need at least forty men. We all agreed that we would target either men who had families to be sold with them or young men without families. Ezrah then smiled and said that we would need a similar number of single females.

So, my attendance at slave auctions became a common sight throughout the eastern part of the state. I was nervous the first few times as so many eyes fell on the new owner of Oak Harbor. I had never thought of being an actor but my new life demanded that I put on another persona like a normal man slipped on a different jacket for supper.

The part of the charade that I detested the most was when Ezrah would lead my new purchases off to the smithy to have their shackles fastened to keep them from running off while I socialized with the other bidders and talked about everything from crop prices to politics. Moriah had trained me to be as arrogant as the men I met at the auctions.

The core of my original Meadows purchase embraced the process and as each new group of slaves would come in, they would begin to interrogate them on their experiences and beliefs. When they felt confident enough that the new slaves could be trusted with the truth of Oak Harbor, they would start their training to play their role.

Each new person had to pledge that they would stay at least six months with the plantation and give fair service. At the end of six months, they were given the option of leaving or continuing on. If they continued on, those that were single would be given the right to marry and start families. Each family would be provided a living space. One of Smithers's men had been a builder back in England and he drew up a plan for cabins that would have four separate living quarters with a loft for children to sleep in. Single men and women would have the separate dormitories to stay in. All of these buildings were kept far away from the plantation house, while the overseer cottages and typical slave quarters would be in sight of the main house.

Some of the Negroes would volunteer to be always present at the slave cabins to preserve the ruse that I ran a harsh plantation. These included demonstrations of corporal punishment whenever an outsider entered the estate. Newcomers were segregated into a separate housing area during their orientation.

On the first day of November, I officially declared Oak Harbor completed. A large celebration was held and every notable person for twenty miles around was invited to tour the new house and its magnificent gardens. My performance of the part of harsh and formal Marse Dupree was convincing and I was declared a most welcome new member of New Bern society.

So, there you have it, my fine sons. You now know the truth of how the world of Oak Harbor came to be. I hope that you, too, will pick up the fight against the abhorrent institution of slavery!

Your Loving Father, Dupree Durant

Zoey was thoughtful for several moments as she looked at the signature of Dupree Durant. She did not know if any of the gold still existed but at one time there was a treasure, and some of it could still be there. Perhaps the next book would answer that question.

CHAPTER 19 • FOUR BODIES

Zoey could hardly concentrate on her classes that Monday. All the excitement from the weekend was enough to distract her by itself but what really made it hard to concentrate was that it was Halloween and tonight she would go to Trunk-or-Treat with Rufus. The day seemed to drag by but the final bell rang and they gathered to board their bus. Neither Rufus nor Zoey had mentioned that evening's event in front of Billy. She felt somewhat guilty about that but she really did look forward to being with just Rufus.

When she arrived at home Meema helped her get into her skeleton outfit and then put on her face-paint. When Meema finished she held up a hand mirror for Zoey to look into. Zoey was stunned at what an expert job Meema had done. While she certainly looked like a skeleton, there was something pretty about her appearance. Zoey hoped that Rufus would notice as well.

At 5:00 the doorbell rang and Zoey started to rush to the door but her grandmother stopped her and made her step back.

"Never let your date know that you are anxious to go," she said with the wink of the eye before she opened the door. "My goodness, Rufus! Don't you look terrifying! Let me see if Zoey is ready," she heard Meema say.

Zoey then came to the door to see Rufus standing there, made up as a zombie. She opened the door and stepped outside with a smile as she noticed the boy looking her over.

"Wow, you look great!" he said as they walked to the car.

Mr. Johnson was standing by the car and said, "Now let me get some pictures of you two escapees from the cemetery!"

They posed for several pictures before they got in the car and headed off to the church parking lot.

Zoey was used to trick-or-treating in the city, where you could quickly get from door to door, but here in the country that was difficult, so it made more sense to have central place where the kids could go and be safe.

They spent the next two hours going around the parking lot getting their treats and laughing at the things that they saw. It felt good to be just two kids enjoying the holiday.

Still, Zoey had a lot on her mind and desperately wanted to talk with Rufus about what Deputy Rawlins had shared and the things that she had read in the first book.

"Rufus, can we find someplace we can be alone?" she asked and noticed that Rufus looked suddenly nervous.

"Come with me," he said as his voice squeaked.

They walked around the side of the church to a spot where there were no people around.

She looked at him and he looked odd for a moment. She wondered what was wrong with him but decided she better tell him what was on her mind.

"I finished reading the first book," Zoey began. "It explains all about Dupree Durant and how Oak Harbor came to be. Dupree was actually a good guy. He hated slavery and used Oak Harbor to help slaves escape to the north. He also married a slave woman and had a son with her that was named Uriah. I know this all sounds confusing but the big thing that I learned is that he did have a lot of gold. That has to be what those guys were looking for." Zoey was somewhat mystified as she saw relief flood over her friend's face.

It took Rufus a minute to regain his composure and say, "Did it tell you where the gold is hidden?"

"Not in the first book but there are still two more to go," she said and then decided she better tell him about what Deputy Rawlins had to say. "Those two guys they caught on Saturday got loose on Sunday morning. The deputy said that he thinks they got released because someone wants to know who got those books out of Oak Harbor. I think he was trying to warn us that they may come looking for me," Zoey said with concern as she looked into Rufus's eyes. "I'm scared!"

To her surprise, Rufus hugged her. His arms felt so good as they held her. He whispered, "I won't let anything bad happen to you."

"Now, what are the two of you doing so far away from the parking lot?" asked Mr. Johnson who seemed to have appeared out of nowhere.

The two teens ended their embrace as Rufus's father scrutinized them.

"I think it would best if you went back to be with the rest of the crowd." Mr. Johnson said calmly but with the hint of a smile.

They stayed for another thirty minutes until the event began to wind down.

When they stopped in the driveway at Zoey's house, she started to get out of the car and go inside but Mr. Johnson stopped her and said, "Rufus, when you ask a lady out it's your duty to see her to the front door."

Zoey was glad that the makeup on her face hid the blush she felt warm her cheeks as she slid out behind Rufus. He then escorted her to the door. They stood there awkwardly for a moment unsure what to do when the door opened and her mom looked down on them with a knowing smile.

"Good night, Rufus. I had fun! See you tomorrow on the bus," Zoey said as she stepped inside and watched him walk back to his father's car.

"So, how was your date?" Meema asked with a grin.

Zoey flashed back on the hug that Rufus had given her to comfort her. She felt warmth flood through veins but this time it was not from embarrassment but from excitement. "I had fun. Would it be all right if I go to my room to read?"

"Okay," her mom said softly as she supposed that her daughter did not want to be grilled about her first date.

Zoey went to her room and changed into her pajamas and removed the makeup. While she did this, she couldn't help but think about the first book by Dupree Durant, which answered his involvement in piracy. She also knew with certainty that he had killed men but she believed that it was either kill or be killed. It amazed her just how violent life had been in those long-ago days. Durant also had to become a deceiver but only to pursue a greater good. The account of his life revealed a man with whom Zoey was coming to admire for his character.

The book also thrust her into a time and culture that was so far removed from her world that she could scarcely believe that they had existed right here in North Carolina. She had learned about slavery and racism in school but Dupree Durant's personal account made it all so real!

After cleaning up she headed straight to her bedroom and retrieved the second book from its hiding place. This one was titled "The Secret History of Oak Harbor" and was written by Dupree Durant on December 12th, 1880. Zoey noticed that after the title the penmanship changed. As she read the opening paragraph it became apparent that Moriah Durant was writing for her husband.

This is the final accounting of the life of Dupree Durant upon this temporal plane that has been my home for the last sixty-two years. My dearest wife, Moriah, is transcribing my final confessions as to what happened since the birth of our beloved son Uriah. She is doing this out of love so that my descendants will have an account of how they came to be and the terrible price that was paid for their position in this world. I do this first, to inspire them to act boldly in their lives to confront and give battle to the forces of ignorance and injustice. Secondly, I desire that they each come to know that who and what they are was bestowed upon them by grace and not merit and that they, too, should extend grace to all they encounter with a heart of mercy.

Zoey realized that this document was being written by a man who was dying. The grief that overwhelmed her came as surprise at first but she realized that Dupree was no longer someone who had died long ago but had become a living person with whom she had shared his amazing life.

At the time of the birth of my dear younger son Uriah, I documented the journey that I took to come to Oak Harbor. That account detailed my involvement in piracy, killing, and deception. I also shared the bold plan that I along with my dearest wife, Moriah, developed out of my loathing for the institution of slavery and, equally as abhorrent, the ignorant belief that race determines the ability and position of any man, or for that matter, woman.

I am writing this journal to set straight certain events that occurred over the last twenty-five years for the benefit of my sons as well as their offspring and, hopefully, for other generations to come. This accounting is spurred by the diagnosis by my personal physician that I will depart this world in the next few weeks due to consumption.

Zoey puzzled over what consumption was but felt compelled to read on.

As my time is short, I will get to the big questions that follow either Oak Harbor or myself. The objective of Oak Harbor was to fight a secret war against slavery. To be successful at this, every member of the plantation had to become actors. I was to portray Marse Dupree. He was an avid proponent of slavery, an avowed racist, a cruel master, a man only capable of loving himself, and most of all an ostentatious man who flaunted his wealth by the lavish parties he hosted at his opulent plantation house.

To this day I am still regarded in this light by most of the people in New Bern.

The reality is that I am none of those things. I am first and most all a man in love with my dear wife, Moriah, who is of African descent and a former slave. I am also a father to two fine young men, Dupree Durant the Second and Uriah Jones. Dupree was born to me by my late wife Bernadette who died in childbirth. Uriah does not claim my surname as he is the mulatto offspring of the secret marriage to my wife. In no way do I approve of the denial of my name to Uriah for I love him in every way and he is the equal to my all-white son! It was only upon the insistence of Moriah and the admitted need to keep my public image up in the years before the Civil War that I acquiesced to this injustice.

After the war I planned to legally claim my son but was again convinced by my wife and Uriah himself that Oak Harbor was still needed to help the formerly enslaved to build new lives. Dupree II has always known that Uriah is his brother and the two are as close as any kin that I have ever known. They have pledged to me that their lineage will always know of the family bond and continue Oak Harbor's mission.

I had hoped that the war would have eliminated the need for Oak Harbor but, if anything, the slavery of the past has only transformed to a new form of slavery where control of education, economics, and opportunity enslaves in the new order just as the auction block, whips, and chains did the old.

This new form of slavery is now enforced by men in hoods who terrorize in the night. It is this reality that requires the true nature of Oak Harbor to remain concealed.

Before the war our effort was to acquire slaves whenever possible and to prepare them for a life of freedom in the Northern States or in Canada. I am pleased that in the years between 1854 and 1861, 427 men, women, and children were sent north. It was this success that necessitated the creation of another legend about Oak Harbor.

People became aware that Marse Dupree purchased every slave that he could throughout the Carolinas.

Yearly, a property tax assessment required the reporting the number of slaves owned. The county tax collector began to wonder why there were not more slaves at Oak Harbor as he was aware of my extravagant acquisitions. The solution was to report that a large number of slaves had died that year. The workers quickly erected a false graveyard while Moriah and the overseers documented false deaths due to injury, disease, and accident.

Despite this massive effort the collector remained skeptical and persisted in inventorying the entire estate to determine if I were evading the tax. This intrusion was only avoided by the quick thinking of Ezrah. He found an opportune moment to fall to his knees and beg the collector to take him away from the cruel Marse Dupree. It was through his pleading that he convinced the collector that I abused my slaves and likely caused their deaths or perhaps murdered them for my own perverse joy. It was a brilliant deception that I reinforced by offering a bribe to keep the whole thing quiet. That is how the rumor of my sadistic treatment of the slaves began. The rumor had the added benefit of keeping people from looking too closely at Oak Harbor. Now my neighbors had a reason for my slaves' high mortality rate and grist for their salacious gossip.

The reality was just the opposite as the population received nothing but the very best care as far as diet and medical treatment. The medical treatment was secured when Elvira agreed to move to Oak Harbor as my guest. She signed over her Meadows Estate to her reprehensible nephew but without any slaves as the few remaining faux-slaves finally came to Oak Harbor. When she arrived, she began to treat any injured or sick person with great skill.

A few weeks after her arrival she prevailed upon me to create a medical training program for any former slave that was inclined to learn medicine. This led to the creation of formal education classes where all former slaves would learn to read, write, and do basic math. All of this was highly illegal but we in the leadership decided they could only hang us once if our charade were ever discovered.

The next development was the suggestion by some of the former slaves that had been trained in various trades to open classes to teach those skills to any willing to learn. Soon we had vocational classes to become a carpenter, seamstress, blacksmith, mason, cook, and numerous other specialties.

As all of this wondrous activity was unfolding, I became concerned that so many field hands were in classes or learning trades that we would have a lack of cash-crops, which would give away our deception. I talked it over with those that had risen to leadership positions. After much discussion a plan was developed to share the profit of the plantation with each member. I suggested that this would be most effective if each person's share was commensurate with the skills they could perform. When paid I would arrange to have each person's funds placed on deposit with the bank in New York that I had become familiar with. Whenever a person decided to leave, he or she would have a sizable resource to begin a new life. The result of this was Oak Harbor becoming one of the most successful plantations in the Carolinas. In fact, the estate was so successful that I only occasionally needed to draw upon that treasure that had come to my possession through treachery to buy more slaves. My continued profligate acquisition of slaves never ceased to astonish my social peers.

So it was as the decade moved steadily toward the fateful Presidential election of 1860, it became clear that big trouble would come if an abolitionist were elected. The South would not allow its peculiar institution to perish. The rhetoric of the politicians, newspapers, and even the pulpit throughout the south became ever more inflammatory. This was probably my most difficult time to stay in character. It took all I could muster to give rousing speeches in support of pro-slavery politicians and to contribute to their campaigns.

Perhaps that is why I did not see the other danger before it broke upon Oak Harbor.

In late 1859 I was coming home from a political rally in New Bern when my driver came upon a disabled wagon blocking the road. He stepped down to investigate when four men appeared out of the brush with guns aimed at us. As I looked them over, one seemed to be familiar but I was having trouble placing him.

"Do you not recognize your old shipmate?" said a voice from my past that sent a chill down my back.

"Meredith Williams!" I said in astonishment.

"You look like you have seen a ghost," he said with a sneer. "I have come for my treasure!"

Meredith and another man stepped up into my carriage while the other two went to the farm wagon. He then ordered my driver to proceed to Oak Harbor. On our journey he told me what had happened seven years before. It was evident that I had not killed him with that blow of the belaying pin! He had been knocked unconscious but somehow did not drown in the river. He was picked up by a fishing vessel bound for New Bern. When he came to, he had no idea who he was or how he come to be in the river.

The captain of the boat called a doctor for him, who determined that other than the obvious fractured skull, which would heal with time, there was nothing physically wrong with him. The doctor said that sometimes a blow such as the one he had taken could cause a person to lose his memory. The fisherman took him on as a crew member since he had nowhere to go nor any money.

"I spent the next seven years working that boat out of Elizabeth City as a deckhand. It was obvious that I knew the sea but I had no practical knowledge of the fishing trade. I began to suspect that I had been a sailor but how I ended up in the river was a mystery," he related.

Then one day he was in a tavern when he heard a conversation going on about ships that had either disappeared or had been wrecked on the Outer Banks. First the mysterious disappearance of the Seahorse was mentioned and how only small amount of flotsam was ever found from her. One of the men then mentioned that the Audacia disappeared at the same time only to be discovered to have been taken by pirates and then wrecked in a small river just off the Neuse. At the end of the discussion the man mentioned that only the captain of the Audacia had survived and apparently was amply enriched by the reward for killing all the pirates.

"I asked if they knew the name of the captain and they said that his name was Dupree Durant," Meredith said with a sneer.

Meredith began to grow dizzy and most of patrons believed that he had consumed too much drink. His fellow fishermen were with him and carried him back to the boat. That night he had a vivid dream recalling all the events back in 1852. The destruction of the Seahorse, the wrecking of the Audacia, the hiding of the gold, and his looking for his crews return before awakening on the fishing boat, had played out in his mind that night as he slept. In the morning he awoke and his name came back to him for the first time in seven years.

The next day he began to search for news of where I was and, more importantly, if I had the gold. I was not hard to locate since my slave purchasing activity had my name widely bantered about. He told me that he had come and observed Oak Harbor from a distance. It was obvious that I had a great deal of wealth.

He enlisted the rest of the fishing boat's crew to arrange for my abduction. "Now you are going to give me back my gold!" he said.

When we arrived at Oak Harbor, the members saw I had unexpected company and took on their roles as slaves or overseers. I sensed that we were being watched closely. Meredith pushed me toward the house where he would be able to interrogate me under torture. When we entered the house, we came across Elvira who could see that something was amiss. Quick as a snake Meredith took her captive as we entered the study. He forced her to take a seat and his companions made my driver kneel on the floor.

"Do you recall the mutiny trial?" Meredith asked with a cruel smile. "Perhaps we should try it again."

Without warning he put his revolver to my driver's head and shot him dead! Elvira screamed as the body thudded on the floor.

He pointed the gun at back of her head and said, "Now that I have your attention, where is my gold?" He quickly added, "Don't try my patience!"

I could not allow any harm to come to Elvira so I told him that I would have to show him its location.

"Get some of your niggers to carry it for us. Must be nice to have a bunch of slaves to do the hard work. May have to get me a few," he said before telling his men to bring "the old lady" along to insure my further cooperation.

We exited the house by the garden porch. I saw Ezrah working there and told him to assemble a work team of ten men with shovels and picks and to meet us at the cemetery.

"You buried it in the cemetery. Very clever," Meredith hissed as we walked through the grounds.

I knew I was running out of time but I wanted to spare Elvira s life. I implored Meredith to release her, for after all, she was just an old woman. He told me that he would do so once the wagon held the gold. Then he asked me how much there was. I confessed that I still had 3,000 pounds hidden.

Ezrah and his work team could be heard moving up behind us as we left the gardens and began to walk the path to the cemetery that had been built just after the opening of Oak Harbor. We were now in sight of the mausoleum that contained the remains of my dear wife Bernadette and that one day would hold my mortal remains as well. We passed through a simpler but larger graveyard that had the faux-graves of the missing slaves.

I opened the gate that separated the white graves from the black and waited for Ezrah and his party to pass. They all walked by as dutiful slaves with their eyes cast down or at least it appeared so to Meredith and his men. I saw Ezrah look at me sideways as he came last and I knew he had a plan. I closed the gate behind us and we passed by his party to take the lead. Just as we turned away from him, I heard the sickening sound of shovels and picks slamming into soft flesh and the screams of agony coming from surprised men. Meredith was just turning and raising his weapon when Ezrah planted a pick into his chest. I shall never forget the look on Meredith s face as he knew he had been killed. The men of the work party went crazy with rage as they hacked the four intruders until one body could not be discerned from another.

I took Elvira by the arm and led her away from that horrific sight. We returned to the house to find more of my people tenderly caring for the body of my murdered driver. That afternoon the dismembered bodies of the four evil men were placed in a hastily dug grave far away from the cemetery as I did not want their foulness to taint that hallowed ground.

The next day we laid to rest my driver with much weeping. I wanted to place his body inside the fenced cemetery near the mausoleum but again I was told that it would be a problem for a Negro to be placed in the ground intended for white members of the house.

"Even in death race determined a man's place!" I thought bitterly.

So, we created a second fenced area that would be for our special slaves that would have permanent markers. From that day forward we carefully separated the true Negro graves from the false ones.

I truly hope the day will come when the fence that separates us will be removed!

Zoey was shaken by the brutal account of Meredith Williams' return. She was trying to get her head wrapped around the violence of that day! It did explain the four bodies found hacked to death at Oak Harbor.

"Time to go to sleep," her mom said as she looked into Zoey's room. Zoey put the books back in their hiding place before turning off the lights.

CHAPTER 20 • WAR, SPIES & GOODBYES

Tuesday evening Zoey told her mom and Meema all about Dupree Durant's account of his life from the first book. They were enthralled by the adventurous life he had lived. She informed them about the contents of the second book and how Dupree, with the assistance of the rescued slaves and a few abolitionist friends, had established Oak Harbor as a refuge and a place where former slaves could prepare for a life as free people. All of that had been made possible by the treasure. She then mentioned that she found it curious that one of the abolitionists was named Bob Smithers and wondered again if he was an ancestor of the Smithers that they now knew.

"Just think, there might be a real treasure still hidden away over there at Oak Harbor," Meema said as she shook her head with disbelief.

"I'm not too sure about that," Hannah said as she was putting dishes into the dishwasher. "The last word so far is that there were 3,000 pounds of it back in 1859. Perhaps that was used up or Durant was just lying to bide time."

"Maybe I'll find out as I read the rest of the book," Zoey said thoughtfully.

"I think we should read it together," Meema said.

Zoey rushed off to her bedroom and retrieved the book. "Let me have it first," her mom said, reaching for it.

Zoey was surprised at her reluctance to turn it over. Somehow the writings of Dupree Durant were very personal to her.

"It's all right, baby," Meema said and Zoey seemed to know that she was reading her thoughts.

She handed the book to Hannah, who opened it to Zoey's bookmark to resume Dupree's account of Oak Harbor's history and began to read aloud.

1860 arrived two months after the appearance of Meredith Williams. We had suspected that the year of fate had arrived. I urged all those that wanted to leave to do so soon for time was running out for their safe passage north. To my dismay few of my friends choose to leave. I warned them that if Abraham Lincoln won the election that the United States would break apart. I felt strongly that only two outcomes were possible if southern states seceded. The first would be that the northern states would say farewell to the millstone that had been tied around their neck and good riddance. The second would be war. Regardless of which happened, the ability to move them would become significantly more difficult if not impossible. Still, the vast majority wished to remain and do what they could to continue the fight against slavery.

On November 6th, 1860 the election was held. Within days it became apparent to the shock of most southern whites that Lincoln had won. As I had predicted, southern states began to secede from the Union starting with South Carolina. In quick order more states left and founded the Confederate States of America. I was somewhat surprised and delighted that North Carolina at first refused to secede. I shall always remember the consternation of my fellow gentry when Governor Ellis's motion to hold a secession convention was defeated by more moderate politicians that wanted time to see if Lincoln could somehow peacefully heal the rift spurred by his election.

In eastern North Carolina the fear of slave rebellions grew more intense every day. I was called upon by the leaders of Craven County to enhance the control of my slaves. Their fear was made even worse by my large population of slaves and rumors of my harsh treatment.

We all put on a grand show of the efficiency of my overseers and punishment methods that kept my slaves in check. I invited the concerned politicians to tour my estate where I was proud to show them my slaves' quarters that included the whipping post with freshly splattered blood provided by a few butchered chickens. Two of my faux-slaves were placed in stocks demonstrating my iron discipline. My overseers, led by Bob Smithers, went around with two Colt revolvers displayed on their hips and a shotgun in a scabbard on their horses as they held their whips ready.

I then took them into the house for a fine supper featuring chicken served by my obedient house servants and the company of Elvira Hale. They praised my diligence and had a lovely evening.

I knew the neutrality of The Old North State could not survive for long. On April 12th the Fire-Eaters of South Carolina fired on Fort Sumter when the United States attempted to resupply the garrison. Lincoln called for each state to supply troops to put down the rebellion. North Carolina would not cross the line of making war on their fellow southerners. On May 20th the state left the Union and joined the Confederacy the next day.

Throughout the preludes to war, Oak Harbor did all we could think of to prepare. We agreed that food production would be put above the normal cash crops of tobacco and cotton. Elvira said that distilled spirits would be of high value in a war economy so we built a distillery and began production. Moriah was concerned that soldiers from both sides may seek to take food supplies and livestock from the estate. We began to actively develop hidden stockpiles.

In August we learned that Union forces had invaded and occupied Hatteras. Immediately the citizens of eastern North Carolina became concerned that they would be the next to fall. I watched with great interest as the defense of New Bern took on urgency. However, that urgency was not a priority in Richmond, which sent minimal resources. This was most likely due to their preoccupation with the defense of Richmond, the need for which had been made real by the First Battle of Manassas.

Nonetheless, fixed entrenchments were prepared for the defense of

New Bern and the railroad. I was invited to tour those works and to view the obstacles and torpedoes set in the river. On the surface they looked formidable but I then observed that the soldiers were poorly equipped and trained.

In mid-March the Union forces came. I wondered just how long the siege would last but when the battle came it was over in a single day.

I pondered how I would be received by the occupiers of New Bern so I decided to pay them a visit. On my arrival I was quickly told that the commander, General Burnside, would not be able to see me. A rather stern captain informed me that if I intended to stay in Union-occupied territory that I would be required to pledge allegiance to the United States. This concerned me greatly. Not because I did not want to but what if the Confederates returned? I had been playing a dangerous game for too long to take unneeded risks. I thanked him for his time and left.

I was walking back to my horse when a gentleman approached me and asked, with a New York accent, "Would you happen to be Mr. Dupree Durant?"

I looked the man over carefully and wondered if I were about to be arrested. He was not wearing a uniform but looked more like a well-dressed gentleman.

"Yes, I am. With whom do I have the pleasure of speaking, sir?" I replied.

"My name is Vincent Colyer. I have been appointed by General Burnside to be superintendent of the poor here in New Bern," he answered.

I was wondering where this conversation was heading when I noticed a young Negro standing just behind Colyer who looked vaguely familiar. As he noticed me looking him over, his smile grew wide.

"Good afternoon, Marse Dupree!" he said.

It was then that I recognized Josiah, one of the former slaves that I had acquired from Elvira Hale. In fact, he was the stable boy who *had witnessed the hasty departure of Thaddeus Hale after my threat of challenging him to a duel. Josiah had excelled at his education after transitioning to Oak Harbor. I recalled he decided to accept the calling into ministry. We had given him as much education as we could and then sent him to New York where a minister had agreed to oversee his training at a seminary.*

Colyer invited me to come to the house he was using as his office so that we might have a private discussion. His job was to see that escaped slaves or, as the army called them, contrabands, were cared for and encouraged to provide labor for the Union Army. Colyer confided in me that one type of labor to be provided was spying. He had learned from Josiah about Oak Harbor and its secret mission to fight slavery. He told me that he would do all that he could to see that Oak Harbor was left unmolested but he would be more likely to succeed if I would agree to send my people out to spy on the Confederates. I wanted to agree but realized that I would have to get the consent of my people at Oak Harbor. Any Negroes caught spying would be executed on the spot. If they were lucky!

As we had this conversation there was a knock on the door. Colyer stood up and opened the door, admitting a colonel who did not give his name at first but who looked me over with great interest.

"Would this be the infamous Marse Dupree?" he asked Colyer with an Irish lilt.

I nodded that I was. He then told me he was Colonel O'Connell. He was in charge of all the spies in eastern North Carolina. He then asked if I had agreed to recruit spies from the occupants of Oak Harbor.

I explained to the Colonel that I would like to make that commitment but that I needed to discuss this with the other leaders back at Oak Harbor.

"I thought you were the Master of Oak Harbor, " he said with disappointment.

"That is only a role that I play. If it is of any help, I will personally *agree to act as a spy for you," I replied.*

He then smiled and nodded.

I returned to Oak Harbor and gathered the leaders. We discussed if it were wise to become involved in being spies for the Union. Everyone wanted to do anything we could to defeat slavery. However, there was concern that if the Confederates learned of our activity and forced the Union out of New Bern that there would be a massacre of every man, woman, and child at Oak Harbor. There was much debate but, in the end, we reluctantly agreed to spying but we would encourage as many of our people as possible to flee to the Union Army to become contrabands. I was confident that Vincent Colyer would see to their safety and needs.

The entire community was called together and informed of what was going to happen. It was made clear that if the Confederacy ever retook the area and Oak Harbor were linked to spying that all of their lives would be forfeit. Only a handful of the people decided to leave. Among those that decided to leave were Smithers and the other pretend overseers. It was not the fear of being caught as spies but rather their desire to go and join the Union forces. It was with much sadness that we watched them depart, for they had become dear friends.

Unfortunately, this was not the only separation that occurred at that time, for only two days later Elvira Hale went to sleep and never awoke in this world again. She had lived a long and productive life of seventy-eight years. She told me only a few days before her death that other than the years she shared with her beloved husband, the time at Oak Harbor had been the best years of her life. I made arrangements with Colyer to return Elvira to her cherished Meadows where she would be laid to rest beside her husband to await the day of Resurrection.

After the funeral we began to work closely with Colonel O'Connell. Right away we decided it would be best to not have face to face meetings with anyone associated with the Yankee Army. Instead, Josiah would come to Oak Harbor on the pretense of meeting a young female slave. We worked this out by finding a willing girl to be his pretend love interest. Ironically, the two really did fall deeply in love with each other!

Sending the Negroes out was possible but they could only go so far or they would be picked up as runaways. The fear of a slave rebellion continued to dominate the concerns of most white citizens in the south. We focused their efforts on watching the Confederate Army between Kinston and Goldsboro.

Josiah returned a few days after our plans were in place to say that the Colonel wanted a much deeper penetration. He wanted to get a spy into the Wilmington area to gather information on the defenses, blockade runners, and troops stationed there. It was essential to cut off the last Confederate seaport on the east coast that supplied essential arms and munitions to the Army of Northern Virginia.

I knew there was only one person who would be able to get into Wilmington and that was myself. I said that I would do it but that I needed a cover for why I was there. I suggested that I go to Wilmington to offer my services as a spy to the Confederacy. Colonel O'Connell jumped at the offer. He then provided me with several intelligence reports on Union troop positions and concentrations. None of the information was critical but it would provide my bona fides.

My journey to Wilmington was fraught with dangers but in the end I found myself seated before the commanding officer of the city, Major General William Whiting. I presented the information on Yankee positions and strength. He looked at me after reviewing the reports and smiled. I said that I would continue to gather information and return as often as I could.

Later I was invited to have drinks with the Commander s staff and that yielded a wealth of information. It was during this social gathering that I was introduced to Colonel William Lamb who was in command of Fort Fisher guarding the mouth of the Cape Fear River. He invited me to come and inspect the fort and to provide an experienced sea captain's opinion of the defenses.

During my visit the next day, I was able to identify a number of units stationed in the fort and the adjoining areas. I also was told significant information about the guns and their capabilities that guarded the Cape Fear River entrance.

Two days later I was escorted away from Wilmington and wished a safe journey home.

So it was that I became a spy for both the Union and Confederate Armies for the rest of the war.

Oak Harbor remained largely ignored by the occupying Union forces but I also regularly appeared in Wilmington with information on Union troop movements.

This is why some said that I remained a loyal southerner during the war, while others said I obviously cooperated with those damned Yankees since Oak Harbor was not confiscated.

We celebrated quietly when we learned of the Emancipation Proclamation in early January of 1863. It was a bittersweet day to know that slavery was effectively ended in the rebellious south, if the Union won the war. However, slavery would still linger in places like Maryland which had not seceded.

In the summer of 1863, we received word of two great battles. First was the Union victory at Gettysburg where General Lee was defeated for the first time. The second was the capture of Vicksburg on the Mississippi River, which cut the Confederacy in half. The war had shifted decidedly in the Unions favor. We at Oak Harbor began to prepare for a post-war life.

This is where my spying actually benefited our purposes directly. Many whites knew that the south would lose the war. Their fear of retribution by the Negroes gnawed at them. As I met with them, they pulled me into their trust on how they planned to keep "the niggers" down.

What I heard in those encounters was far more terrifying than the open hatred of slaves had ever been. They asked that I support their efforts and if not openly endorse them to do so covertly. I kept careful track of who the leaders were that advocated these abhorrent plans. Thaddeus Hales name was prominent on the list of leaders of the effort to repress the former slaves.

The open war ended in April of 1865. The silent war of Negro oppression was just beginning as the north grew tired of war and looked to move on. That was not true for the south, where the legend of the lost cause was just being born to salve the injuries of defeated soldiers along with the widows and orphans of their fallen comrades.

Most of the south had been destroyed but New Bern had been relatively untouched, at least physically. What had changed was that New Bern now had a thriving Negro community. Some whites would not return because of that. Other whites did return but with more malice than any person should ever have or ever confront.

The years after 1865 were in many ways much more difficult than those that came before but we at Oak Harbor did what we could to help people transition to a new life. To my dismay, more and more of the people at Oak Harbor chose to move away. As the Negroes across the south who were educated or skilled fled the oppression, those remaining were left in crushing poverty. This created an oppressed underclass which was preyed upon by poor-whites who were equally impoverished. They committed cruel acts just so that they could still feel superior. All of this was orchestrated by the gentry and the power-hungry politicians.

I wish I could say that we devised a successful strategy to combat this new oppression but the best we could do was to offer fair wages to those that continued to work at Oak Harbor. Even in doing this we had to be extremely careful, since any Negro that seemed to be doing economically well became a target to be eradicated. The Ku Klux Klan made a practice of visiting any Negro that became "uppity," as they called it. Oak Harbor continues to this very day to provide education and health care to our workers and their families. I fear that it, too, is becoming a target as we become more critical of the injustices that we see around us.

Now that I am heading to my reward, I charge my sons, Dupree and Uriah, and their sons to find new ways to fight the injustices of this world.

As for the treacherous gold that makes free, that secret lies with me in my tomb!

They all sat there silent in thought after Hannah read the last line.

"It sounds as if Dupree hid the treasure and decided not to tell anyone where at the end of his life," Meema said quietly.

"Perhaps the third book will have more to say about the treasure," Zoey thought to herself. However, that would need to wait for another day as she had to get her homework done.

CHAPTER 21 • DEAD MEN TELL NO TALES

Wednesday arrived and Zoey was dismayed by the amount of homework she was assigned that day. There was no way she would be able to delve into the final book. On the bus ride home from school her mind wandered back to a question that nagged her. Bob Smithers had served as an overseer for Dupree Durant until the Civil War and then he and the other white overseers had left to join the Union Army. It was the last mention of him. Zoey could not help but wonder if the lawyers with the last name Smithers were somehow related to the overseer. If they were perhaps, it was from Bob that they had come to know of the treasure rumored to be hidden at Oak Harbor.

"How can I find out if there's any connection between them?" she asked herself just as the bus stopped on the road by her house.

"See you tomorrow!" Rufus said, looking up at her when she began to leave.

She smiled at him and then waived goodbye to both Rufus and Billy.

She came in the door to find Meema just coming out of the kitchen with a glass of tea.

"How was school today?" Meema asked as she gave her a hug.

"It was okay but I sure have a lot of homework to do tonight," she said as she set down her bookbag to get a glass of sweet tea for herself.

"What did you do today?" she asked Meema.

"I went to town and did a little plundering around. They have some interesting shops in town," her grandmother replied.

"Yeah, Mama and I went there one Saturday and we had a lot of fun. I'd better get started on my assignments," Zoey said with a sigh.

Hannah arrived about two hours later and had just changed her clothes when there was a knock on the door. Zoey was concentrating on a math problem and only heard her mother greet someone and ask whomever it was to come in. Zoey looked up to see who it was and in stepped Deputy Rawlins.

"Well, hello there, deputy! What brings you to visit again?" Meema said with a knowing smile as she glanced at Hannah, whose eyes were shooting daggers back at Meema.

"I'm afraid that I have some troubling news to share. I think it would be best if we had a seat," he said with a serious tone.

They all went to the table and sat down. Henry Rawlins looked uncomfortable as he glanced at each of them one by one.

"Today we found the two suspects that got released by mistake. Their bodies were discovered in a car that was submerged in the Trent River," he said quietly.

"Was it an accident?" her mother asked.

"No, ma'am. They had both been shot execution-style," he said looking down at the table.

"Oh my God!" Meema exclaimed. "That's terrible!" Hannah added.

Zoey studied the deputy's face and could see that he had more to say.

Rawlins closed his eyes and said, "There's more. The coroner found evidence that before being shot they had been extensively tortured."

All three of them sat there with their mouths open.

"I'm concerned that their torture and murders are connected to their arrest at Oak Harbor," he said with a hint of fear in the statement.

"Why do you think that?" Hannah asked.

"Based on their autopsies they were killed early Monday morning. Their bodies had been put in the river shortly after that time. The coroner determined that the torture started about four hours after their release on Sunday morning," he paused for moment to let what he had said sink in. "I'm convinced that they had been hired to methodically search Oak Harbor for either the treasure or, more likely, the books that were taken from the study," he said as he looked directly at Zoey.

Zoey felt she was being silently interrogated by his piercing blue eyes. She wanted to look away but then she returned his stare, wondering if he could be trusted. Those two men had been brutally killed by someone and she knew that it had to be someone that knew how to get the men released from jail. Who better to do that than a deputy?

"Do you have any idea who might have hired them?" asked her mom, breaking the staring contest.

"If I were in charge of the investigation," he started to say when he was interrupted by Meema.

"You're not in charge of the investigation?" she asked with surprise.

"No, ma'am. This is a murder case which will be assigned to a detective. I'm just a road deputy," he replied. "Anyways, I would be looking at the two parties that have been fighting like cats and dogs over that run down house. They both have the resources to hire people like the two dead men. In fact, the one that did the killing might not even have been the one that hired them," he said reflectively.

Zoey agreed that they were the most likely suspects but she had to admit that there were others. Moses, for example, could easily be made a suspect in her mind, but Deputy Rawlins could be as well. Then it occurred to her that her mom, Meema, and herself could be suspects as well. Maybe they already were. If those books were found in their possession, they would quickly become number one on the suspect list.

"Is he here to investigate us?" Zoey wondered silently.

"Do you know who the two dead men are?" Hannah asked.

"We put their fingerprints through the system and yes, they've been identified. They both have been in and out of trouble with the law since they were teenagers. Their names were Donnie Tyler and Harold Carter," he replied. "They were not from around here. They lived down south in Whiteville."

They all became silent and lost in their thoughts for a few minutes until Zoey's mom looked at the deputy and said, "I do declare that we have forgotten our manners! Would you like a sweet tea or perhaps a cup of coffee?"

Deputy Rawlins looked at her, smiled, and said "Sweet tea sounds wonderful, ma'am."

"I'll get it, Mama," Zoey said as she stood up. "Would either of you care for one?"

"Yes, thank you, baby," her mom replied as Meema nodded that she would like a glass as well.

Zoey served the tea and returned to her chair. Everyone sipped their tea and the conversation seemed to pause. It was then that Zoey noticed her mom looking closely at the deputy, while he seemed to be studying his glass of tea.

"Is there something else bothering you?" her mom asked the deputy gently.

The deputy looked into her eyes and exhaled loudly and said, "Yes, ma'am!" He paused and seemed to search her eyes. "The last time I stopped by, I told y'all that I didn't believe you were in any danger. Now I'm not so sure about that. Someone killed those two men and it must be about those missing books from Oak Harbor. Whoever is looking for them is likely to be taking a closer look at anyone who has been in that house recently."

"Why would they do that? Maybe the killer got the books from those two dead guys," Zoey's grandmother said.

"I don't believe they ever had the books," he said while shaking his head. "They were still searching Oak Harbor the night they were arrested and they didn't have any books on them at that time."

He then looked at Zoey with those eyes that seemed to search inside her mind and said, "Besides, I know who has the books but I think that should stay a secret for now."

Zoey looked away as she realized that he knew she had the books! If he were the bad guy then why did he not just demand them from her? Deputy Rawlins was no longer a suspect on her list. She was also certain they were not suspects on his list either.

"Why do you think the books' location should stay secret for now?" her mom asked quietly but looking relieved.

"If I took possession of the books, I would be required to turn them in as evidence in an open murder investigation," he said with shrug of his shoulders. "The department seems to be having a problem keeping evidence and even suspects from disappearing that are connected with investigations involving Oak Harbor."

He finished his tea and said, "Thank you so much for the tea! It was wonderful. It's been a long day and I'd best be moving along."

He stood up and Zoey's mom started walking him to the door when she asked, "How much longer do you have to work tonight?"

"My shift ended an hour ago. I wanted to stop by to give you the news before going home," he replied.

"Would you like to stay for supper?" Meema asked.

Zoey watched her mom look a little flustered but then she said, "Now Mom, I'm sure that Deputy Rawlins wants to get home to his wife."

He smiled and said, "I'm not married and I'm also a horrible cook so if that offer is serious, I would love to have supper with y'all."

"Wonderful!" Meema said with a big smile. "Come on back in, deputy, make yourself comfortable, and we'll have supper ready in no time at all,"

"Thank you, ma'am. However, I do wish y'all would call me, Henry," he said with a smile.

"As long as you call me Connie," replied Meema, adding with a whisper, "And her name is Hannah."

Zoey went back to work on her math problems but it was hard to concentrate as she kept hearing snippets of conversation between Henry and her mom, with an occasional word from Meema.

They again gathered at the table and said grace together. "God is Great. God is Good. Let us thank Him for our food. By His hands we all are fed, give us, Lord, our daily bread. Amen!"

Zoey noted that Henry happily joined hands and said the prayer. He was sitting between her mother and herself. His hands felt calloused and strong but warm. She found that she was growing much more comfortable with him.

"How long have you been with the Sheriff's Department?" her mom asked as they began to eat.

"I became a deputy just over ten years ago," he replied. "Was that what you always wanted to do?" Meema asked.

"No, ma'am," he said. "I truly had no idea what I wanted to do when I got out of high school. One day I walked into a Marine recruiting center and walked out as the United States Marine Corps' newest member. I spent eight years on active duty. After I got out, I took advantage of the college aid to get my degree. While I was going to school, one of my fellow students was a deputy and he encouraged me to apply. So, I guess I kind of just stumbled into law enforcement!"

"Was your degree in law enforcement?" Zoey's mom asked.

Henry chuckled and shook his head. "No, Hannah. I've always enjoyed history, so I got my degree in American history."

Zoey wondered what Henry would make of the writings of Dupree Durant. He would probably understand them so much better than she did. She was tempted to start asking questions but she recalled how he said he would be required to turn over the books if he saw them. She decided to remain silent.

"I'm surprised that a handsome man like you isn't married," Meema said. Zoey watched her mom turn red and once again shoot daggers at Meema with her eyes.

"Mom, that's not very polite!" Zoey's mom said.

Henry grinned for a moment, which seemed to make Zoey's mother blush even more.

"I don't mind your mother's question," Henry assured Hannah, then turned back to Meema. "I'm divorced. I got married just after I joined the department. It just didn't work out."

"Did you grow up around here?" Zoey asked.

"Yes, Zoey. I grew up right here in Craven County. My parents still live just a few miles from here. In fact, they're neighbors to a young man that goes to school with you, Rufus Johnson. His daddy and I grew up together," he said with a wink.

Zoey had a strange feeling that either Rufus or his father had given Henry some additional insight into what had been happening.

CHAPTER 22 • LOVE?

On Thursday, Zoey noticed Meema packing her bags to leave.

"Do you have to leave? You just got here!" Zoey said, wanting her Meema around all the time.

"I have to get back to Raleigh. Your Pap is coming home from working on the mountain house later today. You know we miss each other when we're apart!" Meema replied with a smile.

"Well, he should come here! I miss him too," Zoey said as she hugged her grandmother tight.

"I'll see if I can talk him into coming to see your new house soon. Maybe for Thanksgiving. You'd better get ready for school so you're not late," Meema said, shooing her from the room.

Her mother had breakfast ready at the table, smiled, and said, "Good morning! I heard you trying to talk Meema into staying. Don't be too sad, sweetie. She'll be back soon enough."

Just then there was a knock on the door. Zoey walked over and looked out the window to see Henry Rawlins standing there in his full law enforcement attire.

She opened the door and said, "Good morning, Henry. Come on in."

He entered the house and looked toward the kitchen. Zoey watched as her mom suddenly glowed and it was obvious that she was developing feelings for the deputy.

"Good morning! Can I get you a cup of coffee, Henry?" she said as her eyes twinkled.

"That would be most kind, Hannah." He replied with excitement in his voice.

Zoey was rolling her eyes when Meema put a hand on her shoulder and whispered in her ear, "That's the other reason I need to leave. Your mama and Henry need a little alone time to figure things out."

Zoey was trying to understand what Meema was talking about, when she saw them looking into each other's eyes again. It was just like when she and Rufus did that. Zoey blushed as she finally got it.

"I was just getting ready to go on duty but I thought I would stop by and check in on y'all," he said as he accepted the coffee mug from her mom.

"I'm glad you did," Meema said. "I'll be heading back to Raleigh today and this way I will get to say goodbye to you. I also hope that you'll be looking in on Hannah," she paused slightly for effect. "And Zoey."

"Yes, ma'am! I intend to do just that," he said, turning to Hannah. "As long as that's all right with you, Hannah?"

"Of course, it is," she replied with a radiant smile. "Perhaps you would like to join us for supper again this evening?"

"That would be great. You have no idea just how bad a cook I am!"

Zoey ate her bowl of grits as the adults all continued to make small talk. Just as she finished rinsing out her bowl there was another knock on the door. Again, she went to see who was there and when she looked out, she saw Rufus standing there.

"Who is it, Zoey?" her mom asked.

"It's Rufus! I wonder what he's doing here," she said before she opened the door.

"Come on in Rufus," Meema said pleasantly.

Zoey was already preparing herself to be teased by her grandmother and probably her mom as well. Rufus came in and nodded at Henry and the two older women.

He seemed to shuffle his feet for a moment and then said, "I thought I would get on the bus here so that you wouldn't be standing out there on the road all alone."

"Actually, I think that's a fine idea," Henry said, sipping his coffee again. "Can't be too careful, what with the things that have been going on around here. You tell your daddy that we need to get together and do some deer hunting. There's a lot of big bucks moving around!"

Rufus seemed to grow a little taller on hearing the approval from the lawman and old family friend.

"Yes, sir. I'll make sure I do that!" he told the deputy.

"Put your bike in the carport, Rufus," said Zoey's mom. "Thank you for being so thoughtful about Zoey."

After giving Meema a kiss and a hug goodbye she walked to the road with Rufus. They only had a moment to wait before the bus pulled up and the door opened. Zoey went on first and walked to her normal seat. As she did, she caught the eye of Billy who had a strange look on his face as he looked past her at his best friend.

"Uh-oh," she thought to herself as she sat down and Rufus took his normal seat next to Billy.

Billy turned away and looked out the window and there was no more conversation for the rest of the ride to school.

At lunch she and Rufus took their normal seats but Billy went off to sit at a different table.

"I think he's upset," Zoey said. Rufus just sort of nodded and looked over to where Billy sat alone.

"He'll get over it," he told her but Zoey could tell that Rufus was concerned as well.

"I'll be back," she said as she got up and walked over to Billy.

He tried not look up at her, as if he didn't notice that she was standing there.

"Are you mad at me, Billy?" she asked as she sat down across from him.

Billy sort of shrugged and then said, "Looks like he won. Again."

"Won what?" Zoey asked.

"You're his girlfriend now," he said with frustration in his voice.

Zoey knew that had to be the problem. "I hate all this boy-girl stuff," she thought to herself. She tried to think of how she could make things better. She didn't want to lose Billy's friendship but deep down she knew she had different feelings about Rufus. He really was her boyfriend!

"You're my friend too!" was all she could think to say.

"But not like Rufus," he said as his eyes searched her own.

Zoey shook her head and said, "Not like Rufus but you are still one of my very best friends. I don't want to lose you as a friend and neither does he!"

Billy stood up, took his tray, and walked away.

She went back to sit with Rufus and said, "It was a big mistake for you to come to my house this morning. I think we both just lost a friend."

"What happened this morning was going to happen sooner or later. I don't want to lose him as a friend either but there's no other choice in how I feel about you!" Rufus said with conviction.

Zoey felt her insides fill with butterflies as she thought about what this meant. She smiled and nodded at him while she touched his hand.

"I wish Meema had not left today. I could really use a long talk with her!" she thought to herself.

At the end of the day, they all boarded the bus but when she and Rufus got to their normal seats, Billy was in hers.

"I think you're in my seat," Zoey said quietly.

Billy just looked straight ahead. She looked at Rufus who just shrugged and motioned for her to sit next to him. As they rode home that afternoon it felt as if the world had changed. There was something nice about sitting next Rufus. She also felt terrible that this might end their friendship with Billy.

When the bus stopped at the end of her drive, Zoey and Rufus got up and walked off the bus. They were just stepping into her driveway when she felt someone was behind them. She turned and there stood Billy and he was grinning from ear to ear.

"I didn't want all those other kids to start teasing the two of you so I decided I'd better get off here, too," he said as he looked towards the bus continuing down the road.

"Thank you, Billy," Zoey said with a smile.

"Well, I've got a long walk home from here so I'd best get started," he said as he turned to leave and then turned back. "You both will always be my friends!" he said as he walked away.

"Looks like he's gotten over it," Rufus grinned.

They had just started up the drive when Deputy Rawlins pulled up in his patrol car.

"Just wanted to make sure you got in the house okay. I'll see you later for supper, Zoey," he said with a wave as he began to pull away.

"Hey, Henry," Rufus called out. "Could you go give Billy a ride home?"

Henry looked down the road and saw Billy plodding along. "Sure thing! I'll bet his brothers hightail it into the woods when they see my car coming," he laughed. "Those boys sure have a guilty conscience,"

All three of them chuckled about Billy's older brothers that bullied him endlessly.

Zoey reached out and touched Rufus's hand and said, "Thanks!" As their eyes met, they both felt a jolt of adrenaline.

They had about an hour before her mom would come home so they spent time talking about normal things like music, shows they liked to watch, kids they went to school with, and, of course, their teachers. Eventually they began to talk about the murder of the two men. The news about that was now everywhere.

"Henry says that he thinks either Smithers or the Wilsons are involved in the murders," Zoey said.

"I don't understand why whoever hired those guys would torture and kill them," Rufus replied.

"He said that they might have gotten released by the side that didn't hire them and that they were tortured and killed by them to find out what they knew," Zoey said carefully, recalling the discussion from the night before.

"I guess that kind of make sense," Rufus replied thoughtfully.

"On the other hand, maybe it was the one that hired them and they thought those guys must have had the books and were going to double-cross them," she said.

"Sure is confusing, if you ask me," the boy said.

"I wish I knew how they both came to know about the treasure," Zoey said. "I saw the name Smithers in the first book but that man and his family went back north during the war and were never mentioned again. I still can't help but think there's another connection. Maybe it happened after Dupree Durant died."

Rufus had no idea what Zoey was talking about so she

spent the next half hour giving him the most important facts discovered in the second book.

"You know whole lot about how Oak Harbor came to be and even more about the treasure," Rufus said thoughtfully. "It really did exist and it still might,"

"I know, but that doesn't help us figure out who is after the treasure now. I could see that Smithers's uncle could have learned about the treasure as the family attorney. I still think he's the one that stole the money and then killed Jonathan Wilson. On the other hand, I have no idea how the Wilson relatives are involved," Zoey explained.

"Maybe Jonathan told them about the treasure," Rufus said.

"That would mean he was after the treasure when he married Miss Rose. That would be so sad. I get the feeling that she was in love with him all her life," Zoey was saying when the door to the carport opened and her mother came in wearing her scrubs.

"Well, hello you two. Did you have a good day at school?" her mom asked as she set a bag of groceries down on the counter.

"It was okay," Zoey said.

"Rufus, would you like to join us for supper?" her mom asked.

He was just getting ready to answer when there was a knock on the front door and her mom said, "That would be Henry!" with more than a little excitement in her voice.

A moment later Henry entered the room and greeted the two teens.

"Rufus, I didn't hear if you would like to stay for supper," Hannah asked again.

"I think I'd better get home before it gets dark. My mom won't like me riding through the countryside in the dark," he replied.

"I can take you home after supper. I'll be going right by there when I leave," Henry said.

"I'll call your mom," Zoey's mother said, settling the matter.

While they waited for dinner the two teenagers dragged the two adults into their conversation about Smithers verses the Wilsons as the leading suspects. Zoey carefully laid out her line of thought about both. Henry seemed impressed by her thought process.

"You've spent some time thinking about all of this," he said thoughtfully and then paused for a moment before continuing. "I had the same questions on my mind today. There is no doubt that Smithers and his family have had ample opportunity to learn of the treasure and, for that matter, the existence of the missing books," he said with a wink. "It made me think about the other group that we have been calling the Wilson relatives. I did a little quiet checking on them today. The first thing I found out is their name is not Wilson but Hale-Pollock," he said and was about to continue when he saw a strange look on the two ladies' faces.

"I take it that the two of you might have heard that name somewhere before," he asked.

"Let's just say that the name Hale has had something to do with Oak Harbor in the past," said Zoey's mom.

Henry looked at her closely and then nodded that he understood before he continued. "Jonathan Wilson had a somewhat complicated family history.

His maternal grandfather, a man by the name of George Halleck, was executed for murder back in 1926. Jonathan's grandmother was married to another man, named Whitson Hale. She had an affair with Halleck and became pregnant. That baby was the woman who became Jonathan's mother. I actually got a look at the 1925 case file and it sounds as if the husband discovered the affair and went after Halleck. They got into a fight and Whitson Hale was killed."

"I would have thought that would have been self-defense,"

Rufus said.

"It probably was but unfortunately for Halleck, the Hale family was a high up in the Klan. I'm fairly certain that he was railroaded to the gallows," Henry said.

"That's horrible!" Zoey's mom exclaimed.

"Yes, it was. After Whitson Hale's death, Jonathan's grandmother and mother were kicked out of the Hale family by Whitson's father. Eventually the disowned granddaughter met and married a young sailor with the last name of Wilson. Jonathan was born in 1943, six months after his father's death aboard a submarine in the Pacific. Jonathan was an only child," Henry explained.

"If he were an only child then there shouldn't be any relatives," said Zoey's mom.

"One would think so, but Jonathan's mother had an older half-sister that was raised by the Hales. From what I can tell by various court documents, the Hale-Pollock side of the family only came out of the woodwork when Rose's health began to fail," he said.

"Seems like a pretty thin claim to the estate," Zoey's mom commented.

"It probably is a thin claim but under North Carolina estate law the property of a person who dies without a will is divided between any remaining relatives. Interestingly, Smithers is arguing that more time should be allowed to search for Rose Wilson's missing will. He has brought a number of witnesses forward that claim they were told by her that she had a will. He argues that time is needed to thoroughly search for the missing will," Henry explained.

"I'll bet he has the will or has already destroyed it," Zoey said with conviction.

"That could be but sooner or later the court will have to rule in favor of the Hale-Pollock family," Henry replied. "I think

Smithers is just buying time. He is also arguing that under the terms of the trust there is no right by the beneficiaries of the trust to dissolve it. The ultimate heirs are only entitled to the income from the property, of which there is none," Henry explained.

"That's rather self-serving," Hannah remarked.

"Exactly!" said Henry. "If Smithers wins his arguments, he will retain control of Oak Harbor and will have plenty of time to search for the treasure. Obviously, the Hale-Pollock side wants the court to rule in their favor and for the trust to be dissolved so that they can do their own search."

"What a mess!" said Hannah.

After supper they all helped to clean up. Afterwards Henry went out to put Rufus's bicycle into his cruiser.

"I need to have a private word with Henry," Hannah told the teens. "Would you mind staying in here until I come back?" Without waiting for an answer, she quickly slipped out the door to have a moment with Henry.

Zoey kind of shrugged but Rufus snickered as her mom went out the door.

"I think your mom and Henry like each other," Rufus said as he took Zoey's hand into his own.

After the "menfolk" left Hannah and Zoey had a long mother-daughter talk about those certain feelings they were both having.

CHAPTER 23 • THE THIRD BOOK

It was not until Friday that Zoey had the opportunity to open the third book. She was anxious to see what came after Dupree Durant's death as she rode back home from school that day on the bus. Rufus and Billy again got off the bus at her house, but Rufus could not stay since it was his mother's birthday.

After getting some sweet tea, Zoey went to her bedroom and retrieved the third book. She ran her finger over the cover and felt the Latin words impressed into the leather: "Perfide Aurum Liberat."

"Treacherous Gold Makes Free," Zoey said, remembering Meema's translation.

She opened the cover and again read the title: "The Duties of Marse Durant."

The book had been documented by Dupree Durant the Second on February 12th, 1881. She flipped to the next page and again read the oath that each Marse Durant was required to take before signing with the date on which he took it. This all seemed rather formal to her but she took it for what it was.

I hereby swear to administer the duties of the position of Marse Durant to the best of my abilities. To see to the upkeep of Oak Harbor and the preservation of the entire family. To do so with a spirit of love, joy, peace, forbearance, kindness, goodness, faithfulness, gentleness, and self-control. Further, I swear to extend mercy and grace so that others may know hope and peace. So help me, God!

On the rest of the page there were four signatures: "Dupree Durant II on February 12, 1881," "Dupree Durant III on September 18, 1905," "Dupree Durant IV May 22, 1925," and "Dupree Durant V October 16, 1945."

It fascinated her that each signature was in cursive but they each had their own unique style. She then turned the page and found the duties of Marse Durant. Zoey counted them and noted that there were five. She decided that this should be taken seriously, so she read each one slowly.

"It is and always will be the duty of Marse Durant to preserve the family! To that end a census is to be conducted every ten years. This census is to include all births, deaths, marriages, and locations of all blood relatives of the family."

"It is and always will be the duty of Marse Durant to preserve Oak Harbor so that its resources are available to support the family and to lift up the oppressed. The Marse shall document his or her assessment of society and who are the oppressed and who are the oppressors. This assessment should be appended to each census and updated more frequently if needed."

"It is and always will be the duty of Marse Durant to manage the financial assets of the family through the Trust established by the first Dupree Durant. A detailed financial statement shall be included with the Census,"

"It is and always will be the duty of Marse Durant to select and train the next Marse. Each new Marse will take the oath before assuming the duties of office upon either the retirement, incapacitation, or death of his predecessor."

"It is and always will be the duty of Marse Durant to preserve the resting place of his ancestors and the treacherous secret interred there."

Zoey was intrigued by this census requirement, which would be a wealth of information regarding the history of Oak Harbor, if they were what was in the rest of this book. Zoey turned the page and sure enough, in a clear title was written: "Census of the Durant Family as of December 31st, 1880."

That page listed all of the family members starting with Dupree Durant who was listed as age sixty-two but with a note added that said he had died on February 12, 1881. There was the name of Moriah as his wife. Then came Dupree Durant II followed by his son Dupree Durant III, who was born in 1875.

Further down the page was a notation for the Jones family. For the first time it occurred to Zoey that Jones was the family name of Moses.

"Could Moses be directly descended from Dupree Durant?" she wondered out loud.

She quickly began to read on about the Jones branch of the family. Zoey knew Uriah would be listed there but right beside his name was that of his wife, Estelle, and a note that they had a son named Durant Jones, who had been born in 1878, and a daughter named Rosalee, who was born in 1881. It was exciting to think that she was reading about the probable ancestors of Moses!

There were other notes on certain non-family persons who lived on the grounds of Oak Harbor and briefly what they did.

It was then that she saw the name Smithers!

Robert Smithers has returned to Oak Harbor after many long years away. Robert is the son of the late Bob Smithers who played the part of our head overseer during the slavery years. Bob left us after the Union Army occupied the area. It was his desire to fight the evil of the Confederacy that sought to preserve that evil institution. It was not until Roberts return that we learned of Bob's death in the Battle of the Wilderness in May of 1864. Robert is an attorney and we have agreed to engage his services for any and all legal issues.

"Oh my God! The Smithers go way back as lawyers engaged by the Durant family!" she exclaimed.

Then came the "assessment of the oppressed and the

oppressors."

As Marse Durant I am obligated to look at the society that surrounds Oak Harbor and give my impression of who is being oppressed. It is my assessment that the Negro continues to be maligned by the whites around him. The second group that is a target of violence and oppression is the white Republicans that openly embrace reform of southern society and political control.

On the surface it would appear that the animosity is greatest between the poor-whites and the Negroes. The poor-white men, who labor long hours, are constantly told that the black men are trying to displace them. In reality it is their social betters who constantly stir the cauldron by pitting Negro and poor-white against each other. They hire some of both and then they tell the whites that they need to accept a low wage to keep their position because the blacks will work cheaper. They tell the Negro they have to be paid less than the white man or they would be uppity and that would end badly for them. So it is that poor-whites are also the target of oppression.

The men who have political power work feverishly to disenfranchise the Negro and the ever so rare North Carolina Republican. They also prey upon the gentry and middle-class whites by whispering rumors that the Negros are only waiting for the right moment to unleash murder and rape upon them. The only way to avoid this is to keep the white man's foot firmly on the neck of the Negro.

This poisonous environment has given birth to the worst of the oppressors, which is the Klan. It is out of the disenfranchised Confederate veterans, the families of the dead and horribly maimed, and the financially devastated that their members and leaders have come. I am personally familiar with a common example of this.

As a boy growing up here at Oak Harbor there was a wonderful woman by the name of Elvira Hale who was like a grandmother to me. I have nothing but pleasant memories of her. After her death I learned that she had a nephew by the name of Thaddeus Hale. My father found him to be a most reprehensible or, as he would say, odious being.

After the war we found out that Thaddeus was forming Klan groups throughout North Carolina. The war had not been kind to him. Whatever money he had was lost on bad investments and he was forced to sell the Meadows, which had been Elvira's home. Perhaps the worst loss he took was the death of his son at Gettysburg. He blamed all of these misfortunes on the Negro with a hate that has burned his soul away.

Thaddeus is intent on passing on his hate through his grandson, Preston Hale, which is not likely to be a difficult task. Preston forged his papers at the age of fourteen to enlist in the Confederate Army in 1864 and was captured in the Battle of Wilmington in February of 1865. Between the bitterness of that defeat, the death of his father, and the venomous nurturing of his grandfather, for him to be anything other than a dedicated Klansman would be unlikely.

Today Preston Hale leads the Klan here in Craven County. He has approached me and made threats to my life on repeated occasions. I have never met a more contemptible soul.

Zoey's interest was intensified as she began to understand the connection of the Hale family to the Durant family. She still wondered how they could have learned of the treasure.

"Zoey, I'm home!" Hannah called as she entered the house.

Zoey set the book down, eager to tell her mom about what she had just read. However, before she could say anything her mom said, "Henry has asked me to go out with him tonight! He wants to take me to dinner and to listen to a local band."

Zoey knew her mother and Henry were growing fond of each other. He had come over for dinner two nights this week. He also seemed to stop by at every other possible opportunity and often had some tea or coffee with her mom.

"That sounds like fun. Does this mean that you two are dating?" Zoey asked with a giggle as she teased her mother.

Hannah broke into a beautiful smile and quickly nodded her

head. Zoey gave her a quick hug and then looked up at her with her own smile and said, "I'm happy for you, Mama! He's a really nice guy."

"He'll be picking me up in a little while. Zipporah will be coming over to stay with you until I get home, so you be good for her!" her mom said as she rushed down the hall to get ready.

Zoey decided that tomorrow would be a better time to talk about the things she was learning from the third book. While Hannah was getting ready for her date, Zoey retrieved the book and put it back in its hiding place. She decided she was not quite ready to have that book seen by either Moses or Zipporah.

Her mother had just finished getting dressed when there was a knock on the door. Zoey went to open it and saw that Zipporah had arrived carrying a basket of food.

"Good evening, Miss Zipporah," Zoey said.

"I thought you might enjoy some of my fried chicken for your supper," Zipporah said with a smile.

Zoey made a happy noise as she accepted the delicious meal from the old black woman.

"Good evening, Zipporah. Thank you so much for coming over tonight," Hannah said as she walked into the room.

"My, my, don't you look lovely tonight! This fellow must be a special man!" Zipporah said as Zoey's mom smiled at the compliment.

"Thank you, Zipporah, and yes, I think Henry is special," said Hannah with a little color rising in her cheeks. There was another knock on the door. "That will be Henry!"

A short time later Zoey was at the kitchen table enjoying the meal brought over by Zipporah. Zipporah sat and watched her devour the best chicken she had ever eaten.

"It's a pleasure to watch you eat, child," she said with a chuckle. "You remind me of my boys when they were about your age. I used to have to fry up three chickens to feed them and Moses when they became teenagers."

"I didn't know that you had children," Zoey said.

"Moses and I have three boys and a girl. They're all grown up and have young'uns of their own. We have seven grandchildren," Zipporah replied with a proud smile.

"Do they live nearby?" Zoey asked.

"Just our oldest boy, Obadiah. He took after his daddy and is a farmer. The two of them work the land that Miss Rose sold us so long ago," she replied.

Zoey could not but help to think of the possibility of a family connection between the Jones family and the Durants.

"Moses told me about that. He said that the Durant family had always been good to his family. He told me the connection went all way back to the slavery days," Zoey said hesitantly.

"Yessum. My Moses is directly descended from a man by the name of Uriah Jones who was born a slave on Oak Harbor. In fact, the old family story says that Uriah was the first slave born on the plantation after it was built by Dupree Durant," Zipporah said.

Zoey was astonished that Zipporah knew the name Uriah. Could she possibly know that Uriah was the son of Dupree Durant?

"That's amazing that Moses knows so much about where his family comes from!" Zoey said with excitement and watched as Zipporah looked at her with a questioning look. "I have kind of become curious about Oak Harbor and its history since I moved here," Zoey explained in a more normal tone.

"It's not too surprising that he knows his family history, since all of his ancestors are buried up there in the Oak Harbor cemetery," the old black woman replied.

"I thought that the Durant family members were the only

ones buried up there," Zoey said with surprise.

"They're over on the white side and the Jones family is resting on the other side of the fence," Zipporah said wistfully. "As much as things have changed there are still echoes of the past."

CHAPTER 24 • FOUL MURDERS

The next day Zoey was up early, anxious to get back to reading the third book. She retrieved it from its hiding place and began to read. She turned to the census of 1890 which was also written by Dupree Durant the Second. Very little had changed other than notes of some people coming and going from Oak Harbor. The Klan continued to terrorize the local area while Oak Harbor continued to find ways to provide education and employment for the oppressed.

Just after the 1890 census report there was another entry that was rather ominous.

June 12th, 1890. We received word that one of our former residents was lynched by the Klan down in Wilmington. Ezrah was closely associated with my father when he was purchasing slaves and was also involved in the fight with Meredith Williams. Our worst fears were realized in this attack, as poor Ezrah was tortured and questioned about Oak Harbor before he was hanged. We learned this from an eye-witness report from Ezrah s grandson who was hiding in the brush nearby. Of particular concern was that most of the questions asked were with regard to the treasure. Our fears are now that other former associates of my father might be targeted. Uriah and I have met to discuss this with the concern that he could be a target as well. It was decided to send as many of the old residents as far away as possible. Uriah has decided to stay, since Moriah will never consent to leaving Oak Harbor. The two of us did decide to no longer share our true family heritage with any of the Jones descendants, to protect them from Klan retribution. I know that this decision would have distressed my father greatly.

Zoey turned the page.

November 5th, 1893. We laid my dear brother to rest. His body was found bound to a tree where he had been beaten to death. Every bone was broken in his body. I have no doubt that Preston Hale and his son Franklyn are responsible for his murder. The authorities have already told me that there will be no investigation. This is truly a sorrowful day for me!

Zoey sat back and closed her eyes as she tried to process the tragedy and violence that the Durant family experienced. She felt compelled to keep reading.

She turned the page and found the 1900 census. The other notable event of the of the 1890's had been the birth of a new generation of both the Durant and Jones families. Dupree Durant the Fourth was born in the winter of 1896 and in the summer of that year the family welcomed Isaiah Durant Jones.

Zoey found this interesting but was disappointed that she was not discovering any new answers. She turned the page and suddenly the handwriting was different.

It is with great sadness that I report the murder of my father Dupree Durant II. Tonight, he was found on the road about a mile from the main gate. He had been shot in the back of the head. I suspect that Preston Hale is responsible for this murder most foul. Father was in the process of returning from a meeting with our attorney, Robert Smithers. It was Robert's son Richard that discovered Father's body. He had seen Preston Hale leave New Bern just after Father's departure, had become concerned, and decided to catch up with Father. Unfortunately, he was too late.

Zoey was once again stunned at the description of the violence, this one dated September 17th, 1905. She read on and was dismayed by the account of how the murder was considered "unsolved" by authorities. Dupree Durant the Third bitterly recounted how Preston Hale was protected by the local sheriff and judges.

Then on the next page: *"March 2nd, 1906. The body of Preston Hale was found today. He had been hanged by the neck with a sign that said he was a Murderer. Justice is done!"*

Zoey knew instantly that Preston Hale had met the same fate as so many of his own victims and she was certain that Dupree the Third had taken vengeance. After this notation things appeared to settle down at Oak Harbor. There was a note that the Hale family, which was then led by Franklyn, had moved away from Craven County and with their departure Klan activity diminished considerably. She read through the 1910 census but there was nothing in it she had not already been aware of.

In the census of 1920, she learned of the death of the matriarch of the family, Moriah. She passed away in her sleep on April 10, 1916. The record said that she was laid to rest on the right hand of Dupree Durant. There were also significant births recorded in those years. In the fall of 1916, the latest generation of Jones was born when Aaron Durant Jones entered the world. In the winter of 1918 Dupree Durant the Fifth was born. Zoey realized that this man would be the father of Miss Rose.

The decade between 1910 and 1920 seemed to be a prosperous one for Oak Harbor. The Smithers family was mentioned several times in passing, with genuine appreciation for their legal and financial advice.

It was not until 1925 that the next significant event occurred, as far as Zoey was concerned.

It is with great sadness that I report the death of my father, Dupree Durant the Third. He was found crushed under a tractor that was being repaired in the barn. It was Richard Smithers and myself that found the body. He will be laid to rest in the family cemetery. Now I must assume the responsibilities of Marse Durant.

Zoey continued to scan the book for other events but most of what was written was about the Great Depression and looming war in Europe and Asia. There was a touching entry just after the

1940 census that was dedicated to Dupree Durant the Fifth, who had become an officer in the U.S. Army.

I am so pleased that my son Dupree Durant the Fifth has volunteered to be an officer for a segregated Negro artillery unit, The 333rd Field Artillery Battalion. I still find the segregation of Negro from white a smear on the honor of those brave men who volunteered to serve. It is known that many white officers refuse to serve in these brave units because they deem it beneath their dignity to be placed in charge of colored troops. This often leads to the worst officers being placed to lead. I am proud that my son will be there to lead and to do so to the best of his abilities. May God keep and protect him!

Further into the 1940's was a tragic notation:

December 28th, 1944. I received word today that my son is missing in action and is presumed to have been killed in Belgium. I shall not give up hope and pray to the almighty God to bring him home to me.

Zoey knew that Dupree Durant the Fifth had not been killed in 1944 and when she turned the page there was a new style of handwriting.

October 16th, 1945. Today I assume the role of Marse Durant on my return from the war in Europe. I have read all of the accounts of our family s history. I also gladly accept my role. My first note is to document the passing of my father Dupree Durant the Fourth. It was reported to me that he drowned while fishing on the Neuse River for stripers. It was related to me by Curtis and Allen Smithers that my father had become quite distressed by the news of my disappearance during the Battle of the Bulge. They suspected that he committed suicide but was able to have his death ruled an accidental drowning. I have trouble grasping any thought that my father would consider taking his own life. There is something not right about all of this.

"Smithers's are involved in yet another death of a Marse Durant!" Zoey exclaimed to herself. "It was a Smithers that found Dupree the Second dead on the road in 1905. The same Smithers was present when Dupree the Third was found crushed to death.

Now two Smithers are involved in the death of Dupree the Fourth," Zoey said to herself.

Zoey did find the census of 1950, which included mention of the birth of Miss Rose in 1946. While the birth of Miss Rose was a celebration, it was followed by the tragic news that her mother and wife of Dupree the Fifth had been killed in an automobile accident in 1949.

There were no further entries. Zoey frowned and began to leaf through the remaining blank pages when she came to a single sheet of paper that was folded in between two pages. Zoey removed the paper and gently unfolded it to find a typewritten entry.

We have been betrayed! Today I received a report from an independent accountant that I had hired to review the Oak Harbors finances. To put it bluntly, the estate is now in debt by over $4 million dollars. I have evidence that Curtis and Allen Smithers forged my father's signature as well as my own to loan documents that go back to the 1930 s. Their actions have been covered over by their bookkeeper who has confessed his guilt and gave a sworn deposition to me. I believe that this was all discovered by my father while I was in the service and likely led to his murder! I also believe that the deception of the Smithers family goes back much further and perhaps all the way back to the murder of Dupree the Second, whose body was found by Richard Smithers who conveniently blamed the murder on a well-known Klan leader named Preston Hale back in 1905. This was the same man who discovered my grandfathers crushed body in 1925.

I have placed the originals of the accounting report, loan documents, bank statements, and other documents in the family vault. I will leave to go meet with authorities in Raleigh in a few short hours. I do not know if I can save Oak Harbor from this disaster or not."

The page was signed Dupree Durant V and dated January 20th, 1960.

Zoey grabbed the book and rushed to find her mother. Zoey spent the next half-hour telling her mom what she had discovered in the third book. There were statements that were quite damning for the Smithers family.

"I think we'd better call Henry," her mom said.

"I think we should ask Moses to come over as well," Zoey added. Her mom looked at her for a moment before nodding her agreement.

CHAPTER 25 • SINS OF LONG PAST

Moses was the first to arrive. Zoey was not looking forward to admitting her deception to him. He and Zipporah had always been so kind to her. Her mother showed him into the kitchen where Zoey was sitting.

"Moses, I have something I need to tell you," Zoey said as her voice wavered with a combination of guilt and fear. "I'm the one that took the books. I found the hidden closet that first day we went in the house. Here they are," she finished as she pushed the books toward Moses who just stood there with his eyes locked on the books.

"I'll need to call Mr. Smithers to let him know we have the books," he said and Zoey could tell that he was not looking forward to doing that!

Hannah spoke up quickly. "You might not want to do that. There is evidence in there that implicates the Smithers family in fraud and murder."

Moses slowly slid into a chair at the table and continued to look at the three books as if they were serpents that might strike at any second.

"There is something else in those books that you need to know about," Zoey said as she looked across the table at him. "Those books prove that you are a direct descendant of Dupree Durant."

Moses's mouth snapped open in total surprise.

Zoey reached for the first book and opened it to the first

paragraph. She then read, "On May 17th in the year of our Lord, 1854 at the age of thirty six I became the father of Uriah by my beloved wife Moriah."

"That is written in Dupree Durant's own handwriting," her mom said. "That proves you are the rightful heir to Oak Harbor!"

Moses sat dumbfounded as he absorbed the first line of that book written so long ago. Finally, he began to speak. "When I was just a little boy I would go up to the cemetery and help my Papaw Aaron take care of the graves. He told me that it was our duty to care for the resting places of those that came before. While we worked to cut the grass and pull the weeds, he would tell me about those that had passed away. He was right proud of his great-grandfather Uriah. He told me that Uriah may have been born a slave but he became a leader of the black folk in these parts. He was an educated man but he chose to stay at the plantation that he was born on. I asked him why Uriah would have done that and he said that Uriah was a part of Oak Harbor just like the Durant family. He could not explain it but it was as if we were just one family and that was why we gave the Durant graves the same care as our own. He told me that it didn't matter which side of the fence we were on."

"In the second book, Dupree Durant talks about the fence that separated the whites from the blacks in the cemetery!" Zoey exclaimed. "He hated that fence and hoped the day would come when it would be torn down." She looked deeply into Moses's eyes and added, "You *are* one family! The whole purpose of these books was to tell your story. Of how Dupree Durant hated slavery and fought a secret war against it and then against racism. And it's a beautiful story."

Zoey pushed the books toward Moses and said, "These are yours. I'm sorry I couldn't tell you about them before."

There was a knock on the carport door and Hannah got up and let Henry in. Zoey noticed her mother gripping his hand as they took their seats at the table.

"Henry, Zoey has read the books that she took from the house next door. Zoey, show him the last thing you found," her mom said.

Zoey opened the third book and removed the paper. She handed it to Henry who quickly read it before handing it to Moses.

"So, it was the Smithers that committed the fraud back in the 1960's and from what it says here, even earlier," Henry said.

Moses finished reading the paper, folded it, and returned it to the book. "I guess they got away with murder," he said sadly. "Those two Smithers brothers have been dead a long time. Even their boy passed away twenty years ago."

"That's true enough, but we can set the record straight about what they did," Henry said thoughtfully. "I'll bet Nathaniel Smithers sure won't like having his family dragged through the mud. But it sure would be nice to have the documentation that Dupree the Fifth had." He turned to Moses and asked, "You ever hear any rumors that there is a vault over there at Oak Harbor?"

"No, sir. I sure never heard anything about there being a vault over there," Moses said as he shook his head.

"I wonder if the treasure is in the family vault along with these records," Hannah chimed in.

"I don't think so," Zoey said and all the grown-ups turned towards her. "If Dupree the Fifth knew where the gold was, he wouldn't have been that concerned about the theft of $4,000,000." Everyone continued to look at her with interest. "The last record of the gold in the books was that there were 3,000 pounds of gold still on hand. If he knew where that much gold could be found, there was no way that Oak Harbor would have been at risk because of what the Smithers had done."

The adults all sat back and mulled over what the teenager had said.

It was Henry that was next to speak up. "I agree," he said. "The theft would have been an embarrassment rather than a threat to the existence of Oak Harbor. From the note we just read, Dupree the Fifth was clearly desperate to save Oak Harbor and felt that he could only do so by recovering the stolen money from the Smithers brothers."

"That's right," Moses added. "There was no way he had any idea that there was any gold left."

"From what I read in the books, the original Dupree Durant was the last person who knew for certain where the gold was, or possibly his sons. He said that he would take the secret to his tomb. I don't think anyone knew anything about the treasure after his death," Zoey said.

"Still, there must be a safe over there. He said he put the records in a safe," Hannah said with certainty.

Moses closed his eyes for a second and then opened them wide, "He wrote that he put them in the family *vault!* That's not a safe—it's the mausoleum up there in the cemetery!" He smiled and began to laugh. "A mausoleum is a vault that holds the family's tombs!"

"Can you get in it?" Henry asked.

"I have to go and get my big key ring over there at the house," Moses said. He looked at the books sitting on the table in front of him. "Zoey, could you put these someplace safe?"

Zoey nodded that she could. She picked the books up, left the room, and returned them to her hiding place below the bottom drawer of the desk.

Soon they were all in Henry's SUV and after a quick stop to get the keys they went on to the cemetery.

Zoey was always fascinated by the sight of the graveyard. It was on a small knoll and she could see the mausoleum at the very top. It was made of limestone with elaborate columns that held up a small portico. In the center were two bronze doors that guarded the resting place of Dupree Durant, Moriah, and Bernadette. Other graves were arranged on both sides of the structure. The style of each grave marker was unique. She knew that at each marker there would be a grave for each Dupree and his respective wife.

Then she noticed the wrought iron fence that was just behind the mausoleum that extended to the end of the cemetery at each side. The same style of fence enclosed both the Negro and white sections of the graveyard. At first it surprised Zoey that the cemetery was so well-maintained but then she remembered Moses talking about how he had been taught to care for the cemetery.

Moses led the way to the main gate of the graveyard, which opened easily, allowing them to pass.

Zoey immediately spotted the most recent grave in the cemetery and walked over to it quickly. There in a black granite monument was inscribed the name of Jonathan Wilson on the right side and Rose Durant Wilson on the left. She noted the date of Miss Rose's death was June 22nd, 2022. Zoey felt Moses come to stand by her side.

"She was a fine lady," he said sadly.

"I didn't realize that her death had been so recent," Zoey said as she felt tears begin to form in her eyes.

Hannah put a hand on her shoulder and gave her a gentle squeeze. "I wish we had brought some flowers for her," she said.

"Miss Rose would have liked that," Moses said softly. "She would have loved you and Miss Zoey here. Y'all are her kind of people." The old black man seemed to gather himself together and said, "We'd best get back to what we came here to do!"

Soon they were all gathered on the steps to the mausoleum as Moses tried different keys to unlock the door. Zoey noticed that "Perfide Aurum Liberat" was engraved into the stone header above the doors. Then they heard the clang of the lock opening. He pushed the doors open and allowed the fresh air and sunlight to fill the interior.

Zoey took in the sight of the old tomb that held the remains of the man she had come to know through his writing. There was a marble bench in the middle of the entryway, a place where those that came to pay their respects could sit and reflect on those that rested there in peace. On the other side of the bench were three crypts. The center crypt was the final resting place of Dupree Durant. It was labeled, simply, "Loving Husband and Father." The crypt on the left side as Zoey was looking at it was marked "Moriah Durant, Loving Wife and Mother." The crypt on the other side was labeled "Bernadette Noble Durant, Loving Wife and Mother." Above the crypts was a stained-glass window that had a Celtic cross in the center. At the top of the cross was written "Christus Gratis" and at the bottom, "Mors Nos Non Tenet."

"Great, more Latin that no one speaks anymore!" Zoey moaned to herself, desperately wanting to know what the words meant.

"The top words mean 'Christ Makes Free' and the bottom translates as 'Death Does Not Hold Us,'" Henry's voice said from behind her.

"You know Latin?" Zoey asked.

"Just a little. I told you I was a history student," he said with a grin. "Kind of a beautiful place in here."

"I have to admit that I've never been in here before," Moses said looking around. When he saw the name Moriah on the crypt, he walked to it and let his fingers run across her name as if he were touching her face. "My ancestors are in this room. Two of them," he said reverently, running his fingers over the name of Dupree Durant.

"I don't see any place to hide any papers," Hannah said as she looked around the room.

Zoey also studied the room, looking for any likely hiding places. One thing that did catch her attention was the fact that the crypts were up off the floor as if they were lying on a platform. Her eyes followed the bottom below that platform and then she saw "Perfide Aurum Liberat" chiseled into the stone centered below the crypt of Dupree Durant. On each side of the motto were bronze medallions, each in the shape of a magnolia bloom.

"Well, I don't see any place to hide documents in here," Henry said with some frustration.

Zoey suddenly turned around and found herself looking back out the two double doors. It hit her like a bolt of lightning that the only place that could not be seen when the doors were open was behind them! As quickly as she could she ran to the doors and closed them. The room became shadowed but the stained-glass window provided enough light into the room for them to see clearly. There behind the door sat an old envelope that was several inches thick.

"You're a genius!" Henry told Zoey as he stepped forward and reached for the envelope.

There were about three inches of documents on the inside that were just as described in that note from Dupree the Fifth.

"No gold but this sure will upset Mr. Smithers," Moses said with glee. "I think it's time for me to start making some calls," Henry said.

CHAPTER 26 • SINS OF TODAY

Everyone was quiet as they returned to Zoey's house, thinking about what they now knew. Zoey was thrilled that so many mysteries had been solved about Oak Harbor but something continued to nag her. There was no doubt that the Smithers's family committed the fraud that decimated the Oak Harbor trust fund. It was also apparent that Curtis and Allen Smithers had committed the murders of the fourth and fifth Duprees. There was also a very real possibility that Richard Smithers was the true murderer of Dupree the Second, as he was the one who had discovered the body. It was becoming hard to view these events as mere coincidence. With all that said, there was nothing that tied Nathaniel Smithers to any wrongdoing.

Unspoken in the background were the two unsolved murders that occurred in the last week. The two men who had been searching Oak Harbor were now dead after being tortured. Someone was more than willing to kill to gain access to the treasure.

They once again gathered around the table and it was Henry that opened the conversation. "I'll put a call in and see if I can talk with the sheriff about what we've found."

"I know that I'm just a kid but can I say something before you make that call?" Zoey asked.

"What's on your mind, sweetie?" Hannah asked.

"I know that we've learned a lot about members of the Smithers family. There's no doubt that they committed fraud and murder but the ones that did the things we can prove are all dead. On the other hand, two men were murdered last week but just because Nathaniel Smithers grandfather was a criminal doesn't prove that he is," Zoey said as she looked at the adults one by one.

"Zoey, I thought you were a detective with the way you look at things but now I think you might be more like a prosecutor," Henry said. "You're right. What we have should let Moses take possession of Oak Harbor but other than giving Nathaniel Smithers some embarrassment for what his dead ancestors did, it changes nothing."

"I don't see Nathaniel Smithers giving up on Oak Harbor that easily, either," Moses said, shaking his head. "He's a smart lawyer and I'm sure he can make the Oak Harbor case go on for years. Not to mention that other group that wants control. You can bet they'll try everything they can to throw out our evidence."

"Are you all saying that we have to catch the murderer before we disclose what we discovered?" asked Zoey's mom.

"It seems that way," Henry said as he took her hand with a gentle smile. "Maybe I can have a talk with the detective investigating the murders and tell him that a confidential informant of mine has given me some history that implicates Smithers as having a motive to kill the two victims. Maybe an interview with the detective might shake things up when Smithers is confronted by what we found in the tomb." He looked at Moses and asked, "Would you mind if I borrowed the books for a day or so?"

Moses looked at him, shrugged, and said, "I don't see why not."

"I'll go get them," Zoey said, racing down the hall.

Zoey knelt down by the desk and removed the drawer. She reached in to get the books and as she did the book with the letter from Dupree the Fifth slid off the top of the stack and back into the desk. Zoey set the other two books on the floor and looked into the space to get the third book. While she was pulling it out, the paper slid out of the book and back into the space. Zoey was feeling clumsy and carefully looked into the space to find the paper. She saw it and reached to get it. When she was pulling it out, she saw something she had never noticed before.

With the paper out of the desk she looked in again to confirm what she had seen. Below the drawer was what at first appeared to be a plywood bottom. However, when she looked more closely there was what appeared to be a picture hanger attached to the plywood. It kind of reminded her of what her grandfather called a D-ring. She reached down and pulled the tab up which made it like a handle. As she lifted, she could see there was something below the false bottom.

"Mama! Henry! Moses!" she called out.

"What is it, honey?" her mom replied as Zoey heard them rushing to her bedroom.

"I think I found something," she said as the adults crowded into her bedroom.

"Let me see, Zoey," Henry said as he knelt down to take her place. "Well, I'll be! There's a false bottom down here."

In a flash the piece of plywood was removed and handed up to Moses who looked it over. Then Henry looked up at everyone else and held up a large thick envelope. On the outside was written "Moses Jones."

"This would belong to you," Henry said, handing it to Moses.

Moses opened the unsealed envelope and pulled out two documents. The thicker of the two was the Last Will and Testament of Rose Durant Wilson and the second was a personal letter from Miss Rose written to Moses Jones.

Moses read the letter aloud:

To my Dear Cousin, Moses Jones.

If you are reading this document, I am now resting up in the cemetery with our ancestors and my dearest Jonathan. It is time for you to become the Master of Oak Harbor or least what is left of it. The appropriate title for you is Marse Durant. Unfortunately, my father died young and I was never given the training that I should have had to become the Mistress of Oak Harbor. I did know that my primary responsibility was to see to the welfare of my entire family.

I don't know what has become of the two books written by the Dupree Durant, but search for them! My father allowed me to read them and it was truly inspiring to know of how we and Oak Harbor came to be. My father told me there was a third book that he would allow me to read when I had finished high school but alas, he died when I was but fourteen.

I'm afraid that tragedy is all that Oak Harbor has known in my years. I pray that your years will see Oak Harbor restored and perhaps our family's amazing history revealed. And, God willing, perhaps you will find the treasure, for it truly does exist but the secret of its whereabouts died with Dupree the Second.

With much love and affection, Rose.

Henry quickly read the will and smiled as he looked at Moses. "Even old Nathaniel Smithers won't be able to deny that you're the sole heir to Oak Harbor!"

"I think I'm going to need a lawyer!" Moses said as he skimmed the will.

After a few calls, the first being to Zipporah, Moses left to meet with an attorney Henry recommended. They would determine the best way to introduce the will to the Probate Court on the following Monday.

Henry spent the rest of the day with Hannah, reading the books from Oak Harbor. To Zoey's delight they were both as impressed as she had been by the tale of Dupree Durant.

The next day Henry came by again and told them that he had photocopied excerpts from the book and sent them to the detective that was investigating the murders.

"I don't know if it will do any good but I thought he should know the background of the Smithers family," he said.

Later Hannah asked Zoey if she would like to go meet Rufus for a bike ride. It was not so much a question as an instruction! Zoey could tell that her mom wanted some private time with Henry and she was happy to spend the rest of the day with Rufus and Billy.

On Monday Henry and Rufus came over for supper and they had just finished cleaning up when there was a knock on the front door.

"Now, who could that be?" Hannah said as she walked to the door. In an instant she reappeared and looked like she had seen a ghost. "It's Nathaniel Smithers!" she whispered.

Henry went to the door and Zoey noted the concern on his face.

"Mr. Smithers, what can we do for you this evening?" Henry's voice said calmly.

"May I have a few words with the Morgantons?" the cultured southern voice asked.

"I suppose that will be all right," Henry replied showing him into the living room.

Zoey watched as the man she distrusted so much stood before her and her mother. She was surprised that he appeared so calm for a man who was such a likely murder suspect.

"Good evening, ladies," he said with a gentle smile and a small bow.

Rufus stepped close to Zoey's side, sending his message to the old lawyer that he was being watched, and Henry took up a similar station by Hannah.

"I shall not take too much of your time this evening," Smithers began. "I wanted to share with you the unusual events that I have experienced today. It started when I received word that there was a certain detective who wished to interview me with regard to information that had come to his attention concerning my family and Oak Harbor."

He shook his head slightly before he continued. "Let me assure you that I am quite familiar with my family's checkered past. I have no idea why certain of my ancestors lost their moral compass while others were honorable men. Unfortunately, none of us can undo the evil that was committed by people to whom we are related and are now long dead," he said with genuine remorse in his voice.

Zoey wondered where this was all going. It was then that she noticed that Henry and Rufus seemed to have moved closer to Smithers.

"Are they getting ready to pounce on him if he tries something?" she wondered to herself.

"You see, my father discovered, to his unending shame, that his uncle and father had defrauded Oak Harbor," he continued. "He also found evidence that implicated them in three murders. His discovery of these facts was after they had both died. My father carried the guilt of what they had done with him all of his life and he did all that he could to correct the wrongs they had committed. Unfortunately, the funds they had taken had been lost on land speculation and other bad investments," he said as a tear trickled down his face. "When my father was dying, he instructed me that I was to represent Oak Harbor pro bono and to see that no further harm came to it or to any member of the Durant family."

Smithers seemed to gaze back across the years and said, "I made a vow to my father on his deathbed that I would try to make amends for the evil our family had done. It has been a burden that I have gladly borne since that day." He smiled wistfully before he went on. "Today, that burden has been lifted from my shoulders. After I met with the detective, I was thrilled when I got my second unexpected call of the day. I was informed that Rose Wilson's Will had been found and that Moses Jones was the rightful heir to Oak Harbor. I can now be at peace that Oak Harbor will remain in the Durant family," he said with a genuine smile.

Everyone was greatly surprised at what Smithers had just said.

"You see, my family has always been well aware of the Durant family history," he added. "After all, my ancestors were here from the very first day but then you know that from the books that Miss Zoey discovered next door," he said with a warm smile at Zoey.

"The final thing that I would like to assure you is that I had nothing to do with the unfortunate demise of those two men, whom Deputy Rawlins had arrested. I suspect that we shall soon hear of an arrest of the true killers," he concluded with satisfaction.

Zoey could not help but ask the direct question that was on everyone's minds, "Who did those men work for and who got them out of jail?"

Nathaniel Smithers smiled softly while shaking his head and said, "I was the one who got them released from custody, my dear. They were working for me. I hired them to search for the books."

The lawyer could see that both Henry and Rufus were ready to tackle him to the ground if he made a sudden move. He slowly raised his hands in a "whoa" gesture and said, "As I've already stated, I'm not the killer nor did I have anything to do with the killing of those men. You see, I knew that there were books that documented the history of Oak Harbor. Those books would prove that Moses was the direct descendant of Dupree Durant. My goal was to see that the estate and the family was preserved long enough to find those books so that it would not fall into the hands of Franklyn Hale Pollock!"

Smithers looked at each person in the room with a subtle

smile before he continued. "Franklyn is the person seeking to take control of Oak Harbor. He is the second cousin of Jonathan Wilson, once removed. Members of the Hale-Pollock family have long been the villains in the story of Oak Harbor. I could not allow them to gain control! However, without the will of Miss Rose the court was bound to award at least a portion of the estate to him and his son, Whitson Hale-Pollock the Second."

"Are they the ones who killed those men?" Zoey asked.

"Yes," replied the attorney with absolute certainty and then added, "I was quite alarmed when Donnie Tyler and Harold Carter did not report to me after their release. I was concerned that they had indeed found the books and were going to sell them to the other side. I had several…" he paused, searching for the right words before he continued with a smile and an unsavory emphasis on his next words, "…of my associates search for the missing men. They managed to apprehend a fellow who performs certain, how should we say, unpleasant tasks for Franklyn and his son. Even as I met with the detective this morning, the man confessed to my associates that he and Whitson had murdered the men on Franklyn's orders."

"Speaking as a deputy sheriff, I doubt that a confession coerced by your associates would be admissible in court," Henry noted.

"As an attorney, I would agree with you. However, he was also kind enough to provide a video of the interrogation of poor Donnie and Harold," Smithers said. He appeared to have sucked on a lemon before adding, "A most unpleasant piece of evidence that has now been delivered anonymously to the detective I met with this morning. I shall take up no more of your time and I do wish you all a pleasant evening." Smithers gave a slight bow and then showed himself to the door.

"I sure never saw that coming!" Zoey said as the others nodded their heads in agreement.

Three days later they were greeted by the news that Franklyn and Whitson Hale-Pollock had been arrested for the murders of Donnie Tyler and Harold Carter. A third man had been arrested as well, had confessed to the crime, and was prepared to testify against the father and son.

CHAPTER 27 • RETURN TO THE TOMB

"Zoey, are you ready?" Hannah called from the living room.

"Coming!" Zoey answered from her bedroom.

Zoey stepped into the hallway and could see her Mama, Meema and Pap waiting for her by the door.

"Could you carry the broccoli salad?" her mom asked as they prepared to walk across the road to where they would have Thanksgiving dinner with the Jones's extended family.

Of course, Henry would be there, as would Rufus and his family. Zipporah had insisted that everyone that could be there should come. Even the Thornton family pledged to be there. Zipporah had cooked two turkeys, a ham, and slow-cooked eastern Carolina barbeque. The other families signed up to provide salads, side dishes and desserts.

With the help of Henry and his sons, Moses had erected an enormous pavilion for the families to gather under, with an assortment of picnic tables and benches.

The entire scene resembled a festival.

Zoey's mom and Meema immediately jumped in to help Zipporah in any way that they could.

"Hi, Zoey!" Rufus said with a big smile and to her delight actually took her hands in his and added, "You look beautiful!"

That made her blush but she also felt a thrill at his approval of her outfit.

"You two need to knock that stuff off around us poor single guys," Billy said as he joined them.

"Don't give us that! We saw you put a move on Mary Beth at school last week," Rufus said with a chuckle.

"That's right! I've seen the way she looks at you with her big, round eyes," Zoey added with a giggle.

"You think she really likes me?" Billy asked with genuine surprise.

"Just talk to her and let her see what a nice guy you are," Zoey said with sincerity. She wanted Billy to experience the same happiness that she and Rufus felt.

Zoey could not help but think how much her life had changed in less than two months. Her mom and Henry were in a growing relationship. Hannah had always been happy but Henry seemed to bring a side out of her that Zoey had never seen before. Then there was her own budding relationship with Rufus. They were great friends and loved many of the same things. He truly cared about what she was going through and she wanted nothing but the best for him. Just a few days before, they had shared their first kiss. It made her head spin and her stomach tingle. The whole experience left Rufus speechless.

"Maybe this whole boy-girl thing will be fun," she thought to herself.

There was also the resolution of the mysteries of Oak Harbor. The true history was now known to at least all the people that mattered. She had heard that Moses was working with an agent to have the history of Oak Harbor made into a novel. He said that a Hollywood studio would like to buy the movie rights!

Nathaniel Smithers was sharing documents from his family's archives that elaborated on some of the events the Durants had described. The murder of Dupree Durant II was well documented in Richard Smithers's journal.

Richard believed that his family had been inadequately compensated for their role in Oak Harbor. This led him to seek revenge by going after the treasure, which he had been told about by his father. He cooperated with Preston Hale to force Dupree to divulge the hiding place of the treasure. They took him captive and tried to get him to talk but he refused. Dupree then pushed Preston Hale aside and told him to "go to hell, little man" while walking away. That was when Preston shot him in the back of the head.

Richard Smithers continued to harbor his lust for the treasure. While his journal was less clear as to how it happened, he was also responsible for the death of Dupree Durant III. He then passed his obsession on to his two sons, Curtis and Allen. The two brothers decided that embezzlement of the trust fund was easier to do than to find a treasure that no one had seen since the 1850's. They mostly did this by forging loan documents to get money for various investments that would make them rich. Unfortunately, most of the investments went bad and they spent close to twenty years running a Ponzi scheme to cover up the original crime. When they were discovered, they murdered Dupree Durant IV in 1945, Dupree Durant V in 1960 and finally Jonathan Wilson in 1969.

Despite all of these mysteries being solved, there was one that had defied every attempt to be resolved: "Where is the treasure?"

All of this was running through Zoey's curious mind when she heard the deep molasses voice of Moses ask, "Are you two enjoying yourselves?"

"Yes we are, Moses. This is quite the party!" Rufus said happily as he squeezed Zoey's hand.

"How are you doing, Moses?" Zoey asked.

"Fair to middlin'," he replied with a smile. "Oak Harbor will be moved into my name come the first of the year. I also just signed a deal to turn the books you found into a novel and the publisher thinks it will do well. I just hope we can start bringing in some money to begin fixing the place up." Zoey could see concern grow on his face before he added, "Zipporah wants to turn Oak Harbor into a wedding venue but that's going to take a right fair chunk of money!"

Just then the bell rang announcing that it was time to eat dinner. The crowd gathered in the serving line and Moses stepped on top of a stepladder and banged a pot for everyone's attention.

"First of all, thank y'all for coming to the first Oak Harbor neighborhood Thanksgiving!" he said loudly as people began to cheer.

"We hope that this is the first of many!" he shouted. "Now, if you would, please join me and bow your heads as I say grace over this awesome gathering and delicious food!" Everyone grew quiet. "Heavenly Father, we gather in your name to thank you for the bounty of this land, to celebrate our community, and to ask that you would continue to bless this country that we love! And all God's people say Amen!"

The crowd said "Amen" as one.

Zoey and Rufus watched as the people began to work their way through the serving tables overfilling their plates. The teens waited until most of the people had made their way through the line before they joined in the organized chaos.

After the meal, people broke into smaller groups. Some of the older men pitched horseshoes while younger ones played tag football. Others played various card games. Zoey and Rufus found a quiet place where they could sit on a garden swing that faced Oak Harbor.

"I think Moses is a little more worried about taking control of Oak Harbor than he lets on," Rufus said as he looked toward the old plantation house.

"I agree. You weren't there when he read that letter from Miss

Rose. I know he was happy but I think there was another part of him that was feeling overwhelmed by what it will take to put Oak Harbor back into shape and keep it that way. I wish we could figure out where that treasure is!" Zoey said.

"You really believe that it's still here?" he asked as he squeezed her hand.

"It's here, I'm sure of it. Meredith Williams came for it and Dupree was leading him to it up by the cemetery. He admitted that there were still 3,000 pounds of gold. After that he said that he would take the secret of the treasure with him to his grave," Zoey replied as her mind wandered over all the things she had read in the books.

"Actually, I think what he said was 'as for the treacherous gold that make free, that secret lies with me in my tomb' if I remember right," Rufus said as he yawned with drowsiness from the large meal.

Zoey suddenly jerked upright as his words sank in. "I know where the treasure is!" she said in wonder.

She wanted to run and reveal the treasure but knew that it needed to wait until the next day.

"You know where it is?" Rufus asked, suddenly wide awake.

"Yes!" she replied before she kissed him, driving any further conversation out of their minds.

The next day Rufus met Zoey at her house. They quickly rode their bicycles over to Moses's house where he and his sons were busy taking the pavilion down.

"Good morning, Moses!" they said in unison as he walked over to greet them.

"Now what are the two of you up to this fine day?" he asked with a knowing grin as he recalled the two of them kissing on his garden swing the day before.

"I know where the treasure is," Zoey said with more calmness in her voice than she felt.

The old black man looked at her and asked, "Are you going to let me come along to find it?"

"You have to. We need to get into the mausoleum," she said softly.

"I'll get my keys and meet you there!" he said as he headed toward his house, hardly believing that it could be true.

The two teens pedaled as quickly as they could to the cemetery. They arrived before Moses. Zoey looked at the cemetery, remembering her last visit just a few weeks before. It seemed unchanged at first but then she saw that one thing was decidedly different. The wrought iron fence that separated the white and black graves was no longer there. She smiled as she knew that Dupree Durant would have been pleased.

Moses arrived just a few minutes later. The three of them walked to the mausoleum. Moses quickly inserted the key and Zoey noted that the lock turned far more easily this time.

Moses looked up, smiled at her, and said, "I did a little oiling. I plan on putting flowers on their crypts. That includes Miss Bernadette. We's all family!"

Zoey smiled and gave him a hug for his thoughtfulness.

They pushed the doors open and Zoey walked forward to stand in front of Dupree's crypt. She then looked down to see the Latin inscription, "Perfide Aurum Liberat," with the bronze magnolia blooms on each side. She knelt and gripped the two bronze nobs and tried to pull but nothing happened.

"I was sure that this would open right up and the gold would be on the other side," she said with frustration.

"Let me see," Rufus said as he joined her on his knees.

Rufus began to twist the bloom on the right side and it began to turn. Zoey tried the one on the left and it also began to turn. They continued to turn until they both came to a stop. Rufus looked at Zoey and smiled and with a nod they both pulled and the panel of stone came free. The teens bent down to the floor and looked into the darkness where they saw the light streaming in through the open doors being reflected back out of the darkness. Rufus reached in and had to pull really hard until a gold ingot slid out of the opening. He held the bar out for Moses and Zoey to see. It was about ten inches long by four inches wide and two inches thick.

He handed it to Zoey who was surprised by how heavy it was. She passed the gold bar to Moses who held it like a baby.

Rufus was already looking back into the hole. He began to count. There were eight bars with their ends sticking toward the opening and they were stacked fifteen high except for the one he had already pulled out.

"There are at least one hundred and twenty bars like that one!" Rufus said with excitement.

"This thing has to weigh at least twenty-five pounds!" Moses said as he hefted the ingot.

Zoey sat back and smiled as she did the math and realized that they had found exactly what Dupree had written in his journal, over 3,000 pounds of gold! She got up off of the floor and watched as Rufus began to free the bars from their hiding place and stack them one by one on the floor.

She looked at the cover to Dupree's crypt and smiled, saying, "Thank you, Marse Dupree, for helping to change us all! Oak Harbor is in good hands and will continue to fulfill its mission!"

EPILOGUE

It had been eighteen months since the discovery of the Oak harbor treasure. Zoey approached the front gate of Oak Harbor. The wrought iron gates were now wide open. Discreetly out of sight was a guard station just in case someone decided to skip paying the entrance fee. It only cost ten dollars to come in on foot and visit the gardens and walking trails.

However, the way that most people chose to come in was on one of the horse-drawn carriages that accommodated six people at a time. They were then taken on a guided tour of the main house, the slaves' quarters, and the overseers' quarters. Along the way they would meet reenactors who would answer their questions. The ride took them through the countryside from the visitor center some two miles away. Officially, Zoey was a volunteer but in reality, she had become an unofficial member of the Durant family.

She marveled at the change to the old plantation since she had first set foot on it with Moses in what seemed like another age. Where the yard had been overgrown with brush there was now a manicured lawn that would make any groundskeeper envious. The circular cobblestone drive had been repaired and was now neatly maintained. The vines had been cleared from the statues, allowing visitors to see the recreated Roman gods and goddesses that watched over the arriving guests. The live oaks were now trimmed and shaped with dead ones removed and replaced with new mature specimens. She looked towards the house with its freshly restored exterior. The bricks had been cleaned and damaged bricks had been replaced. Any rotted wood had been repaired and all of the wood surfaces were regularly painted as needed.

Soon Zoey arrived at the main door, which was opened for her with a bow by the "butler" in his 1850's-style servant's clothing. Oak Harbor was now a living history site that helped visitors to understand the nature of the antebellum south and how Oak Harbor had used deception to fight racism and slavery.

The inside of the house had been restored just as meticulously as the outside and the rest of the grounds.

Zoey always made a point to stop and admire the portrait of Marse Dupree in the dining room. Even though he had died more than 130 years before her birth, she felt closer to him than any man in her life.

"Well, except for Rufus," she whispered to herself. She still blushed as she thought of him.

Zoey turned the other way and walked back toward the study.

As she passed the front door, the next tour group was entering the house. She worked her way to the study and opened the pocket doors to find Moses sitting behind the desk with the fully stocked shelves of period edition books behind him. She smiled as she looked at the fully restored scale on its pedestal. The scale once again served as the trigger for the hidden storage closet to open. Inside that closet were reproductions of the three volumes she had found there on that fateful day. The originals were on display in the museum at the Welcome Center. Those books had allowed her to discover the gold which, at the time, she and everyone else considered the treasure of Oak Harbor. But Zoey knew that the true treasure which was discovered in those books was the history of the Durant family and the heroic Dupree Durant who chose to fight a secret war against slavery and racism.

Moses smiled warmly at her as she entered the room, "It's good to see you, child!"

Zoey went up to him and gave him a hug and a kiss on the cheek.

"So, what did you want to see me about?" she asked as they both set down.

"Zipporah is going to need your help. I'm afraid we are going to have a really big wedding coming up this fall for a very important couple. They want to take over Oak Harbor for an entire week! There are going to be formal dinners, receptions, and a grand ball. The ceremony is to take place in the formal garden just like Jonathan and Rose's so many years ago. The couple wants to use the Durant suite for their honeymoon. They also need to accommodate a girl about your age in Miss Rose's room for the whole week. Do you think you can help take some pressure off of Zipporah? You know how she frets about such things," Moses said with a serious tone.

"You know I'll do whatever I can to help Zipporah!" Zoey said trying to reassure Moses. "Just who is this couple? Are they celebrities?" she asked and wondered just who could afford such an extravagant affair.

Before Moses could answer there was a knock on the door.

"Ah, that will be the couple in question as we speak," Moses said as he stood to open the doors.

Zoey stared at the couple as they entered the room. She wanted to laugh, scream, and cry all at the same time but then she just ran into her mother's loving arms.

The End

AFTERWORD FROM THE AUTHOR

I do hope that you have enjoyed my story The Mystery Next Door.

The story was inspired by my nine-year-old granddaughter's request that I write a book that she could read. The request was made after I published my first novel "A Songbird in Flight" which included the topic of human trafficking. Probably not an appropriate subject for her to read about until she is a little older.

Her challenge was accepted!

From the beginning I wanted the main character to be a person that my granddaughter could identify with. I went so far as to ask her to supply me with the name for the main character and she gave me Zoey Morganton.

After that it was up to me to wrap a story around a thirteen-year-old girl.

I began to toy with certain story lines and eventually settled on a mysterious house that was located next to Zoey's home. I cannot speak for how other authors approach writing but for me I start to write and let the questions that form in my mind guide me to the development and evolution of the story.

In this case, I was confronted with a mysterious run down house. Why is it there? Who lived there? Why is it abandon? Why are there people searching the house at night?

Out of these questions was born the back story of Oak Harbor and Dupree Durant. Looking at the time of the house being built it was obvious that the story would have to tie into the Antebellum South through the period of Reconstruction and into the twenty-first century. By the way, many people do not know what Antebellum means. Antebellum is Latin for "Before War" so it really means the period before the Civil War. Therefor the subjects of slavery and racism would be an integral part of the storyline.

As the author, I began to wonder what would have happened if a man who detested slavery and the racism that supported it, found himself with unbelievable amount wealth?

As I explored this theme, I began to think of other examples of ordinary people who did extraordinary things to save others. There are many stories from World War II where people helped Jews to escape the atrocities of the Nazis.

What about a white person seeking to set slaves free in North Carolina?

There were many abolitionists in the years leading up to the Civil War and not all of them were above the Mason Dixon Line. In North Carolina there were Quakers and others who did not support slavery. Many of these would not cross the line and actually break the law. However, some did such as Abigail and Joshua Stanley who used a wagon with a false bottom to smuggle slaves up to Ohio from their farm in Guilford County. I suspect that there were others whose stories have been lost to time since what they did was illegal or worse punished by mob justice.

After doing just a little research, a tale about a man with a Quaker background forming a scheme as described in this book is plausible.

The vast majority of characters in this book are fictional. One exception to this is a man by the name of Vincent Colyer who was appointed Superintended of the Poor in New Bern by General Burnside after its occupation by the Union in 1862. Later he wrote a report that was instrumental in the formation of "Colored Troops" as part of the United States Army. There were also rumors that he helped to recruit former slaves to act as spies for the Union during his time in New Bern.

One final thing on the subject of racism, I have chosen in this book to use certain terms that today are found to be offensive. The term "Marse" is now looked at as a derogatory word since it was used by slaves as a word for Master. When an author decides to write about events that are set at a point in time, they cannot ignore the terms that would have been used by people in those days. The head of a plantation would have been called "Marse" or some other equivalent. I chose deliberately to carry that term forward into the twenty-first century and ultimately to bestow it on a man descended from slaves. This is a point of irony on my part as in reality there was never a "Marse" at Oak Harbor. The entire enterprise was a fraud and the title of its chief perpetrator should be a badge of honor for the heir of his legacy!

I would also like to point out that I used a racial epitaph that I personally find deeply offensive, as does most of polite society. However, this is like a swear word being used where it naturally would fit in a dialogue. To avoided using it when describing an offensive statement by a racist would be a disservice to the reader. Besides if it offended you that speaks well of you.

Again, thank you for reading my book and please tell others about it if you did.

Michael Rodney Moore

ABOUT THE AUTHOR

Michael Rodney Moore

Mike retired from the world of finance where he spent forty years as CFO and Treasurer for small to medium sized banks. Mike and his wife, Debbie relocated to the tiny community of Little Switzerland in the mountains of North Carolina. Since his retirement he has engaged his love of telling a good story by writing fictional stories. In 2022 he self-published his first novel and found the entire process both challenging and exhilarating. He looks forward to continuing this new stage of his life.

In addition to his passion for story-telling, Mike enjoys history, motorcycles, cooking, and music.

BOOKS BY THIS AUTHOR

A Songbird In Flight

Veronica Tillman was a woman trapped in a life of quiet desperation. She had been Roger Culpepper's mistress since she was eighteen. He had seduced her with a life of unimaginable wealth and privilege.

Being a kept woman is not a secure life and would end whenever Roger decided to throw her away like a piece of trash. So, she submitted to whatever he demanded and hoped that he would continue to be entertained by her.

This was her life, or at least it was until she had learned of just what Roger Culpepper, in the service of Percy Brigston, was really doing. She could no longer tolerate the thought of him touching her. She shivered as she recalled the look on that young girl's face. It would haunt her forever!

She was determined to stop them or she would die trying.

Made in the USA
Middletown, DE
01 March 2024